# Haunted Futures

WITHDRAWN

### Edited by
### Salomé Jones

GHOSTWOODS

# THIS IS A GHOSTWOODS BOOK
4 5 6 7 8 9 10 11 12 1 2 3

**Executive Editor**: Salomé Jones
**Cover Design**: Gábor Csigás
**Copy Editor**: Tim Dedopulos
**Image Credits**: *Cover images* **Road-Sky-Clouds-Cloudy** by Ryan McGuire (https://www.pexels.com/photo/road-sky-clouds-cloudy-215/); **Earth, Blue Planet** by Wikilmages (https://pixabay.com/en/earth-blue-planet-globe-planet-11015/); **Purple Abstract Blur** by Nic at littlevisuals. co [ RIP, Nic :-( ] (https://www.pexels.com/photo/purple-abstract-blur-bokeh-1755/). *Fonts* "**Nexa Rust**" font family by Radomir Tinkov, Svetoslav Simov, Ani Petrova & Vasil Stanev via FontFabric Type Foundry (http://www.fontfabric.com/nexa-rust/), "**DejaVu**", a retool of *Bitstream Vera*, is Copyright (c) 2003 by Bitstream, Inc (https://www.fontsquirrel.com/fonts/dejavu-sans), "**Courier New**" by Howard "Bud" Kettler via IBM and Monotype, and especially "**Garamond**" by Claude Garamond via Christophe Plantin and Adobe. All artworks, fonts, and textures appear under license.
**Gábor Csigás can be found at gaborcsigas.daportfolio.com**

ISBN: 978-0-957627-18-5

This edition published May 2017 by:
Ghostwoods Books
London
United Kingdom
http://www.gwdbooks.com

Obviously, we can't stop you pirating this book, but we hope you don't, unless you're in serious financial trouble. Ghostwoods Books is an independent, fair-opportunity publisher, and 50% of all proceeds, before our costs, go to the authors. The rest is used putting our books together and keeping us going. No shareholders. No fat-cats. No rampant profiteering, we promise. If you have pirated this book — and if you enjoyed it — please consider buying a copy and/or putting a rating and brief review on your preferred book site!

If you are interested in writing for Ghostwoods Books, please head over to **http://gwdbooks.com/about-us/submissions** for details of our submissions policies.

# Haunted Futures

*Tomorrow is Coming*

Edited
by
Salomé Jones

# DEDICATION

*To the future – yours, ours, everyone's.*
*May it be haunted by only the most delightful specters.*

SF/FAN
HAUN

# TABLE OF CONTENTS

## EDITOR'S NOTE

*"Imagination is more important than knowledge."*
– Albert Einstein

Unlike certain other forms of art, fiction is rooted in the passage of time. For something to happen, there has to be a moment for it to happen in. Just like in life, we can sometimes guess what the future of a story holds, but we can't predict it with complete accuracy. Just like in life, understanding that future – finding out what's going to happen – is what pulls us forward.

In speculative fiction, that future is not limited to what is currently possible in our real world. Its writers build pictures of what might happen in a given set of more or less unrealistic circumstances. So in many ways, a science fiction anthology is the result of a group of creative people brainstorming about possible futures. The ideas do not necessarily predict any aspect of reality, but they explore possibilities and consequences that we might not get a glimpse of if we limit ourselves to strictly pragmatic, real world thinking.

For this anthology, I asked writers to interpret the phrase 'haunted futures' as a story. We received over four hundred submissions in response. I have selected the best written and most interesting of them here, for your enjoyment. Although they are all very different, there are certain similarities to many of them, similarities that were often also present in the stories that didn't make it in. Do these subtle trends reflect our current social preoccupations, or could they perhaps hint at possible directions for the real future? I leave that question for you to answer to your own satisfaction.

The fifteen stories in this anthology range in time from the very near future to unimaginably distant epochs, and spread across the palette of speculative genres. The writers are from all over the world, and not just the English-speaking parts. Some are award-winning famous names, while others are relative newcomers. All are excellent.

The true common ingredient for all of these stories is imagination. It is an incredible thing to see how varied human imagination can be – so many different interpretations of just two words. Haunted futures. But maybe the future doesn't have to feel haunted. If this process has shown me anything, it's that we're not as doomed as it may at times seem.

Salomé Jones
13 January, 2017

# YOU'RE WELCOME
by Felicity Shoulders

*Internal Record 24601CEB2_13042*
*Account: Darla Tierney*
*Date: 8-4-2019*
*Communication Type: Shipment/RetReminder*
*MiniStatus: Active/3/B; 18/F/0/0/NoCalTeen6/E\*FJ/*
*Res3-Dig3-Med2; Return 41%*
*Financial: Employee Family Plan/Marit Tierney*
*Client-facing text:*

> **_Selected for you, Darla_:**
> *1 Beachy Free swim cover-up, turquoise snake, size M, one-time selection*
>
> *As always, if you don't love what Genie got for you, follow instructions <u>here</u> to reseal the eco-friendly carton, and leave it for pickup with your empties.*
>
> *You're welcome!*

*Client response: Apparel item #1 Return 8-7-2019/no reason selected/packet open/2*
*Adjust: <u>Reposition on apparel/media matrix</u>; -1*
*trendweight:apparel/CA*

"What is this thing?" Marit holds up a little tube of thin aqua fabric. "It can't be a dress? But it's too long for a shirt. It's not like I'm tall, but Genie couldn't possibly think this is a dress, could they?"

Darla looks up from her reader and frowns. "Don't like to speculate on what computers are thinking, but that isn't yours. Pink packets are for you, coral ones are for me. They think that's enough dress for me," she says and turns back to her book.

"That's ridiculous," Marit says, most of her attention on stuffing empty pink packets back into the carton for recycling. "The Midwest is cold, why would they send that to you?" She can hear the fretting tone in her voice—she does *try* not to worry—but at least it's aimed at her employers' algorithms for making bad predictions, not at her daughter for potentially freezing to death.

"Okay, yeah, that's a point." Darla puts down her device and pads over to look at the skimpy little dress and pluck the shipment statement from inside its wrapper. "Oh, it's a swim cover-up. So... still no points for Genie, swim team doesn't mean sunny lounging—even less so out there. Little less silly than as a dress though."

"Do you like it?"

Darla holds it up and purses her lips. "Nope. I wouldn't use it much, and it would look silly with my swimsuits. Back to the magic workshop it goes! Tell the elves to work on their wishes!" She starts to ball the thing up, then notices her mother's glance and folds it to stuff back into the coral packet.

"Maybe it'll send you some weird stuff for a while," Marit says, trying to cheer herself up. "Freshmen are fickle. I joined the show choir one week, the movie society the next, and I actually went out for fencing. Fencing! Sharp things! Electrical shock hazards! Thank God I didn't get in."

"Yeah, well I'm not you." Darla raises her eyebrows. "I don't need weird beach-wear or a sword. Tell your gnomes I'm planning on being the same old Darla." She gathers up her reader. "*And* tell them it's sexist to give us variations on 'pink' and Dad 'blue.' Not to mention pointless, when he's in China half the time."

"They'll roll out individual color selection next year, I think. It's been requested a lot—you think this is bad, imagine if your mom were colorblind, instead of just bad at telling pink from coral. I'd open all your packets and know all your secrets!"

Darla rolls her eyes as she starts up the stairs. "That assumes

9

Genie knows all my secrets. I like to think I'm a *little* more complicated than that!"

"Don't we all?" Her mother sighs.

*Internal Record 24601CEB0_37020*
*Account: Marit Tierney*
*Date: 8-20-2019*
*Communication Type: Confirmation*
*MiniStatus: Active/4/B; 46/F/M/1-18/NoCal13/INT*/*
*Bk4-Dig2-Med1; Return 20%*
*Financial: Employee Family Plan/Administrator*
*Client-facing text:*

> *You have temporarily raised the budget for sub-account*
> *"Darla" to level 4. The gift message to Darla will read:*
> *"Happy first month at college from Mom & Dad! Here's a*
> *little something to help you settle in." Thank you -- and You're*
> *welcome!*

*Client response: Message read 8-20-2019*
*Adjust: None*

Marit doesn't like being home alone. Sean's absence is usual, even comfortable, but only with Darla here to tease her out of her thoughts and occupy her evenings and weekends, to make more noise than the house ticking down the years. Single motherhood, even part-time, is saintly: an empty nest is just hermitry.

She thinks about getting a dog. Genie is a dog-friendly office to say the least—there's even a running joke that the company sends out doggy beds and food bowls to staff to get them to rescue dogs, whether the algorithms predict they want one or not. The first month of Darla's absence goes by dog-less however, and Genie doesn't try to change that. Audiobooks queue for download and cartons arrive full of spices and devices for the experimental cooking she likes to do while picky Sean isn't there. Nothing to do with dogs. She's a little smug at Genie's lack of discernment: see, they aren't infallible! Or rather, *I'm unpredictable.*

Finally she stops desultorily web-searching for dog pictures and gives in on the game of algorithmic chicken. She tells her home assistant she is 'mildly interested in dog ownership' and the next packet includes a book for first-time dog owners. Whether it's the number of chapters on training or the book's ominously laminated pages, Marit starts to wonder if she's being hasty. Her daughter *has* only been gone a month, and a dog is a huge commitment. Maybe she and Sean will take road trips when he gets home, go dancing, enjoy the empty nest the way they're supposed to—things that aren't fair to a needy child-substitute with fur.

Genie seems to agree with her, since no further dog-related selections appear on her doorstep or in her download queue for the next while.

In video chat, Marit tells her husband, "Maybe the company servers picked up some chatter about Doug bringing his beagle puppy in last week—I think rushing out another baby before I hit menopause would be less trouble than that thing, honestly. Or Genie just knows I get nervous."

"Hon, I'm pretty sure I could throw a rock in Shenzhen and hit someone who knows you get nervous. Not exactly a well kept secret, even among those who haven't got access to your email. Your jitters are legend."

"Very flattering. But a dog is a big decision! I'm only being responsible. Even if I want to go ahead, shouldn't I wait until you're home to help me pick a breed?"

"Nah, I'm fine with dogs, and, apart from my grandmother's demon-pugs, they're fine with me. Promise me there will be no pugs, and I'll be fine with whatever you choose."

Genie isn't hooked into their video calls as far as Marit is aware. But when she gets home from the Humane Society with Sebastian, there's a carton on the porch with tooth-friendly treats, a rope toy, and a walking harness adjustable to retriever-mutt size. Well played, Genie—almost eerie, predicting the precise length of her hesitation. She reads over the manifest and narrows her eyes at the slogan 'We know what you need!' blazoned under the logo's tail of magic sparkles. "Sassy program," she says and puts it aside to deal with Sebastian eagerly snuffling in the open box.

*Internal Record 24601CEB0_43165*
*Account: Marit Tierney*
*Date: 10-26-2019*
*Communication Type: Shipping/DigReminder*
*MiniStatus: Active/4/B; 46/F/M/1-18/NoCal13/INT*/*
*Bk5-Dig2-Med2; Return 20%*
*Financial: Employee Family Plan/Administrator*
*Client-facing text:*


### Selected for you, Marit:


<u>*Limited Release: Erotic Tales*</u> *edited by Farrar, Germaine,*
*one-time selection*

<u>*Sous-Vide Cocktails*</u>* *by Vaughan, E.G., one-time selection*


*\*This is an enhanced cookbook! Access each recipe as an*
*interactive audio-experience with your home assistant, thanks*
*to our <u>new corporate partners</u>.*


*You're welcome!*

*Client response: Book #2 reviewed 4 stars 10-27-2019/<u>review</u>*
<u>*text analysis*</u>
*Adjust: +2 to Bkweight:cookbook/ +0 freq:cookbook*


"You're so fucking brave." Connie often praises her friends extravagantly, though in a tone Marit thinks of as 'habitual.'

"I'm not brave for having a husband in China. There are plenty of people with spouses in China."

"Well, yeah. China's full of 'em."

Marit sighs and pours from the shaker. "Anyway, if I were 'brave,' I'd visit him from time to time, right? Step on a plane? See the world?"

"They could drug you up and wheel you on Hannibal Lecter-style. With an IV full of—what is this I'm drinking?"

"That started with celery-radish vodka, and then I improvised."
Marit shrugs. "Lymphy Mary?"

"Sounds like food. They can give you an IV full of this stuff
on top of the latest mother's little helper, and you'll be in Shanghai
before you know it."

"Sean never goes to Shanghai. And we're okay without me
visiting. This works for us, as I've told you before."

"I just don't know *how!* I've been between boyfriends for two
weeks and I'm already antsy. How do you survive three months?
Six? How does he? There's your real courage, letting a man—" She
trails off and becomes very interested in her drink.

"What? Come on, Connie, tell me what ghastly sexist thing
you were going to say."

Connie shuts herself up with a long sip and a longer hum
of enjoyment. "He must run up a hell of a porn tab, that's all I'm
saying."

Marit rolls her eyes. "I don't know what he watches alone, and
he doesn't know absolutely everything that comes from Genie for
me in extra-opaque packaging. Some of it, obviously. Not all."

"Well, is *he* getting anything naughty from your Big Blue
Brother?"

"How would I know? I can't pull his manifests out of the
recycling when he's in China. We've got separate subaccounts, we're
not one of those creepy two-headed beings that share everything
down to an email address."

Connie raises her eyebrows. "You work for them. I *know* you
can peek. Something to do with databases—Remy bragged about
it when we were dating."

"Yeah, well, he would've had access to the production
database, and I—" She stops, thoughtful.

"Yes? Oh my poor virtuous Marit, are you being tempted?"

"No. If I wanted to be unethical, I could snoop on Sean while
he's home. Why would you want me to be unethical at work too?
If your ex-boyfriend hadn't jumped ship, I'd tell the HR twins on
him."

"Oh god, 'boyfriend' is dignifying it remarkably. Let's stick with
the one syllable. Yeah, Remy wasn't a sterling guy: used customer

data to spy on his dates, when he could. If you guys had better market penetration, maybe he would only have dated Genie users, and I would have been spared that brief indignity!"

"But since you've already taken that bullet, might as well be part of the penetrated market too. Then you would know about the latest old lady music and advances in comfortable bra technology without asking me all the time."

Despite a wince at the idea that they are now 'old ladies with comfy bras,' Connie doesn't rise to the bait. "Why would you hang out with me if I didn't need your help? I'm like a hungry baby bird, squeaking for your book recs. But mostly for your weird cocktails, come on," she says, pushing her empty glass across and pointing at her gaping 'beak.'

Marit obliges—one of the advantages of a distant husband and a daughter at college is that her best friend can get sloshed and sleep in the guest room with total impunity.

As if reading the turn of her thoughts, Connie says, "How's the next generation? Does she mix up a drink as well as her ma?"

"Oh gods, I hope not! She's just eighteen after all! The stuff she feels she can tell me sounds fine, but there's so little of it I fill in all the gaps with dread. And even the safe-for-parents Halloween party pictures she posted yesterday made my skin crawl. She didn't make swim team, but that's probably all to the good, for her studies. Although I wish she'd told me instead of letting me go on assuming she was on the team until the first meet results came out. Still no major."

"And yet you're not worried?"

"Of course I'm worried, I'm alive! But my worries are one thing I can keep off her plate."

"Virtuous mama."

"She's brilliant, she's talented, she'll be great," Marit repeats like a mantra.

"Yeah, well, maybe she'll rebel by being mediocre! Romance?"

"She admitted to a crush once, but said he was 'too cool to notice her.'"

"Upperclassman?" Connie's eyes narrow. "Hope he stays not noticing."

"I don't know, I thought Sean was too cool for me once. Little did I know his big sister did all his clothes shopping."

"The old-fashioned version of your product. Fashionable siblings that dress you... as a service!"

*Internal Record 24601CEB1_36544*
*Account: Sean Tierney*
*Date: 10-30-2019*
*Communication Type: Shipment/DigReminder*
*MiniStatus: Active/3/B; 47/M/F/1-18F/WCTransient7/ESTJ/Res1-Bk3-Dig3-Med3; Return 27%*
*Financial: Employee Family Plan/Marit Tierney*
*Client-facing text:*

> ### Selected for you, Sean:
> *3 Basics Extra-Wax dental floss, cinnamon, recurring selection*
> *Doodles for Meditation by Flores, Anna, one-time selection*
>
> *And check your queue for 007: The Sean Connery Collection and more -- we know what you need! You're welcome!*

*Client response: none*
*Adjust: none*

--

*Internal Record 24601CEB2_21208*
*Account: Darla Tierney*
*Date: 10-30-2019*
*Communication Type: Shipment*
*MiniStatus: Active/3/B; 18/F/0/0/UnTyped/E\*F\*/Res3-Dig3-Med2; Return 68%*
*Financial: Employee Family Plan/Marit Tierney*
*Pilot Programs: MD1*
*Client-facing text:*

**_Selected for you, Darla_**:
*1 Triple-A Skater Skirt in Black/Silver, Size 8, one-time selection*
_Nice Girls Finish Last_ *by Harmon, Gretchen, one-time selection*
_Crime and Punishment (Spark Notes)_ *by Notes, Spark, one-time selection*

*You're welcome!*

*Client response: none*
*Adjust: _New potential type matches identified_; narrow index selections; send interest questionnaire with one-month bonus level (Resistant 3)*

She could do it, actually, Marit thinks as she stares at the airport and her dormant phone screen by turns. Could get item numbers for Sean's Genie shipments. She has analytics reports all the way back to before she was even hired. She could cross-reference some of her own selections that had been shipped in a carton with Sean's when he was home, figure out his subscriber UIN....

She stops drumming on her steering wheel and slaps it instead. "Dear God, Marit, stop thinking about it! If you wanted to know anything, you'd ask like a grownup." She isn't really tempted, but it's pleasing somehow to know that she could. Virtue in self-denial? Or simple smugness that Connie's greasy ex couldn't do anything she can't do. In theory, of course: she isn't about to try it out just to see.

The sound of sirens whips her head around before she's aware, and she cranes to see the fire engines, tennis-ball yellow instead of red, careening toward the airfield. Her mind generates worst case scenarios by unvarying habit: Sean's flight should be safely down, but another plane could crash into it on the runway—wait, she hasn't gotten the automatic message that the flight's landed. She forces herself to focus on her phone and breathe more or less normally as she punches up the app: still 'in transit', 20 minutes over flight time. Could just be a headwind, she tells herself.

It isn't. She spends hours waiting, dodging luggage carts and nasty coughs in the terminal and forcing her anxious inquiries on harried employees, making do on comforting texts from Connie. Darla, by contrast, responds to the news that her father's flight has belly-flopped down at SJC with "Wow! Sounds intense!" Well, they did say no one was seriously hurt, and she's probably busy.

Finally Sean wanders out of the emergency services limbo, looking handsomely rumpled, and grabs her into a hug. "Never been happier to be home." He holds onto her, kissing her temple for punctuation.

"Were you scared?" Marit asks, voice wobbly as if she's still trying not to cry.

"Of course! But it happens—" He trails off, perhaps realizing he was going to say something particularly unreassuring. "It's not routine, but it's not the end of the world, I gather. I fly a *lot*, something was bound to happen. But now I've had my one in... twelve-thousand, and I'll be safe forever." He smiles, shifting his arm so he can keep it around her and walk, both.

"That's not how statistics work!"

"You got me. But it is vastly unlikely: you know, no one better, how much flying I've done, and this was the first problem. If you ever decide to get back on the Pegasus, think how small your chances will be of even a hiccup." He looks at her, from face to hands, then changes the subject. "In the best hackneyed fashion, though, the whole thing made me think: maybe I should stay home more. Especially now you're by yourself."

Marit smiles, pleased and effectually distracted by the idea, though she's still jittery—his arm across her shoulders makes her realize how tense and hunched they are. "Having *one* of you in the same time zone as me would be a glorious luxury."

"That was my plan, work abroad for years so you'd think I was something special when I got back," he says with a broad smile. He checks his watch for messages and frowns.

"What?"

"Just thought Darla might have responded."

"She saved her distant stage for college, maybe? Or it's her phone—she did say her battery was kaput. But that doesn't explain

17

why she hasn't committed to dates for Thanksgiving—we're going to have to take out a loan for the ticket at this point," she jokes feebly.

He squeezes her shoulders. "You smell incredible, by the way."

"You like the smell of fear? That's creepy, Sean."

"Nope, I like the smell of wife. And... baking?"

"If I'd known, I would have skipped the comfort food and just made us a pitcher of Long Island iced teas."

\*

The scare is good for them, Marit has to admit—or would admit if she were that frank with anyone except the mirror. Usually the first day or two back would be awkward: her hyper, him dead asleep on his feet or otherwise. The next few would be the honeymoon phase. But the belly flop of Flight 7989 pushes past Sean's jet lag and puts them in honeymoon territory on day one, eating molasses cookies in bed. The next few days, they drive out to Half Moon Bay, take Sebastian to Fort Funston. They actually go dancing.

Unfortunately, they get to Phase 3, 'I don't live alone?,' correspondingly early. There's a disjointed evening where Sean refuses to admit he's ever eaten and approved gnocchi in the past, and Marit calls him a philistine not quite as teasingly as she meant to. He withdraws to the living room to watch a long movie about Soviets and Nazis dying in the snow. When he staggers upstairs, she stays up and makes herself a refreshingly strange mixed drink out of cloudberry liqueur and pineapple juice.

Phase 3 is normal, Marit reminds herself. Usually Darla makes the awkwardness comic somehow, perhaps by narrating it as if they were a nature special, or threatening to stay at Tracy's until they get their act together. Tracy's moms report she's very happy at Pomona: joined a choir, talking about med school. But Darla wanted to go far away. Marit thinks she understands: she did her laundry at home on the weekends in college, and later felt she'd missed some step, some adventure.

There's snail mail, she recalls suddenly, swishing her glass. Left unopened after the first salvos of the gnocchi fight. She sorts through and finds a letter from Darla's school, probably another plea for donations—or every parent's favorite, a request to be written into the will—but she cuts the envelope open with nonsensical eagerness to touch something real from her daughter's world.

It's definitely something real: NOTICE OF ACADEMIC PROBATION, the header reads. It's mostly boilerplate, and she wonders how many of these they send out. This happens to lots of freshmen, doesn't it? This isn't the crushing end of the world it seems? She sets the trembling paper down and sips her cocktail, which seems less interesting and more foul. She gets up to pour herself a Scotch instead.

She wants to wake Sean, but can just imagine that conversation: "What do you expect me to do about it *now*?" Darla's asleep, too, or should be. Only Mom up late drinking. Such a bad example, she thinks and laughs hollowly. Even Connie is likely slumbering— owlish Marit is left alone to wonder what the hell her little Honor Roller is up to.

So of course she and her rocks glass end up at the computer, VPNed into work and poring over analytics reports. It's a little harder to do than she thought, even when she wasn't sure it would work. But, of course, it does work.

Everything Genie sent to her daughter in the four months since they packed her off is listed, albeit awkwardly and at one query's remove. Category and item UIN. Housewares, to be expected; music downloads, a lot of them, innocuous enough.

A sudden uptick in a clothes subcategory: lingerie. Pretty racy lingerie, Marit discovers, looking it up. She tries to tell herself her burning cheeks are from Scotch, but she knows it's guilt. Undeterred, though, she clicks on. Self-help books on love and dating, the kind of titles she can barely read without wincing. Some about 'passion' and arguing that make her heart double over with fear. And an odd category she doesn't recognize until she parses the company-internal doublespeak: the prescription pilot program—video chat appointment with a doctor, pills in your shipments. Feeling like the ultimate rat, she clicks down that trail. Anti-depressants. Not content to be a horrible mother and an unethical employee, she is now probably breaking Federal regs.

19

She clicks on a few more things in a misguided attempt to... what, feel *less* nosey? More justified? Darla is 18. She's allowed to have sex. And doctor-patient confidentiality. These reports don't list what got returned, she tries to tell herself, but all this stuff got sent for a reason.

Marit sifts back through the early picks—*Wuthering Heights?* Isn't 18 a bit old for dirtbag tragic romance? Biographies of rockers. Nothing she recognizes as Darla, her bright-eyed girl who bought medieval mysteries and listened to her dad read Sherlock Holmes over video chat every night her eighth grade year. Kerouac and Burroughs? Who is this? How could she change so quickly? How did Genie know and her mother didn't?

Shame and liquor boil up her throat and sublimate to anger. Whatever, honey, you've got to find yourself at school, sure. But college is costing us too much for you to just check out of class! If you decided you didn't want to go, why didn't you tell us? Maybe we could have afforded to have two kids after all!

Marit picks up the phone, earlier resolutions forgotten. 4 am there? Oh well, Darla sure hasn't earned her beauty sleep.

It rings and rings, and it isn't her daughter that finally answers but a young man, muzzy with sleep. "Umm, Darla Tierney's phone?"

"Who the hell is this?" Marit snaps involuntarily.

"Who the hell is *this*?" the boy bristles, sounding more awake. "It's 4 o'fucking clock in the morning!"

"I'm Darla's mother!"

"Oh sh— sorry, ma'am. Laura thought it might be Dar calling, so we answered—"

She goes cold and hot successively in mortification. Laura, the roommate. Darla's double is one room, not like the little detached cubby off a quad *she* had as a freshman. She can remember the room, now, from the video messages Darla sent home at first. "Why would Darla be calling her own phone?"

"I—uh, better hand you to Laura."

A lot of flapping around, a little whispering. "Hi, Ms. Tierney? This is Laura, Darla's roomie. She left her good phone here plugged in—it won't hold a charge."

Marit's recovered enough now to be more polite. "I'm terribly sorry for calling like this: I totally forgot I might wake you up too, and Darla's never online these days—I'm so sorry for waking you, I just... got some news."

"S'all right, Ms. Tierney." The tired mumble made the name sound like 'Miz T', as if she was the girl's coach or neighbor. "Did the school just tell you 'bout Dar?"

"Yes, I just got—" No need to be prim, her roommate has to know, right? But still, she hedges, ashamed on Darla's behalf— "Notice about her grades. Is she out? I do need to talk to her."

"They didn—I thought somebody would have told you." A pause. "She's gone."

*Internal Record 24601CEB1_42382*
*Account: Sean Tierney*
*Date: 11-14-2019*
*Communication Type: Shipment*
*MiniStatus: Active/3/B; 47/M/F/1-18F/WCTransient7/*
*ESTJ/Res1-Bk3-Dig3-Med3; Return 24%*
*Financial: Employee Family Plan/Marit Tierney*
*Client-facing text:*

> ### Selected for you, Sean:
> *2 Stress Relief Honeybush Tea, 24 bags per box, one-time selection*
> *2 Espresso Anywhere instant coffee packs, extra strong, one-time selection*

*Client response: none*
*Adjust: +1 to weight:travelfood until stress markers <2*

*--*

*Internal Record 24601CEB0_37020*
*Account: Marit Tierney*
*Date: 11-14-2019*
*Communication Type: Shipping*

*MiniStatus: Active/4/B; 46/F/M/1-18/NoCal13/INT\*/*
*Bk5-Dig2-Med2; Return 48%*
*Financial: Employee Family Plan/Administrator*
*Client-facing text:*
   **Selected for you, Marit:**

   <u>Homemade Gelato: Tradition and Beyond</u> *by Wick, Yukiko,*
   *one-time selection*
   <u>Milkshake Uglies</u> *by Boy, Gastro, one-time selection*
   <u>Light in the Dark: True Stories of Hope and Redemption</u>
   *edited by Penfield, Gene, one-time selection*

   *Client response: Book item #1 Return 11-17-2019/no reason*
   *selected/packet unopened/1*
   *Book item #2 Return 11-17-2019/no reason selected/packet*
   *unopened/1*
   *Book item #3 Return 11-17-2019/no reason selected/packet*
   *open/3; debit item damage to account*
   *Adjust: <u>Reposition on nonfiction matrix</u>; tag data for analysis in*
   *client crisis study; widen input scope*

Gone, with no word or message left behind. Sean flies out to talk to the disapproving roommate, to those girls and boys who will admit to knowing anything. 'Dar' left school with her boyfriend, Rob, without even telling the registrar—hence the academic probation.

She doesn't have her own credit card yet, and cashed out her debit account before she left. Laura doesn't know the number of the prepaid 'dumbphone' bought in place of the battery-dead one, and by the time Sean finds the number, one slip of paper in the strata of her desk, the minutes are all used up. No knowing how they're living, or where. One of Rob's friends mentions, apparently in all sincerity, 'riding the rails' as one of the young couple's ambitions.

Sean and Marit decline Thanksgiving invitations and wait for their daughter to turn up on their doorstep, instead. They make the meal, complete with cranberries only Darla likes, and then watch it get cold together. Marit can't sleep until dawn comes most nights, since Darla is a night owl like her. But no one comes, and no one calls. Not a postcard or a message. Sean tries, with persistence and reason and emotional appeal, with their suburban respectability wielded like a club, to instill a sense of urgency in the police. He starts a social media campaign to gather news or get her to call, enlisting her high school friends to spread the word. They wait.

Marit lets her Genie shipments pile up until the day before they come to pick up empties and rejects. Mostly she has no patience and no interest for their selections, and piles them back into a single carton unopened unless something about the feel—the soft squish of comfortable clothing, for instance—intrigues her.

It isn't touch that stops her with one compact packet, though. It feels like a paper book, usual enough for her selections. She stares at it, trying to figure out why it's interesting.

The wrapper, the tinted corn-plastic wrapper, isn't quite pink like the others in that shipment. She finds a name for the orangey shade while her fingers are already pulling it open greedily: coral. This packet is for Darla. Her subaccount hasn't been cancelled, and the college must have returned some shipments and given the home address as forwarding. But why now? Why did they send something *now?*

The police haven't found anything—if they've even looked, she thinks bitterly—but perhaps Genie has? Has Darla finally logged onto something, appeared somewhere in the scope of Genie's data-gathering agreements?

She turns the book over, trying not to get her hopes up, to expect 'the Dumpster-Diving Guide to Des Moines' or anything so ludicrously actionable. She stares at the bulging outline on the cover, the title and long subtitle awkwardly laid out inside the figure. Her eye rests on 'Know Your Options'.

"How the hell does this mean she's pregnant? All we can be sure it means is you forgot to take her off the goddamn account," Sean says when she shows him. "Probably it's just that 82% of National Merit semi-finalists who ditch school to run off with psychotic weirdoes—"

"Psychotic? Who said he was psychotic? Did you not tell me—"

"Disturbed, then. How do you know the algorithm didn't shoot this off at random, based on some pregnancy actuarial table deep in its convoluted bowels? It means nothing, Marit. Less than nothing. It means you'll grasp at anything."

"Why wouldn't I? Why won't you?"

"I would do anything to get our daughter back. Are you saying I don't care?" He exhales a gust and visibly settles. "But chasing ghosts or software bugs isn't *going* to get her back, it's just going to drive us out of our minds. She's out there, and sooner or later she's going to need us and call. Or someone's going to call us and let us know where she is, at the very least. Everyone knows we're looking—" He gestures toward his computer where he made the site for their search.

"I don't find the 'thoughts and prayers' of your cousins in Poughkeepsie that reassuring," snaps Marit, but she sounds so miserable he apparently doesn't take offense. She puts her hand over her eyes. "Maybe I'm already out of my mind, but I think it means something. She gave Genie medical permissions, so maybe she went to a connected clinic? Used her Social?"

"When did we give them authorization for medical info?" Sean frowns, and Marit tries not to look guilty.

"She did it before she went to school. I didn't have to sign or agree—it was after her birthday."

"God, they'll be in our brainstems next. Can't you find out if they know something real, Marit? I don't want to—I can't spin stories out of nothing. Not and keep going."

So she doesn't talk to him about the next shipment, although she can't help but obsess over it: a warm pea coat in mustard wool. Dreadful color, she thinks, petting it fondly. Darla would have loved it. Will love it. But she can't find out why Genie sent it, any more than she can find out about the pregnancy book. Her analytics are all fulfillment side, not predictive, and her carefully correct email to the head of Predictive pleading for info—'exigent circumstances'—gets a reply from the CFO's lawyer husband. No way in hell, she translates. She tries to tell the PI service Sean hired about the packets. "Wouldn't they just send a coat because it's December?" they ask. "Did they send her one last year?"

The investigators are not impressed by her strong contention that the coat is meant for a cold climate, not the South Bay, December or no. Couldn't her employer have realized the school address was dead but still sent a Midwestern coat, they ask? She reminds them that they said the trail went cold in Chicago, and gets the coat out of the closet to brush with meditative fingertips.

*Internal Record 24601CEB0_98513*
*Account: Darla Tierney*
*Date: 12-10-2019*
*Communication Type: Shipment*
*MiniStatus: Inactive/4/B; 18/F/0/0/UnTyped/E\*F\*;*
*Return N/A*
*Financial: Employee Family Plan/Marit Tierney*
*Pilot Programs: MD1*

*Client-facing text:*

### *Selected for you, Darla:*
*1 Timbertrails 100% Silk Sleepsack, sea blue, one-time selection*

*You're welcome!*

*Client response: None*
*Adjust: None; selection return feedback unweighted for client profile Darla Tierney*

Marit doesn't even check the name on the address labels now, just rips open the cartons. Sean is annoyed when they prove to be for him, but almost as many of the packets are Darla's as his now— very few are desultory attempts to draw her mother's interest.

Darla gets gloves, sweaters. A quick-drying small-packing towel. A rather dear hat with ear flaps, which Marit thinks Darla would have pronounced 'twee' and too young.

She is cold, Marit thinks, folding the clothes away though Sean insists they should send them back and cancel Darla's subscription

25

already. Her daughter is cold, somewhere. Marit wonders if she's still pregnant—or if she ever was. Perhaps she had only used a chain store discount card to buy a test. Why would she not call, if she was? There was nothing she could have done to lose their help.

Then Marit opens another dense little coral-wrapped rectangle, smaller than the pregnancy book. Obviously not a book though, the way the weight holds together as she unwraps it, without the subtle shifts and shears of pages. A slip of paper falls out and she retrieves it from the curious dog: it's a cheerful reminder that Genie also delivers selections digitally. Shit, she hadn't thought—she'll need to pry into the databases again to see those clues.

For a moment, her spirits lift, thinking perhaps Darla *has* been picking up her digital selections: consumption is proof of life. But no, she's sure Genie wouldn't have included the slip if the items were being downloaded.

She lets the paper go and her attention falls heavily back onto the box in her hands—another turn and the wrapper falls free. A beginner French course, a little phrase book embedded in plastic next to a solid-state audio player.

French? Darla took Mandarin. Marit pads into the bedroom clutching the thing. "She's in Canada," she breathes to Sean, too quietly to wake him, then louder.

"Canada? What?" He blinks up at her silhouette against the bedroom lamp as he listens, then scrubs his face with his hand. "Does she have a current passport?" She hears the 'even' although he didn't say it. "Wait, probably so. Costa Rica. She came with me to that conference." He looks for a moment like he wants to argue, then sighs. "All right, we'll tell the investigators."

"And the cops? FBI?"

"All the investigators. We'll sound crazy together." After a discreet pause, he asks, "Can we try to sleep?"

She pauses and then smiles, her face so tight it feels creaky, and pulls off her clothes to curl in around him, chill skin to warm.

*Internal Record 24601CEB0_71002*
*Account: Marit Tierney*
*Date: 12-22-2019*

*Communication Type: SignatureShipping/RxPilot1*
*MiniStatus: Active/4/B; 47/F/M/1-18/NoCal13/INT*/*
*Bk3-Dig1-Med1; Return 30%*
*Financial: Employee Family Plan/Administrator*
*Pilot Programs: MD1, SP*
*Client-facing text:*

### **Selected for you, Marit:**
*0.5 mg Lorazepam, one-time selection**

*The New Way to Beat Your Fear of Flying by Gonzalez, Dr.
Peter, one-time selection*

*\*Please read all included cautions and directions. Insurance
billing insert also enclosed. We're happy our Prescription
Program was able to get you what you need. Together, we're
always making Genie better -- thank you and you're welcome!*

*Client response: Rx caution links opened; no returns*
*Adjust: narrow selection scope*

The Feds promise to hand Darla's information over to the RCMP,
but all the usual warnings are reiterated—their daughter isn't a
minor, there are thousands of missing women and girls—with
added reservations about the source of the parents' information.
Marit asks if they might subpoena her company's records. The
silence before the polite demurral turns Sean's ears red.

"We look like idiots," he mutters afterward.

"Yeah, but together, right?" Marit says with neither sarcasm
nor conviction.

Marit can remember Darla the child, and the teenager.
The expression of her large eyes under straight, rather heavy
brows. How she would eat anything once, and screech with
laughter if she hated it. A few years' interest in origami, to fill
her twitchy hands. But Darla the woman, who she had started
to know? Marit's idea of her is gone as surely as the rest of her.

Convolved too closely with tales of 'Dar,' who ripped her tights with a razorblade and considered going freegan, who played with a lighter while she waited for the boy in the apparently crappy band. Too headily spiked with secondhand report and fears both primal and cultural: my child is freezing in the woods. My child is strung out in a brothel. My child is alone. My child is with a boy who can't protect her. My child is with a man who hits her. She is dead in a ditch. In a shallow grave. In a morgue. She hates me for failing her. She is happy in spite of my absence and will never need me again.

Darla is the unknown future, but at least she spins out these physical signs and portents, haphazardly wrapped and delivered to her passive, cowardly mother.

Sean can't read the signs, or trust them; but then, he has no passivity to reproach himself over. When a laminated map of Paris and a backpacker's guide to the hostels of France arrive, he throws up his hands: How could she be in Europe? No, Marit, she couldn't stow away, this isn't a Victorian novel. There are security measures now. He talks about terrorism and human trafficking while she wonders if she could fly, for Darla.

What Sean does seem to reproach himself over is having started to believe her, when it was Canada: he's angry 'at her' in a way that is transparent to Marit and can't touch her. "Our daughter isn't a damsel in Dickens, she's a real modern girl who knows our phone number. She'll call, and I'll be here when she does, wherever the Mom of La Mancha has gone off to." Marit remembers all this very vividly, and the look of his face when he said it, the bones showing through the skin where it was taut, the wrinkles gathering to either side. His voice, though, sounded very young.

The anxiety meds were the last shipment before the flight, after the more conventional preparations of travel blazer and guidebooks. "Genie really does know me," she said drily to the empty room when it suggested she chat with a doctor about a prescription. She did have to actively clue it in that she was planning this trip—buying a ticket was a pretty blatant sign—but that's just further evidence they know her. They do send her more normal, tourist-oriented guidebooks than she feels appropriate, but what else is there? Most women her age take a sabbatical and travel to find themselves, not missing persons.

She wonders, not for the first time, how much the algorithms can really parse of a situation like theirs: unusual, she hopes. Genie had asked her a month ago if she would talk to a doctor about anti-depressants, which means she must have signed medical auths herself, somewhere among her employment papers. Maybe she signed over her college transcripts, too? At least, she doesn't remember writing any emails in her rusty but serviceable French, but *she* receives no phrasebook.

She is bringing a second, smaller suitcase, a sort of talisman prepared for Darla's recovery. Worn, left-behind clothes from her daughter's room, toiletries sorted out of the jumble of boxes Sean shipped back from the dorm, and a few of Genie's brand-new selections—even the warm, twee hat.

> *Internal Record 24601CEB1_54225*
> *Account: Sean Tierney*
> *Date: 12-25-2019*
> *Communication Type: Cancellation acknowledgment*
> *MiniStatus: Inactive/3C/B; 47/M/F/1-18F/*
> *WCTransient7/ESTJ/Res4-Bk3-Dig3-Med3; Return 31%*
> *Financial: Employee Family Plan/Marit Tierney*
> *Client-facing text:*
>
> *December 25, 2019*
>
> *Dear Sean,*
> *We're so sorry you've decided to end your Genie subscription. We hope this is only temporary. Please remember Genie is always learning and growing, coming up with new ways to anticipate and delight you... and to get you more for your subscription dollar! If there's any specific way you can see for us to do better, feel free to click here and let us know.*
>
> *We've included some links below to our more limited plans,*

> *and of course, you can always rub the lamp again at <u>our</u> <u>website</u> or app if you change your mind.*
>
> *Thank you for being a Genie customer—and You're Welcome!*
>
> *Client response: Message read 12-25-2019*
> *Adjust: Schedule return invite with one-month bonus level offer*
> *3/25/2020; Schedule discount offer 6/25/2020 (Resistant 4,*
> *projected 2)*

Marit's head aches—jet lag, maybe. If it were stress letdown from not being dead in a fiery smear across Charles de Gaulle, then surely the new stress of dealing with the dubious French police would have done away with that. Or is that not how stress works? It could be the anxiety drug, according to Genie's helpful list of side effects.

The wind is blowing chill and welcome down the Boulevard du Palais, and she walks into it. She has ibuprofen in her many-pocketed purse, along with hand sanitizer, an external power pack for her phone, travel spray deodorant in place of pepper spray, and many other useful items, but she doesn't stop to fish it out, letting the cold on her forehead be enough.

Paris is so strange: the realness of it, stone facades and famous buildings dimensional and physical though they should be paintings or movie backdrops. The apse of Notre-Dame looming into sight behind the next ornate, oddly lovely headquarters of some aloof and unhelpful branch of government. It's dizzying, the dislocation of it, of being here, of having flown. All that grounds her is the thought that Darla might be here too.

A scent of cut flowers, brief but thick and rich, reaches her as she walks under bare-branched trees. Strings of Christmas lights, useless in the bright day, outline some of the buildings like the dark trace of a sketching pencil.

Of course the police wouldn't tell her where young homeless congregate—*sans-abri* they call them in French, 'without shelter,' almost poetic. Don't want an American matron losing herself as well as her daughter.

She reaches the Seine and looks out, resisting the momentary lift of her heart at the breadth and beauty. She does turn to walk along the water, like a *flâneur* in an old painting, but she makes sure to check under the bridge as she passes, just as she looked down every alley on her way to the police prefecture. She has a list of hostels, a stack of pictures of Darla. She doesn't need official help.

Her phone rings in her pocket, interrupting the momentary warmth of self-sufficiency that is recently her closest approach to happiness.

"Hi, honey," she answers. "Sorry I forgot to let you know I landed safely. Guess I was too amazed myself. Not sure my white knuckles would have let me—"

"Marit."

"What." She stops walking, talking, moving her face.

There is a silence, or a breath, difficult to discern compressed across a continent and ocean. "They found her. They found Darla."

"Who? Where?" she cries, and a little old woman scowls at her. "I'm on the Île de la Cité, it's the exact middle of Paris, but I have apps and schedules, I can get anyw-"

"In Seattle. She was in Seattle. She was never in France." His voice is strained but gentle.

Marit hangs onto the low stone wall with her free hand, then pulls against it as if gravity has gone sideways. The dislocation is worse than ever. Darla was never here. "Is she—is Dar—"

There's no answer, just ragged sobs, and she puts the phone down on the limestone and takes her hand away. So much wiser than throwing it into the water. Good decision, Marit.

She can barely hear her husband weep, just faint breaths like a dog sleeping, or a small child. People are looking at her as they pass. A young man glances from her to the phone as if thinking about snatching it. She is in Paris, and Darla is dead in Seattle. Or perhaps between Seattle and Mountain View, if they have already shipped her home to Sean on a truck or a train or a plane—however much of her there is, after however long she has been dead.

The childless mother hears a voice, a small angry voice, and steps back to the phone. "Are you even there, Marit, goddamn—"

31

"I'm here, I just don't know why."

"Well, you better figure that out, then. Unless you just want to come home and help me bury our daughter." The call ends, and Marit looks at the phone, the lock-screen one of Darla's senior pictures, smeared into rainbow glints by a wet cheek-print.

At first she thought she would have no room for the fear of flying, but courage by numbness is denied her. She is prepared, though, even if she is a coward, a failed mother, and probably a bad spouse. It is with the pleasant floating feeling from Genie's drugs, like just enough booze but not too much, that Marit suddenly, with newborn conviction, opens her laptop in the darkened, hurtling cabin. The German business traveler beside her grumbles in his sleep.

Hunched over the glare, she pays her 10 euro for wifi and VPNs into Genie's network. This time, she pulls up the customer UIN easily: her own. She scrolls down in the relevant internal reports, past the fateful date, and watches her shipments get marked 'returned', space out, dwindle, separated by notes for mailings and enticement offers. Then, suddenly, a flurry of selections. The day of the pregnancy book she can almost pinpoint. She recalls there was also a packet for her, though she doesn't remember what was in it. And there, the first of many, is a pilot program reference she's never seen before, with a zeroed out price. The book about unplanned pregnancies. A coat. A very sweet warm little hat. "It's a story they told you," she says aloud on the wuthering plane, "to make you want things." Maybe they send all unhappy middle-aged women to Paris. The German whimpers, disturbed by her words. She stares at the Genie logo, the arc of the smug little shooting star—*We know what you need!*

"But all I needed was Darla." She whispers it, but too loudly. Then she starts to sob, louder still, becoming the bright center point of a silent growing ring of mortification and rage.

# RETIREMENT PLAN
## by Pete Rawlik

The room was stark, utilitarian. The walls and floors were concrete, and the wear marks in the floor looked old. Somebody had painted the walls white once, but most of that had flaked away, leaving only a few patches here and there. Nobody seemed to care enough to repaint it or even scrape the last vestiges of the old stuff away. On the ceiling, a glowball floated, bathing the room with pale, cool photochemical illumination. The main feature was an old table with two matching chairs, orange plastic over steel frames. It was rare to find a set of anything from the old world. At the table were two women. One woman was in her seventies, iron gray hair pulled back in a tight bun. She was wearing an industrial one-piece uniform, pea-green in color. A name—Doolittle—was emblazoned on her breast pocket. The other woman was younger, exactly forty years old. Her hair was shaved close to her head, which made it difficult for other people to tell the exact color, and she wore a sundress with a blue and white flower print. Although they sat across from each other, neither woman could bring herself to look at the other one.

The older woman spoke in a gruff, raspy manner. "My name is Liza. I don't have your file. Lost in transport, I suppose. Can you tell me your name, and what you did on the inside?"

The younger woman looked down at the floor, and made herself remember.

*About six weeks after she had arrived at the refugee camp, the doctors came and lined everybody up for examinations. The camp had grown up in the shadow of Palm Beach International Airport. The airport itself, with its computer networks and communications infrastructure, had been turned into a military base. Tanks and armored vehicles lined the access roads. The makeshift camp was like a tick swelling in the hotel parking and car rental lots that encircled the facility. Tarps and canvas and sheets of plastic had been strung up to provide shade from the brutal sun.*

*The place was mostly women and children. Every few days a truck would come by and drop off food—rice, vegetables and corn, but some milk and meat too. Before they left, the supply people always asked for men to volunteer and go west to work the farms. Those who went never came back. So when the doctors came and lined up all the women for examinations and began sorting them into groups, the only people that were left were either too old or too young to do anything about it. A few tried to get the military to intervene, but they just walked away.*

*The trip west in the school bus was long and hot. The air-conditioner was broken, and the girls weren't allowed to open the windows. The shocks on the bus were shot, and it seemed like the driver hit every possible pothole. Like the driver, the guards were all older women, and they carried nasty-looking assault rifles. They never said anything, just glared and motioned with their guns.*

*An hour west and the suburban blight turned to fields of row crops, with men working them. Some of the men drove trucks, or combines, or other odd pieces of equipment, but most were just laboring shirtless in the sun. Once, there would have been hats and sunscreen. Once, this work would have been done almost exclusively by Hispanic migrants or Bahamians. Now displaced Anglos, and Blacks, and Hispanics all labored together, under armed guard. Their faces screamed that hope was a commodity that was no longer affordable —that it wasn't even for sale.*

*Another hour, down roads that were more dirt than asphalt, and they turned off and passed through the gate of a fifteen foot tall barbed wire fence. There were two fences actually, with dogs in between. Some signage had been torn down, and on it she had seen the word prison. The driver welcomed them to The Palm Beach County Women's Complex. They were careful not to call it a prison. They never called it a prison. But there were fences, and dogs, and armed guards.*

*The Matron Superior was a tall lean woman with a cruel twist to her mouth and a shaven head. She explained it all to them. The world needed to be repopulated quickly, with the right kind of children. Those children would only be bred from superior parents. It was an honor to serve. In return for their service they would be housed, clothed and fed. There was a library, and they had established courses in electrical and mechanical engineering and repair, as well as other vocational classes.*

*It was two days before the first men arrived. They put her in a room with a man who had to be twenty years older than her. He wore a uniform of some sort. He was strong, stronger than she was, stronger than she could hope to fight against. She let him touch her. She let him undress her. She went down on her knees.*

*It was a full minute after he started screaming before they were able to unlock the door and pull her off of him. The guards were so concerned with getting the soldier to the infirmary that no one bothered to secure her or the room. Nude, she wandered out and down the hall, passing through the common room and then into the showers. The other girls all stared at her as she scrubbed the blood off her face and chest and let it spiral down the drain. When the guards finally showed up and dragged her away there was still blood in her hair.*

The younger woman looked up and stared at the older one. "They call me Red."

Liza Doolittle sighed. "Ok Red. This would be easier if I had your file, but I don't, so I'm going to ask you some questions and I need you to answer. How many kids did you have?"

"Eighteen."

"Did you contract any STDs?"

She nodded. "Syphilis, twice, from the same man. I responded well to antibiotics."

"What did you do while you were inside?"

"Electrical and mechanical engineering, mostly old tech. It's what we started with at the Complex. In the last five years I've been working on integrated systems. Glowball arrays, trucks that run off of plasma capacitors, flux generator banks to power old style electrics."

Doolittle smiled. "What do you remember, Red? From before?"

*She had been sixteen when the aliens had come. She had been a maid at one of the beachfront resorts in Fort Lauderdale. Like everyone else, she had spent that day divided between doing what she was expected to do, and snatching glimpses of the news reports about the alien ships that had suddenly appeared in the sky. There were dozens of them, and they had spread out over the world and taken up positions over major metropolitan areas. There had been one to the south, over Miami. She could remember seeing pictures, but she couldn't actually remember the ships themselves. Even afterwards, when she had seen pictures in history books and lectures, she could never describe them. The ships had attacked simultaneously, devastating the population centers of the world. Billions died almost instantly, vaporized by plasma backwash. More than half the world's population gone in less time than it took to drink a cup of coffee.*

*She survived because she was in the basement doing laundry when the shockwave from the south moved up and the building collapsed down on top of her. Six hours later she crawled her way out of the rubble through a ventilation shaft to the parking garage. She spent weeks on the streets, scavenging food and bottled water. She knew there were other survivors—she could see and hear them. The war against the invaders was an aerial one, and some of that took place in the sky right above her head, missiles and strange blue bolts of energy screaming back and forth while she hid and prayed for it to end. It wasn't until the scavenging party found her that she learned the war was over, and that humanity had won.*

*Victory was at a terrible price.*

*She had vague memories of the actual reports, but her knowledge of the state the world was left in came from books she read years later. They actually couldn't count the dead—it was easier to estimate the living—but the way you got there didn't matter. There were about six billion dead. Seventy-five percent of the world's population gone. The urban areas were in fiery ruins, and the surrounding Sub-Urbs had been shattered by blast waves. Government services were in tatters. The new federal government established itself in Memphis, and conscripted all commercial aircraft, crews and support staff into the military.*

*Everybody talked about winning the war, but nobody ever talked about how the war had actually been won. Even the historians were vague on the subject. She had spent years pursuing that bit of information, but no one would or could answer her question. There was speculation, of course. Some said virus, but whether that was biological or digital no one could say. Others said that the ship engines were vulnerable at a ventilation shaft. There were even legends about a plucky group of teens who infiltrated the command ship and killed the alien queen which meant all her forces had died instantly. There were lots of stories.*

*None of them seemed to be true.*

"Not much," Red said. "The psychiatrist said I had suffered severe mental trauma."

Doolittle nodded, her movement seeming sad and familiar, well-practiced. "As a retiree, you have certain rights. You can see your children if you wish. The younger ones, that is. The older ones, sixteen and up, have been sent to other population centers to prevent inbreeding and nepotism."

Red's eyes opened wide. "How can there possibly be nepotism?"

"The Sisterhood keeps detailed breeding records. The lines can be manipulated. There have been scandals. Some men, some women, favored over others, even when their scores and ranks weren't any better than the rest of their peers. Maybe there were family bonds, maybe some Sisters just adopted a particular person or gene line and made it theirs. It doesn't have to be a purely genetic relationship. The war damaged everybody, even the women that joined the Sisterhood." She paused and sighed. "Did you want to see your children?"

*Red saw Mary cowering in the corner, weeping through black and blue eyes. The child had been ripped from her arms and was being cradled by a guard in the crook of her arm, her left hand between the child's legs, stabilizing it as it squirmed and cried for its mother. In her right hand the guard held a Billy club that was dripping blood. Clumps of Mary's hair were still stuck to the side of it. Red kissed her own child and tried to close her eyes and not think of what would come later.*

"No." Red choked back the sadness that was welling up inside of her. She was trying not to speak, not to let this woman know that all she wanted to do was scream. "Do you know what the women inside called the Complex? We called it the Baby Farm. The men who came to visit called it the Sex Factory. For us, babies were the primary reason we were there. For them, the babies were just an unfortunate byproduct. So no, I don't think seeing my children would be a good idea."

"I appreciate your honesty. A lot of retirees feel that way. We can get you some therapy if you want." She changed tone. "I'm obligated to tell you that you have the option to notify the community that you are available for courtship and matrimony.

Many of the older men in town already have wives, but the younger men, eighteen to thirty, are mostly bachelors. If you do decide to make yourself available, you'll have to notify the Sheriff."

Red must have looked puzzled, because Doolittle felt the need to explain. "The ratio of men to women in the general populace is about fifteen to one. That makes you a rare commodity. Men aren't taken out to the Women's Complex until they've proven themselves as fit members of society. They don't even qualify until they're twenty-five, and most don't go till they're thirty. There's a whorehouse over on Palm Beach—Maralago—but they have their own set of rules, and most can't afford that anyway. That makes you worth fighting over, worth killing over, and worth dying over. Men are going to flock to you like flies to shit."

"And if I don't want that?"

"You have other options. You can marry a woman. Hell, you could marry into a collective, men, women, or both. If marriage is not your thing you could homestead alone. There's a federal voucher with your name on it worth one hundred acres of farmland. You can redeem the voucher in any municipality in the country, as long as they have land to give. You can trade it for other kinds of property too, including waterfront or forest, or even suburbs or urban. The bank will always give you cash value for it if you want. You could move into town, open up a shop, fix things. We need people who can fix things. We need people that can figure out how to make the human tech work with the Mechtech."

"Mech?"

"Sorry, plasma flux technology. We call it Mechtech."

"Why?" Red was rubbing her fingers together.

Liza Doolittle shrugged. "It's just this thing. We call them Mechs."

"Them?"

Doolittle closed her eyes. "The ships, the invading ships, we call them Mechs, short for mecha or mechanicals."

"Don't the aliens have names?"

"I'm sorry, I don't understand."

Red stared at the woman and annunciated as if she were talking to a child. "You call the machines that we got from the invasion 'Mechtech,' which is a reference to the ships. Why aren't they named after the aliens—the invaders, the ones who were in command? What was the name of the species that attacked us? What did they call themselves?" She paused to let her words sink in. "It's a simple question."

Doolittle shook her head. "It's not as simple as you think." She laughed a little. "Do you really want to know?"

*It was ten years after the war when the first glowballs arrived at the prison. Light bulb manufacture had ceased years before. There had been enough back stock to last for a while, but when that ran out, requisitions for light bulbs were eventually met with glowballs. The basketball-sized things generated a chemical light that was recharged by exposure to the sun. They floated around rooms, semi-autonomous, always just out of reach, using an artificial gravity generator to push them away from things. There was a kind of hive mind that kept them rotating in and out of the sun as needed. They could respond to simple commands like On and Off, Brighter or Dimmer. They were the first and most accessible example of alien tech anybody in the Complex had ever seen.*

*It took Red three tries to bring one down so she could take it apart and figure out how it worked. She had to corner one, and then use broom handles to hold it in place while someone else bashed it with a rock. The part designs were unfamiliar but the concepts were pretty similar. She had expected to find something half circuitry and half biological, but except for novel designs, the components were all pretty much identifiable. There was the globe of photochemicals, and the gravity generator which knocked her on her ass when she re-established power flow, but other than that she understood how it worked. She even found the onboard digital repair manual. It was written in Portuguese of all things, but there was an English translation, and even a basic tutorial. Later, as new alien tech came in, she always made sure she understood how it worked. It wasn't a formal education, but it put her one up on everyone else in the Complex.*

"Yes, yes I do."

It took a week to get her off planet. First there was the drive to Canaveral, straight up the interstate, but not in a truck, in a ground-effect vehicle—a recycled VW Bug welded onto alien technology that generated enough gravitic lift to fill a skirt and then coast down the road. Not that there was much of a road. Humans didn't use wheels anymore, so they didn't need asphalt

39

or concrete highways anymore. Slowly but surely, the once-great roadways were being reclaimed by the Earth. Life took hold in the cracks and pores, it put down roots, it gathered dirt and debris to itself, and found a way to live, to grow, and to thrive. Where a ribbon of black asphalt death had been, there was now a stretch of green where deer and birds and raccoons lived and fed and played, with only the occasional vehicle to whiz almost silently by, scattering them back to the forest.

Canaveral had remained relatively unscathed during the war, probably because it had been abandoned a decade earlier. The historic American spaceport had survived because it had been deemed irrelevant by a political administration that didn't value science. Now it was a temple to the very thing it was created for. Ships based on Mech designs, flat disks of various radii that could be merged to form spheres, departed and arrived almost on an hourly basis. Red could see them now, could see how they fit together. She remembered how they had moved through the sky during the war, sleek, quiet, and deliberate, like sharks in the sea. It was jarring to see them, but there they were—still sharks, but broken now, and serving humankind.

The inside of the transport disk that took her and Doolittle into space was strange. The design was more than just inhuman, it was inorganic. There were no corridors or rooms, just gaps between great blocks of machinery and circuitry. Human control panels and furniture were shoved into corners and grafted onto the machines like medical equipment plugged into a human body. It was the second clue to the true nature of the attackers that Red divined, and she quickly confronted Doolittle with her suspicions.

"The ships were autonomous. There were no invaders, no aliens, just the ships, robot ships. Why? What did they want?"

Doolittle sighed. "At first, after it was over—after we defeated them—we thought they were an advance force, drones to do somebody else's dirty work. Then we thought they were berserkers, robots programmed to seek out and destroy sentient life. Now we think they might be something more, something entirely different."

As they broke through the atmosphere, Red caught sight of the orbiting dry-dock and what was being constructed inside.

It was a ship, massive and magnificent, and despite some Mech considerations it was clearly human in design. If the Mech ships were sharks then this was a whale, a human whale.

"We call her *Leviathan*. She's the first of a dozen planned. We've started a secret shipyard in orbit around Mars. We're going to terraform the planet, too. There's a long plan, it will take hundreds of years, but we're moving off of Earth. Well, most of us."

"You said the Mechs weren't berserkers but something different. What did you mean?"

"We've reviewed the programming traces that were left in the Mech version of computer memory. They are tens of millions of years old, maybe more. They seek out life, sentient life, and then wait for it to develop a post-industrial, pre-space culture. Then they devastate it. They take it to the brink to clear away the past and give the survivors a blank slate—a chance at a new life, a new way of living. We didn't defeat the Mechs. They stopped. They destroyed our world and then just went into a hibernation mode, waiting for us to take them over." There was sadness in her voice. "The people who we have thinking about this are calling them Darwins because they force life to evolve, to become something more, to move off planet and out amongst the stars."

Red moved her eyes away from *Leviathan* and back toward the planet below. From out here you couldn't see the damage that had been done to the world. Probably because there hadn't been that much damage done to the actual world. The damage had been done to the human race, and the world itself was healing. Humanity, what was left of it, wasn't a burden anymore.

She reached out a finger and touched the window, but from her point of view she was touching Florida, her home, her prison. "Its not just the Complex. It's the whole world, isn't it? The whole world is a baby factory."

"It may have been for a long time." Doolittle came up behind her and stared at the planet slowly spinning beneath them. "We think the Mechs were watching us, maybe even influencing our development for millennia." She put a hand on Red's shoulder. "We set up the Sisterhood and the Complexes to salvage what we could, to protect young women from the dangers of a world in upheaval. It was a terrible thing to do to you, but it was necessary. Your time in the Complex was horrible, but it might have saved your life."

Red looked at Doolittle, and saw her own sadness reflected guiltily in the eyes of the other woman. "You have no idea what it was like. How horrible it was. To be forced to do that, to become nothing more than a machine for babies—did you have to be so inhuman, so inhumane?"

"The world was in chaos, order needed to be restored." There was a touch of doubt in her voice. "Yes, what you were forced to do was monstrous, and I assure you that the people who devised the plan have paid for their sins. But you weren't the only one to suffer. Some of us sacrificed just as much, if not more." She rolled up her top. There were small scars on both sides of her abdomen. "I have DiGeorge Syndrome, a genetic disorder with only a low level of expression. Still, just possession of the faulty genes was justification enough for sterilization." She lowered her shirt. "It was a terrible world, and in a few short hours it was all wiped out, but we survived. We survived, not only as individuals but as a species." She stared out the window at the world below. "We're almost finished here. Another month or two, and *Leviathan* will be done. We'll be heading to Mars, and then... who knows. Care to leave all this behind?"

Somewhere in the depths of Red's mind there was a tiny glimmer. It was small and weak, but it was there and it looked a little like Mars, and a little like hope, and nothing at all like Earth.

# SPLIT SHADOW
by SL Huang

Isadora Trast split herself when she was twenty-one years old.

In the throes of major clinical depression, Isadora lay empty, the only desire she had left being to crawl out of her own skin and scrape the leftover husk free of her soul. Fortunately for Isadora, she was deemed a good candidate for just such a procedure. The doctors mapped her brain and very carefully designed the incision, neuron by neuron.

Then they split Isadora in two.

The half of Isadora who considered herself the real Isadora, the true one, woke up cured. She took a deep breath and looked around and burst out crying, because the world was beautiful again, and she loved her sister again, and she wanted to go out and feel the sun on her face and travel to places she'd never seen and look at beautiful things and hear music and have a boyfriend and get her PhD in mycology and live and love and grieve and *feel* again In other words, she wanted to live happily ever after, and for the most part, she did.

This story is not about Isadora.

Modern medicine was a miracle. Neural splitting had created a treatment where none existed for the most recalcitrant of mental and neurological illnesses. But it left an inconvenient side effect— namely, the other half of the person.

Most so-called shades—to the great relief of a populace who would rather not think about them—died within a few hours of the splitting. After all, the doctors excised as little as possible, and usually too little of the original brain imprinted to make any sort of whole person.

Sometimes, however, the procedure ended with both a healthy, cured person and also with a copy who was the most desperate, sickest parts of them trapped in an identical body. This result was undesirable and, when it happened, entirely awkward for all involved.

Isadora's shade was one of the ones who lived.

She woke up in the hospital and knew immediately what she was. She had all Isadora's memories, after all. She woke and sagged under the desperate weight of nothing that sank against her from toes to chin, and *knew*.

The standard treatment for someone with major depression was splitting. But Isadora's shade was already only half a person—the bad half. The depression couldn't be split out of her; it was all she was.

"I hate it when they live," she overheard one of the hospital orderlies saying to another outside her room.

"She won't last long," the orderly's companion answered. Grimly.

Isadora's shade supposed that was true. People died of depression. People died of depression when it was a lot less severe than hers.

(It wasn't really fair to call it suicide, was it? When you died of an illness? She supposed she didn't care. She'd be dead.)

A doctor came in and explained what Isadora's shade already knew. Her other half got to go on, healed and whole, and live.

Isadora's shade didn't even have her sister anymore to drag her up and demand she go see a doctor because, *by golly, you're too important to me, Izz*. She had no friends, no family, no one who cared whether she lived or died: all of those people were celebrating a newly-healed Izzy.

Isadora's shade supposed she'd have to go by Dora.

"You're free to go," the doctor said. His mouth puckered down, twisting shut on the pessimism of her future.

"No," Dora said to the ceiling. "No. I need help."

The doctor's face folded in even more. "Miss, we can't split you again. It wouldn't..."

"There are other treatments," Dora said. "I know there are. The cases who aren't bad enough to split, they still do medicines. Behavioral therapies."

"Miss," said the doctor. "The state you're in... The severity means it's unlikely you'd respond well—or at all—to any more traditional treatment."

Dora did not have the will to argue her case. Fortunately, she also did not have the will to move. "I'm just going to keep lying here," she said. "Someone will admit me eventually."

The doctor opened and closed his mouth a few times. He couldn't exactly make the argument that she wasn't sick, which she assumed he'd have to do to get her forcibly removed. He was too professional to say what she knew he was thinking: that she was only drawing out the inevitable end of a meaningless existence.

Being cruel to herself.

Dora supposed she probably was. She couldn't bring herself to care at the moment.

*

They admitted Dora to the hospital. They put her in a double room that looked like the barest example of a college dormitory. She didn't have a roommate; the other bed stayed empty.

Dora lay on her bed and figured this was all right. She wouldn't have been able to handle finding somewhere to live on the outside, anyway.

She lay on the bed a lot. For most of every day.

She got assigned to a therapist. She rather suspected every word he said was slanted toward convincing her to give up, for her own sake, because as far as the mental health profession was concerned, she had already been cured.

Maybe she was just making assumptions. But who cared? Who was going to stop her?

Requesting another therapist seemed like too much work anyway.

They tried a cocktail of medications, then adjusted it and tried another.

Eventually, some days Dora felt the motivation to get up and dress. Her therapist slowly started to seem like he wasn't just chattering at her irrelevantly, but saying things she had a hope of applying to her life.

One day, she realized she had room for a goal again. But only one, so she decided working on the depression eating her brain was a pretty good one. The next seventeen days in a row, she got up out of bed.

On the eighteenth day, they discharged her.

\*

Dora's therapist, who turned out to be not nearly as out of touch as she'd pegged him for at first, had helped her make sure her disability paperwork was in place before he signed off on her discharge. He'd also carefully waited until she'd had the stamina to make calls about a small apartment. She moved two blocks away and continued with daily appointments. Every few weeks she missed one, when she couldn't get herself out the door.

"I'm never going to get all the way better, am I?" she asked her therapist one day, a few months later. "This is what I am."

He paused. "Do you know the history of mental illness?"

"A little. Not much."

"Before splitting, for a lot of patients there was no cure," her therapist told her. "But just because there's no cure for something doesn't mean we can't treat it. I don't think... I think splitting has in some ways done us a disservice, with this sense of black and white, cured and not cured. Plenty of physical conditions are chronic ones that require management, and yours is no different." He leaned forward, resting his elbows on his knees and folding his hands together. "Dora, you can manage this. You can build a good life through it. Don't let it define you."

*But it does define me*, Dora thought. And then, because she felt rotten and she wanted him to feel rotten, too, she said it aloud. "It does define me. It's literally who I am. Thinking I could become a whole person—how can you tell me that isn't hubris?"

He shrugged. "We only call something hubris when people fail. The rest of the time we call it impressive."

*

Dora kept up her routine, because she didn't really have anything else to do. But she also started making it out to the library once every month or so. She took out books, brought them back to her small apartment, and read them. Slowly. Sometimes they went overdue, and she paid the fines out of her disability checks.

"I think I might have space for another goal," she said to her therapist. "Not something big. But I want to want something, other than getting better."

"That sounds like a fine idea," he said.

"I want to help other shades," Dora said.

Her therapist hesitated. "That is very, very admirable of you, Dora. But... I think you should be prepared. Many shades are difficult people, and—some of them don't get any better. Make sure you're prepared. Don't invest in others at the expense of yourself."

Dora nodded. "I'll try to be careful. I just... I need some more meaning."

"Then I think you should do it."

*

Dora had seen a signup sheet for use of the library classroom. She asked the librarians if she could hold a support group there. They gave their blessing, so she wrote "support group" on the sheet and posted a notice online.

She meant to buy some cookies for the first meeting, but she ran out of energy.

When the appointed day came, she sat alone in the classroom, waiting. She didn't know whether she wanted people to show up or whether she wanted nobody to show up so she could go home and lie watching TV for nine hours.

A young white man wearing a brightly-colored scarf poked his head in. "Is this the group for second-class citizens?"

"For shades, yes," Dora said. She got up and came to shake his hand. "I'm Dora."

"Billy. So what happened to you, darling?" He said the endearment like she was his sister in confidence, not like a come-on.

"Depression," Dora said. "I am depression personified." It made her want to giggle for some reason. She wasn't sure she'd ever laughed, not since being Dora. "What about you?"

"Oh, I'm gay," Billy said.

For a long moment Dora thought he was making a joke, one she couldn't figure out. Splitting was strictly regulated and reserved only for the most severe medical conditions. Back-alley procedures, people exchanging stacks of cash for the mutilation of their own brains... Dora had assumed those were ghost stories. "You mean you were split because...? But that's illegal!"

"Of course it is," Billy said. "And most days if you ask me, my bastard of an original got the rotten end of the stick, taking me out of him. But then other days I wonder if there is literally anything else to me than a sexual orientation, and I want to kill myself." He choked. "Oh! Oh my god, I wasn't thinking. I'm the worst! I'm so sorry!"

"It's okay," Dora said. She continued to think about suicide, probably always would, but it was passing thoughts now, like an old touchstone she held onto for security. "I'm okay. Don't worry about it."

A black woman came in and hesitated with her back to the wall, her posture very straight. She was almost run over by a middle-aged lady who burst in right behind her.

Emboldened by meeting Billy, Dora stepped forward. "Hi. I'm Dora. Depression."

The middle-aged woman shook her hand enthusiastically. "Myrna. I'm an alcoholic."

The black woman came over, too, unsmiling. "Liddy," she said. "I was in the war."

Dora cleared her throat. She hadn't really planned out a next step. "Why don't we all sit down?"

\*

"Do any of you, um, check up on your originals?" Billy asked.

"They don't want nothing to do with us," Myrna said. "Don't want to remember we exist. Why should I care about her? I don't wanna see her running around all happy, not even thinking about booze. It's shit."

Billy hunched his feet up onto a rung of the chair. "Maybe it's different with my guy. I'm pretty sure he screwed himself. I mean, what did he get from it anyway? It's not like cutting out the gay was going to magically make him straight. I used to *be* him, and trust me, he doesn't have latent lady-love lurking below all the queer. I'm not even convinced he doesn't still like men—he just gave me all the flaming bits. So I keep looking him up, hoping to catch him being miserable."

"It sounds like you're the person and he's the copy," Liddy said quietly. "If so, you're luckier than the rest of us."

"Lucky?" Billy's voice went small. "I'm a ball of everything William Raymond hated about himself. He hated me so much he paid thousands of dollars for black-market surgery to cut me out of him. These pieces he built me out of—they shouldn't even make a whole person. I'm a stereotype. A caricature." He hugged his knees and hunched over them. "I don't think I'm lucky."

Myrna laughed hoarsely. "Well, you know what they say. Living well is the best revenge."

Her voice echoed awkwardly in the room. Her words weren't slurred, but Dora was sitting next to her, and could smell the liquor on her breath.

"Let's make a pact, then," Dora said into the silence. "We live well." The words sounded so absurd that she hastily amended, "Or, we live. And if not always well, we still live, and make our own lives."

"I can dig that," Billy said. His voice was still small.

Liddy nodded.

"I'm already living well," Myrna said. "I'm living the life. It's all uphill from here."

Dora swallowed. "Let's exchange phone numbers. For support." She made sure to meet Myrna's eyes. "Call me day or night, okay?"

*

They kept meeting in the library. Sometimes one of them missed. Sometimes all of them missed. A few other shades joined them, and the group grew. Sometimes Dora called Billy or Myrna or Liddy at two in the morning, and sometimes one of them called her.

"We sort of... muddle through," Dora told her therapist. "It's good. I think."

Five months later, Dora got a call from the hospital. In the first heart-clenching moment, she felt sure it was about Myrna. But it wasn't.

Dora, Myrna, and Billy all rushed to the emergency room. Dora had an instant to hope Myrna had called a taxi to get there before they were all occupied with accosting the staff for details of Liddy's condition.

The staff refused to give them any information, of course. They weren't family.

"She doesn't have any family," Dora said. "She's a shade. We're all she's got."

"She's a shade?" The nurse looked down at the chart, and her face smoothed out in understanding. "Right. Of course," she added, almost to herself.

Myrna punched her.

Thirty minutes of crisis control followed. Dora dragged a screaming Myrna back while Billy tried to talk down the furious nurse, who was shouting about being assaulted. Dora left him to it and pushed Myrna in the direction of the cafeteria, where she plied her with buckets of coffee. "Here. Sober up."

"I'm plenty sober," Myrna snapped. "Did you hear what she said about Liddy? Our Liddy? If she'd said that about one of my kids, I—" Her voice broke. Her kids weren't hers anymore.

"Enough people think shades are dangerous," Dora said. "Don't give them an excuse." She didn't say what else they both knew: too many people thought shades should be locked up, or put down. If the nurse pressed charges, no prosecutor would ever assume the best of a shade—Myrna could go to jail tonight, for a long time. Dora tried not to think about it.

Tried not to think about anything.

"She better not die," Myrna said. "She better not, you hear?"

*

Liddy didn't die. Dora and Billy crowded in around her bed as soon as she woke up—Myrna had been temporarily banned from the hospital, fortunately without the involvement of the police.

"Hey," Billy said, as soon as Liddy's eyelids twitched open. "We're here. Hey. You're okay."

She closed her eyes again and turned her face away.

"You're in the hospital," Dora tried. "They said you were in a car accident. Do you remember?"

"I remember," Liddy said, after a long moment. "Stupid. I hit too slow."

Billy grabbed Liddy's hand and started speed-talking, his soothing words belied by the horrified way he pelted them at her. Liddy lay stiff, still facing away from them.

Dora stumbled blindly out of the room and called her therapist at his home.

"We're all an inch away," she sobbed hysterically into the phone. "An inch away from killing ourselves, or losing control, or—"

"Breathe, Dora. Just concentrate on breathing for a minute. Let's just get through tonight."

"Why?" Dora demanded recklessly. "There'll always be another tonight. And another, and another."

"But there will be days that aren't," her therapist said. "And you deserve them the same as any other person."

*

Liddy never talked about that night.

Dora tried to insist on staying with her after she got out of the hospital, but she refused. The suspense before she walked into their support group the next day made Dora's throat knot up until she couldn't swallow.

But then Liddy limped in, laid her crutches against a chair, and sat down, like it was any other day.

51

They talked, and Liddy said nothing, and said nothing, and responded to everyone's questions with "fine," until Billy finally lost it on her. "I can't take it!" he screamed, on his feet. "You can't—you can't do this to us, I can't be just sitting here waiting for something to happen to you, I *can't!*"

"Okay," Liddy said.

"If you're going to—if you're—you need to tell me, so I can stop *caring* about you, because I can't—you can't ask us to live like this," Billy pleaded.

"I didn't plan it," Liddy said. "It was just... that moment."

"Do you have a lot of moments?" Billy asked.

"Sometimes."

"Are you at least back to, to—to *not* having one?" Billy had started crying, but he didn't seem the least bit ashamed.

"Yeah," Liddy said.

Billy sat back down. And that was the most Dora ever heard Liddy say about it.

*

Myrna died two and a half years later, the week after they celebrated her fifty-second birthday. Dora thanked any god that existed that Myrna did it at home, alone with her bottle, instead of on the road where she might have taken someone with her.

"What's this going to do to me?" Dora asked her therapist, the day after it happened, while she was still waiting for the reality to hit her.

"You'll grieve," he said. "You've been managing for a long time. I think you'll be able to grieve, and recover. And I'll be here to help you. Call me any time."

"I'll take you up on that," Dora said.

Almost everyone from the support group came to the funeral. There were over fifty of them now. A lot of people cried. Dora wondered if they were sobbing for Myrna, or in fear of their own lack of future.

Dora stood up to speak. "Myrna Elise Johnson lived every day for over three years," she said. "She lived. Every. One. Of those days. She lived."

She sat down.
Liddy stood up. Started clapping.
Slowly, everyone else did, too.

*

While shelving books as a volunteer at the library, Dora met a young man who smiled a lot and liked reading terrible thrillers. They went out for coffee, and then for dinner. On the third date she told him she was a shade.

Her mouth dried up as she did it.

"Oh!" he said. "Oh. Does that, I mean. Does it mean anything?"

"No," Dora said. "I just thought you should know."

She broke up with him after a few months, because he bored her and was unimaginative in bed. "I'm so used to being afraid other people will judge *me*," she told her therapist. "I thought I'd be grateful for anyone who wanted to talk to me."

He smiled. "Welcome to the world. Where you get to be as judgmental as everyone else."

Dora laughed. She did that now, sometimes.

*

Liddy met and married another vet, a woman who hadn't been split. They moved to Arizona. Dora and Billy took road trips to visit them.

"You're pregnant!" Dora said, one hot desert day when Liddy opened the door with a belly as big as a house.

"Twins," Liddy said. "Janice's brother is the donor. I wasn't sure a shade could—but the doctors said they didn't see why not, and Janice said we should try it."

"I'm just hurt you didn't ask me," Billy said. "How am I going to pass on my dashing good looks now?"

"We hope... we talked, and we'd like you both to be godparents," Liddy said. "Will you?"

Billy crowed and tackled her with a hug. "That's better than asking for my jizz! Of course, you goose!"

"I'd like that, too," Dora said.

*

Dora kept volunteering at the library, and one day they told her a part-time paid position had opened up. They asked if she would like it. She said yes.

She showed up on time, mostly, and went out to coffee with her coworkers after. Some days, at least.

*

On a crisp fall day in late October, Dora got a call telling her that her therapist had passed away.

He was healthy. Still young.

He hadn't ever been split.

Heart attack, they said.

Dora curled up at home and cried and didn't move for three days. She missed work and ignored all phone calls and wrapped her dirty pajamas around her as if that would help. As if anything would help.

Billy came banging on her door.

"Go away," she shouted.

"No," he said, and kept knocking.

Eventually she dragged herself up and opened it. He barged in, wrinkled his nose, and started picking up her apartment. "First things first, hon. Have you been taking your meds?"

"Yes," she said, sulkily.

"Good. Now let's get you through a shower. I'm not taking no for an answer."

He shooed her into the bathroom, and when she came out red and warm as a lobster, he'd remade her bed and tidied all the dirty dishes and trash. "I fully approve of feeling sorry for yourself, under the circumstances," he said. "But you're not going to do it alone."

Dora's eyes went mushy with tears. "There was no *reason*," she sniffed. "He wasn't split. There was no reason."

Billy pulled her to him and crushed her in a hug. "I know, baby. I know."

*

Billy contacted the library, and they told Dora to take some bereavement time, that it was fine.

The hospital referred her to a new therapist. Dora sobbed her way through the first four sessions.

"At least I'm crying," she said, during the fourth one. "I can't do anything; I'm lying in bed all day, but at least I'm crying. I haven't stopped caring yet. I'm not back there."

"You're not," her new therapist said. "You're not back there at all. It's okay for this to take some time."

"I don't want to break," Dora said. "Sometimes I slide, you know? I'm always fighting, I'm always afraid, and it's so *hard*. I never know if the next time will be the one I don't come back from." She wasn't sure her tearful babbling was even understandable. "I don't want to break, but sometimes it seems like that would be easiest. Get it over with. Be done."

"Grief is normal," her new therapist said. "You can allow yourself to grieve. Do you feel like you're backsliding?"

"I don't know," Dora said. "But it's there, waiting for me. I'm built to fail."

"There comes a point when where you come from, or what your brain chemistry is, doesn't matter as much as how you live," her new therapist said.

"That's an awfully fancy way of telling me life is what I make of it," Dora said bitterly. "I don't want platitudes."

"They aren't platitudes when they have truth in them, Dora. I can already see how much you build up the people around you. You tell your friends each day, each minute, each second is an accomplishment, and I know you mean it. Let yourself see *you* that way, too."

"I don't want this much pain," Dora wailed. "I don't want it. I want to be numb again."

"No," her new therapist said. "No, you don't."

She was right, and Dora hated her for it. She contacted the hospital and requested a change. Irrationally hating and firing her first new therapist for the crime of not being her old one at least seemed like something she had control over.

*

Billy came over every day to check on her. One day, she texted him not to come because she was going in to work.

*FUCK YEAH*, he texted back. *You go, girl.*

Showering was too hard, but she combed her hair.

\*

Dora's new new therapist was an older woman whose office sported a lot of homemade crochet. For some reason she reminded Dora of Myrna, even though there was no resemblance. Maybe something in the voice.

The echo was pleasant rather than painful.

"It feels like a constant treadmill," Dora said to her. "Life. I'm getting through this, I'm going to be okay—for now—but it's exhausting, and there'll always be the next one, and I can never stop running. The only happy ending for me is to keep running until I run out the clock. It's *exhausting.*"

"I'm not going to tell you this isn't difficult, what you're doing," the new new therapist said. "You're right. You might not ever be able to relax. You might always be fighting. But think about the things that make it worth all the difficulty."

Dora thought of her friends, her job, the books she'd read. She thought of laughing at jokes and learning new facts about interesting funguses. She thought about Billy, and Liddy and Janice, and Myrna.

She *had* built something worth the trouble. The idea was almost surprising.

\*

Dora decided to get a cat. He was fluffy and brown and huge, with a smushed-in face and a purr that could wake the neighbors. She named him Mushroom.

She managed to keep her apartment cleaner, for Mushroom's sake, and when she slept, he curled up on her chest like an enormous vibrating motor.

His weight was warm. It pushed aside the other weight, the one that sometimes made it hard to stand.

\*

The support group continued, but Dora stopped going. It had a life of its own now; it didn't need her, and she felt better looking forward, living in the world.

She tried to up her hours at the library to full time, but could never quite manage it without starting to wobble. That was okay. Part-time was good.

She and Billy still had coffee every week. Dora was dating the assistant manager at their usual shop, so they got free pastries along with the coffee, which Billy happily took full advantage of.

One day Billy came in with a newspaper. "I'm trying to decide if you'll want to know this or not," he said, after the usual pleasantries.

"Know what?" Dora asked.

Billy hesitated, twitching his nose. "Do you ever think about your original?"

"No," Dora said honestly. That life didn't seem like hers. That life *wasn't* hers. "Do you?"

"Oh, yeah, I still plug him in to the old search engine sometimes, make sure hetero life is making him crazy," Billy said blithely. "But I, um. I might have looked in on yours a couple times, too. Is that—do you mind?"

Dora considered. "I guess not. She seems pretty alien at this point. What's she doing?"

"Well, she died," Billy said.

"What?"

He smoothed the folded-over newspaper on the table, the obituary page on top.

*Dr. Isadora Trast,* Dora read. *Aged forty-six. Respected scientist and professor. Loving wife, adored mother.*

"How did it happen?" she asked.

"Skiing accident," Billy answered. "Kind of a freak thing, they're saying."

"It sounds like she was happy," Dora said. She found she was glad for that. "This feels so strange. I wasn't supposed to be the one who lived."

"You both lived," Billy said, with a smile.

"Yeah," Dora said. "Yeah. We did, didn't we?"

Sunlight slanted through the window and across their table, warming her skin and transforming the passing dust motes into stars. Dora folded the paper shut and picked up a croissant.

She remembered a funny story from the library she wanted to share with Billy. And after this she'd go to work, and then home, where she'd watch a movie with her boyfriend while drinking a mug of hot chocolate with Mushroom on her lap.

The buttery flakiness of the pastry melted on her tongue.

# FUTURES PAST
by Thord D. Hedengren

It was like I'd never tasted air before, all dry and heaving. The memory of breathing came shortly afterwards and left me gasping for more, filling my lungs. It hurt, it burned, it felt like I was being torn apart.

Then my eyes exploded, or so it felt. The world thawed as I did, the medical technicians of Samarhead Cryonics pulling me back to rejoin the living.

"Don't speak yet, Mrs. Terrence," a man said. I couldn't see him, and his voice reminded me of water. "You have a tube in your throat. Your vision and hearing should be back to normal shortly."

"She got it," said another voice, out of sight. Well, not that the first one had really been in sight, but there was a silhouette, a person shape. I assumed it was him.

A third person approached, said something I couldn't hear to someone I couldn't see, and then stepped into my field of vision. My eyes were slowly starting to remember how to pass information to my brain, and I saw more of her.

"Mrs. Terrence, you're alive and well," she said. "We have successfully reinstated your bodily processes. For a little while, you'll feel vertigo, your sight and hearing will be impaired, and you'll feel strange while breathing. It's all perfectly normal. We're going to remove the tube from your throat. It'll be slightly uncomfortable, so try to relax."

A doctor, clearly. She commanded a stern voice, one used to being obeyed. Whilst I mused over it, they pulled what felt like a chain of razorblades out of me.

"Welcome back," said the stern doctor. "The emergence crew is ready for you now. Have a good long life, Mrs. Terrence."

They rolled me out of the room. Flickering lights in the ceiling, a long corridor, weird whooshy noises – it was like I was in a cheap horror movie. For a moment I was afraid, frozen stiff (and not in an ironic sense), but then I realized that this probably wasn't an abandoned hospital where criminals unfroze people from a cryonic state to torture them to death, nor was it really sporting flickering lights. The theory gained additional ground as my vision returned, and what had seemed horrifying and distorted a moment before became crisp and clean. When they rolled me into the emergence chamber, my eyesight was back to normal.

"Welcome," said a friendly voice belonging to a sharply dressed woman. Beside her was a tall man wearing an equally sharp suit, and trying to fight a smile which wanted to split his face in half. "We're so happy to have you, Mrs. Terrence," the woman continued.

I was left with the two of them, lying on my bed.

"Everything is as instructed," said the man. His voice was giddy.

"We'll be right outside," said the woman. "Just let us know if you need anything. Take your time. You might feel dizzy, but when you feel up to it, do get out of the bed. It's been long enough, hasn't it?"

I wanted to ask how long it had been, but they left in a hurry, and I couldn't find the words until after the door had shut behind them.

The white room had grey butterflies painted on the walls, and soft light came from the ceiling. It was a pleasant room, smelling faintly familiar, a reassuring place to return to reality in.

I sat up. The world span a turn or two, but then settled down. I coughed and looked around. I wondered when my ears would stop bubbling. The floor was both soft and hard, like a mattress made of concrete. My naked feet liked it, and my toes tried to grip it for some reason. I got up and nearly buckled, but found my balance in time.

There was a table and a chair in the middle of the room. A box with my name printed on it sat on the table. I fought the urge to walk over there, instead I just stood for a moment.

"Hello?" I whispered tentatively.

"Yes, Mrs. Terrence?" asked the giddy man. His voice came into the room, but he wasn't there. It didn't sound like an intercom, and I could see no speakers. "Is everything alright?"

"Yes," I said. My throat hurt. "I'm a bit thirsty."

"There's water on the table, Mrs. Terrence."

I walked over to the table. A plastic bottle of water sat by the box.

"Drink carefully," said the voice. "Don't hesitate to tell us if you need something else."

The water burned in my throat, but not so much that I considered stopping drinking it. My thirst was very real. I remembered his words though, and found the control to take small sips, consuming just half of the bottle.

I was tired and my legs ached. Some distant memory trickled back, told me that I'd often felt like this before, after running. Why I had been running so much, I couldn't say.

I sat down and looked at the box. Something nagged at the back of the head, reminded me that this was important, that this was the reason for everything.

The box contained letters in thick envelopes. A note at the top said to read the letters in order, starting at number one, then two, three, and so forth. I snorted at that, and then wondered if that was something I used to do. I wanted to ask who I was, out loud, but lingering shame stopped me. I picked up the letter labelled 'One' instead. The paper was thick and warm. It felt luxurious.

*

Dear Sass,

It's very empty without you. I keep explaining that you're just sleeping for a long time, and that it's for you to get better, but I don't think the kids are buying it to be honest. I guess that's what I have to be. Honest. In these things. This is the first that I'm writing to you, and I have no idea how to do this. It took a long time for me to finally sit down. You won again, I guess. I hope it will be a sweet victory for you. You can't know. Neither can I, right now.

I've been appointed grief counsellors, the kids too. I'm not going, but they're talking to a nice man about your "illness". I guess that's good.

I'm sorry, I can't write anymore.

Love,
Tim

*

I was pretty sure I was Sass. It was short for Cassandra, a name I had never liked.

Tim... He was my husband, I realized, with a pang of guilt and longing. We had two kids, Jeremy and Brianne. Where were they? I wanted to cry, or at least I thought that's what I was supposed to want in such a situation. But I couldn't. I felt dazed and numb, unsure of what to do. The only thing I *could* think of was picking up the next letter.

*

Dear Sass,

I can't sleep, knowing you're stowed away somewhere. It's so wrong in so many ways! You know I'm not a religious man, but I keep wanting to talk to a priest or a rabbi or an imam or whatever. Someone who could put this into perspective, because this isn't right.

The kids are asking and asking and asking and it's driving me nuts. I snapped at Jeremy today, and now that's keeping me up too. It's hard enough for me, but how about them? Talk about not fair.

We had no say in this, maybe that's it. Maybe the unfairness of it all is what's eating me inside. I keep wanting to make a glib remark now, about cooking and silver linings or something. I'm too tired for this I guess.

Love,
Tim

--

Dear Sass,

I love you.

- T

--

Dear Sass,

Brianna is growing up fast. She's taking on responsibilities at home, with Jeremy, and the dog too. Shopping for groceries, remembering to plan for laundry, all those things I suck at. She's really helping out. I'm proud of her, and you would be too.

Jeremy keeps asking when you'll get better. Some kid in his school said that when his dad was in the hospital for a long time, he died. He's scared, the poor thing, and he's not managing too well. It's been two months.

Different people are handling this differently. Your mom called and cried for five minutes, then she hung up. I've thrown away so many flowers and condolence letters lately it's crazy. People love you, or at least they used to. They don't know what you've done though, like I do. That'd change things I guess.

I'm considering going to the doctors to see what they can do, get a second opinion, tear up this whole thing. It has gotten out of hand.

Love,
Tim

*

I sat back, puzzled. It took minutes, I thought – I wasn't really sure how long – until I mustered enough courage to speak out to the room.

"What's going on here?"

"It's all according to the program, Mrs. Terrence," said the man. He was clearly monitoring the room.

"What program?" I asked.

"The one you decided on, of course."

"I decided on a box with letters?"

"Yes, Mrs. Terrence. That's not the way we usually do things here, but your situation is special. It's a bit cruel, the letters, but we often use outside media, mostly audiovisual, to help ease the patient back into her life."

It made sense, I thought, and there was nothing there that sounded like a lie. Somewhere in the back of my head, I knew this was according to my wishes. There was more to it than that, but it would have to wait. I turned my attention back to the letters.

*

Dear Sass,

It's been a while. A long time, actually. Where to begin? I went through a rough patch. It got pretty bad. The kids are at your mother's, but I'm gonna get them back soon. It was a mutual decision, it'll be fine. I think.

I'm seeing a grief counsellor. She's nice, makes me think and talk things through.

There are nights where the pills can't knock me out, and I can't take the stronger ones anymore, they interfere with my work. I got a prescription for morning uppers, but that made me shake and I don't like that. I looked like a junkie for a week, then I gave up on it. You would've laughed.

I can't remember how your laugh sounds anymore. There are pictures of you everywhere, but they're starting to seem unreal. It's like I'm living in a mausoleum, and I'm getting used to it.

All for you.

Love,
Tim

*

She's *nice?*

*

Dear Sass,

Journalists showed up on our doorstep today. I couldn't figure out why they wanted to talk to us so badly, and then I understood. It got so bad that I had to take the kids away. We went to the country.

I can't believe it's been three years already. There are stories about you in the papers. I keep them from the kids as best as I can, but I think Brianne suspects something.

Jeremy cries a lot. The tension is too much.

I'm having a hard time with this right now. A really hard time.

- T

*

It hit me like a sledgehammer swung by a giant with the arms of an orang-utan.

*Three years? I've been gone for three years?*

Several times I started to phrase questions to the people behind the walls, but in the end I let them be. I had the distinct feeling that they wouldn't tell me anything anyway, that this was how it was supposed to be, and that I just had to live through it. There was a tight knot in my stomach, and it was creaking with anxiety. I was missing something fundamental, and I was starting to panic about it.

The next letter was thin, just one page. I hoped for the best.

\*

Dear Sass,

I, no we, can't take this much longer. I'm seeking help. I won't write to you anymore.

Love,
Tim

\*

The lump in my throat wouldn't go away with water. But there were more letters. I didn't cry.

\*

Mom,

The doctors say you won't get better unless we write to you, and dad is too tired. I'll write to you, but I don't know what to say.

School is OK. I have to study more math. I'm not sure why I'm telling you this, but you always seemed to want to know. And now I can't take it back. They don't let us take words back.

I'm not playing tennis anymore.

I miss you, Mom. Get better soon. Please.

Hugs,
Jeremy

\*

*Why did you quit tennis, Jeremy? You loved tennis, you used to play it all the time, talk about it all the time. Even your comic books and video games were about tennis. Did you quit because you were too sad to play?*

66

I stood up and stretched, cracked my back, and immediately gasped for air. Stiff. To be expected from someone coming out of a freezer, I supposed. My mind reminded me of that in the darkest way. I walked around the table, strangely blank and calm.

*Why did you quit tennis, Jeremy?*

And I broke.

\*

I came to in a bed. Clean white linen, starch with a hint of coarseness on my skin. It felt familiar, the first thing that had, in what had to be a long time. I knew I wasn't in that previous room anymore, the one with the table and the box. I wasn't in the room I'd awoken in either. This was a new space. I didn't want to open my eyes, but I did it, because who wanted to live their life in the dark?

"Are you feeling better, Mrs. Terrence?"

It was the same doctor, the man in the sharp suit, but not so giddy anymore. He sat there with a glowing piece of glass in his hands.

"Yes," I lied.

"When you're ready then," he said, and nodded towards a door in the far end of the room. He disappeared out the other door. I heard him lock it from the other side – possibly trying to do it quietly, but I could tell.

There was no getting away from it. I wanted to run, I wanted to leave, but I was afraid to ask. What if they'd just let me go? What of the box, the letters, the truth?

I didn't ask why this was happening. I didn't ask anything at all.

In the other room, the box and the letters sat there on the table, where I'd left them. I slumped into the chair, already exhausted. I sat there for the longest time, thinking about nothing at all.

Then I picked up the next letter.

\*

Mom,

Maybe I would understand better if someone told me, but Dad's gone stone-face, and you're not here. I know this is bullshit. I know you're not sick, Mom. I didn't want to play this game, but they say that the more we write – these stupid fucking letters – the more we get to know. I'm not sure I want to know, or would like knowing, but there's not much choice now is there?

Let me make one thing very clear: This is your fault, Mom. You did this. All of it. Your choice. I'm sure of it, not how or why, but I'm sure of it. But no one will tell me.

So here goes. Yeah. Mom, I'm alive and well. I get by without you being here. I've had my period, I'm not a virgin, and I take recreational drugs. You would hate the clothes I wear and the music I listen to. My boyfriend wants to fuck me in the ass and I'm going to let him.

See how much I care?

- Brianne

\*

I felt numb. Choked. Too tired to cry. It wasn't what my daughter wrote, lashing out to hurt me, but how she'd done it. That wasn't her, not my sweet baby girl. I refused to think about how the years without me had changed her. I almost didn't want to look in the box for more letters, but I had to, I must, because if this was the last one, then I'd know nothing more, nothing else, and there would have been no point.

I was finally crying as I picked up the penultimate letter.

\*

I love you.

- T

\*

That felt better. That felt about right. Tim's expression of love felt real, but it couldn't wash away the lingering feelings of Brianne's hurtful words. I reread his letter over and over again, willing myself to believe it, to bask in his expression of love.

I longed for closeness, but I knew I wouldn't get it. I remembered deciding that this was the way it should be, for some reason. All of this was by my design, my choice – and the people in this building, the doctors and who-knew else looking at me through unseen cameras, they were just carrying out my will. In my darkest place, I knew I'd done this to myself, and that it had been a very conscious and calculated decision.

One last letter.

*

Dear Sass,

There's no easy way to say this, but please understand that it had to be done. We, me and the kids, we were in a really bad place. We got help and we found something resembling happiness again. Not a normal life really, just something we could live with. It didn't hurt so much anymore, and then it hurt less. The only fear we had was the requests for letters to you. They came irregularly, and it haunted us.

I tried to drown it. Brianne tried to end it. Jeremy tried to forget it. Somehow we all lived through that, and I'm thanking all gods I can think of that we all failed in our own way.

I love you, but I can't do this anymore. You stole the normality from our lives with your art project, so it's only fair that I take it back. What's not so fair is that I'm stealing the rest of your life in our time in order to do so. When they wake you up, you've been in cryogenic stasis for 52 years. I'll be dead. The kids will have different names and be somewhere else, living their own lives. They won't be your pawns anymore, and neither will I.

I wish you well, we all do, but this is the way it's going to have to be. We have to settle for a past without you. Best of luck in the future.

I loved you.

- Tim

\*

Salty tears snuck into the corners of my mouth as I sat there, smiling widely. Memories started clawing their way back. He'd done it. He'd actually done it!

I looked up, wondering where the cameras were. This was going to be the best installation yet, and who could say what opportunities I'd have to present it in a new day and age? What should've been years had become decades, and my responses – everything the cameras and sensors could pick up – had surely been amplified accordingly. And Tim was a genius, he'd really gotten it! His final decision was the *piece de resistance* of the project. Amazing.

I tried not to think about what I'd lost – no, given up. It wasn't important.

Only the art mattered.

# THE PSYCHOMETRY OF TUVAN CURRENCY
by Tricia Sullivan

"Is a long way to go for meet with journalist who will mock you," Papi says.

"You don't know he'll mock me."

"He'll mock you for being backward. I know."

Candara's sweat blooms with effort. She's so hungry, and she feels the weight of the scavenged dead in her shopping cart as the grade of the road increases. In the brightness of the augmented reality field cast by Candara's dangling ARings, Nani knits and sings little songs, and Papi is carving a microscope out of balsa wood. They walk slow. The ARings are green jade and Candara can't remember the last time she took them out of her ears. They are her only personal adornment, bar the pinkie ring she inherited from Nani.

"If you would stop collecting so much rubbish it wouldn't be so hard to get up this hill. Look at me! Everything I own in one little valise." Nani holds up her scuffed leather carryall.

"I'm grateful for that, Nani," Candara says. And she is. Candara's dead hardly weigh a thing. They have folded their own existence and that of her deep ancestors like a pocket map, and they go everywhere she goes. They only complain 98.2% of the time. They also pray for her and sing for her; sometimes it's only their singing that keeps Candara going. The shopping cart gets heavier by the day.

"You collect too much junk," Papi echoes. "You should only take what is useful."

"It's not junk. It's research for my thesis."

"Was your thesis. Fifty-seven years ago. Now is your sickness."

The cart is piled with coffee mugs, ballpoint pens, wool hats, well-thumbed mobile phones and hand-me-down pocket-knives, each retaining some essence of its owner's identity. Suffering and history and hope have been scribed into their materials by subtle processes. Candara wrote a psychometric signature detection app during her student years, and now she can hear the ghosts calling to her from charity shop windows and junk heaps. Her life's like an ectoplasmic Antiques Road Show.

Everywhere she goes she drags a cavalcade of strangers' ghosts like a bridal train. They dance and revel, lending her field a circus atmosphere. The ghosts are unclaimed by biological family, absent from the global database. Candara can't afford to translate them into permanent archives, and they aren't historically interesting enough for the universities to want them.

She had planned to finance their storage through including them in her thesis on family breakdown, but to do that she would have to finish the thesis. It became impossible to do that because other people's dead dragged on her resources; with an overcrowded AR field she could neither sell her own processing time, nor perform the analysis necessary to complete her academic work. Earning money became a scrabble and her life spiralled down from there.

She could have been an academic. Now she's the crazy cat lady of the unclaimed dead.

"You're a servant to phantasms," Nani sniffs.

"These ghosts are as real as any abstract system that we live in—more real, because they once were flesh and blood. Surely it is currency itself that's the phantasm, Nani."

Candara's out of breath from saying all that. She pauses, taking off her knit cap because her head is sweating. A group of passing tourists edge around her, no eye contact. Except one, who puts a coin in her upturned cap, thinking she is begging. She scrunches the cap and stuffs it in her pocket, mortified.

And Nani says, "If you had some currency you might not smell so much."

"You can't smell me, Nani."

"I can. You smell of B.O. and you smell of dead things."

It's an old gripe. Every time Candara picks up a new item from a boot sale, Papi says, "You can't save everyone." He says, "In this life you have to look out for yourself."

Finally Candara reaches the café. The journalist is already there, conspicuously chatting to people no-one else can see. She recognises him because he is slightly famous.

"—dangers of AR," he is saying. "It enhances lives but also destroys them. Yes, Candara Vasylenko... promising historiographer until her life was progressively destroyed by AR hoarding addiction. Well, I think it's important—"

"You could be like him." Nani prods Candara with a knitting needle. The journalist's skin is ripe, his hair shines; he is a vision in Fair-trade cotton and important conversations.

This man is carrying nothing. He can afford an AR driver so powerful that he can interact with the living no matter how far away they may be, and with the abstract—no matter how far-fetched. Interestingly, he has blocked his own dead. He's spiritually unencumbered. No reconstructed great-great-grandparents hanging on him. No illnesses or recreant DNA, either; even his gut bacteria are in perfect working order. He has no imprinted objects entrusted to him—no family wristwatch or cufflinks, nothing handed down. Of course, unlike Candara he has no need to wear earmuffs for those occasions when the objects' ghosts spontaneously scream in remembered agony.

"—Saba, I'm telling you, the story is more compelling than it sounds. My personal involvement? I don't see how that's necessary..."

When Candara's grandchildren were small she taught them to make a spine out of marshmallows and biscuits. It was flexible and sweet. There is no more cushioning in Candara's spine; it is coiled and stiff now as a dry leather whip. No more sugar. She holds her head as high as she can.

While she is standing there, still panting and contemplating her own smell, the wagon-train of her adopted dead comes to a staggered halt behind her, with sagging carriages bumping into donkeys bumping into children bumping into old ones in their wheelchairs until the vectors of their motion collapse into a sort of Brownian cloud. Buses and cars pass right through them, no probs. The wind of this lifts Candara's shawl. It brings café smells: cinnamon and coffee.

"You're hungry," Nani observes, sharply. "You forget you're not dead yet."

Candara has two teeth left. One is a lower molar and one is a lower incisor. The incisor has taken to slipping over her thin upper lip and jutting out in a yellow curve. It makes her look stubborn. That and the little white beard: the gifts of a long life.

She is older now than Nani ever lived to be, but Nani bosses her anyway. "If this man could see you as you once were, ah what curves you used to have! And your hair! He would be not so full of himself. I'd like to get in his field and show him—"

"Nani, please don't!"

"Don't what?"

"Don't mess with his perceptions."

"You need to eat."

"Not like that."

"Is a fair transaction," Nani sniffs. "Besides, he mistreat his dead."

"How do you know anything about his dead? He's blocked them all."

Nani makes an impatient noise that is exclusive to the dead. "My point exactly. Go on. Let me help you. Is what I'm here for."

"I'll make my own way," Candara says, scratching a louse bite. But the journalist turns his head and catches sight of her. The look on his face.

"Told you," says Nani. "Ask him for money. You need to eat."

"Good evening. I'm Gerald. Are you Candara?" The slightly famous man pulls out a chair for her. Oh, he has beautiful pores. So clean. "You look faint. A beautiful woman should not fall in the street."

Candara doesn't sit. It would be too hard to get back up again.

He orders wine and the waiter brings bread and flavoured oil and a candle. Candara's reek rises around her; other café patrons move away. The slightly famous man moves closer, pupils wide. He seems in a trance, as if he doesn't know where he is. Even after all these years she recognises the expression of a man who thinks he's in love.

"You should turn off the app you're running, Gerald," she tells him. "There's a fault in your AR."

She positions her hand near the bread, getting ready to seize it and run. She hopes to get some of it in her mouth before she is caught. Even a mouthful would be better than nothing.

"Forgive me for staring," he breathes. "I know it's inappropriate, but I can't seem to stop myself. You are incredible."

Candara rolls her eyes. Nani is so predictable. Voyeuristic, too. The lascivious dead.

"I do apologise," Gerald says. Then he begins to wank. For a few moments no one notices, but he's not subtle about it. After he gets going he forgets everything and stands up, legs apart, fly down and cock in the air, head thrown back, arm jamming up and down in a frenzy. He gives no indication that he's anywhere other than the privacy of his own fantasy.

This sort of thing wasn't unusual in the early days of AR. Now it is passé, a bit pathetic. Either his hardware is faulty, or he has hyper-extended from his body to the point where he's easy to hack.

People move away, more annoyed than shocked. With an obligatory air, a tourist takes video. Candara is the closest person to the unfortunate wanker but no one else seems to notice her or her wagon train.

She grabs the bread and is just about to chuck it in the shopping cart and push off when everything goes horribly wrong. Trouble is, Gerald is whacking off so hard in AR that he rips his actual member off.

From the department of new problems: the slightly famous man stands holding shrinking meat in his hand, staring down into its sightless eye as his face whitens. The hole that his penis used to plug is as wide as the body of one of those single-sized wine bottles, the kind Candara has on special occasions with fishcakes and tinned peas. His burgundy drains into the gutter.

This doesn't happen every day. People are running around. The man's knees give and he falls. Someone tries to stop the

75

bleeding with a tea-towel from the café. There is blood all over Candara. As the slightly famous man lies face-down on the road he stretches one hand toward her, the one with the penis in it. He flops it in her direction.

"Sorry," he says. "Been under a lot of pressure..."

Then he faints.

"Nani, this is unacceptable," Candara says.

"I didn't do it! I didn't do it!" Nani hisses, lifting up her yarn to avoid the blood. "I swear it wasn't me."

Candara steps over the little red river best she can, but the train of her shawl drags in the body fluid and paints the dry pavement behind her for several meters. In this momentary interaction between her field and his, his blocking app must slip. It must miss a beat, because all of a sudden the man's dead and his neverborn possibility-children are rising up in Candara's AR field like just-add-water freeze-dried cartoon Martians. They sprout from the bloodstains and run after her with the hollow vitality of beggars. *Please save us*, they say in tiny voices. *Take us with you.*

She pulls Nani's old shawl over her hair so she won't hear them. An ambulance is screaming. The vehicle passes right through Candara's collection of scavenged objects and her old men muttering over their chessboard. She legs it—any moment she'll be arrested, she knows how these things go. Gasping, sweating, joints protesting, she pushes the trolley away from the scene.

Still the slightly famous man's dead chase after her. One lady is dressed in her Sunday best, pillbox hat on her head with its miniature veil. Well-thumbed black rosary. She has papery Celtic skin and a quavering voice that has screamed after dozens of children to put on their coats. She tugs at Candara's shawl.

*"Don't blame your Nani, darling. We had to do something. He has turned us away for years. He fed off us and gave nothing back. We only want a place to shelter. We heard you're easy. Look at all these possibility-children. Surely you want them."*

Candara shudders at the proposition. Like ancestor, like son.

"She not want." Nani is standing there between Candara and the blood phantom. "My granddaughter she can't take on no more. Look at great big shopping cart she pushes!"

The slightly famous man's ancestor peers inside at the ghost-laden objects.

*"Oh, my,"* she says. *"What heavy archives you have. It's just that the lad was such a disappointment. We hardly know where to go."*

Nani clasps the other ghost's hands in her own. The other ghost is wearing hundred-year-old white gloves, but Nana's hands are fleshy and muscled with work, and even in death you can feel the heat of them. The other ghost blinks in dismay at such bald intimacy.

"You take it all much too far," Nani says in her nice voice that isn't really nice. "And of all the body parts not to attack! You better hope they can sew back on or you got trouble."

*"Just hear me out,"* says the other ghost. *"If Gerald doesn't come up with a story soon, his boss will sack him."*

"Good," Candara retorts. "Then Gerald will have to give his fancy AR drive back. He won't be able to block you anymore."

*"He wouldn't be a credit to us anymore, either,"* says the dead woman, her blue eyes snapping. *"So maybe we can help each other. You can give him his story, and he can arrange to store your dead."*

"I can't give him any story. I'm just a person."

*"You're the story of a man who got seduced by a woman who looks like a decrepit, ugly goat. You prowl the city, pretending to be an innocent young girl and then making heterosexual men rip off their own... Well, you saw what happened."*

Candara starts to laugh but ends up coughing up some rubbery phlegm.

"You're telling me you made him rip off his own cock on purpose? *To get attention?"*

*"We did what we had to do."*

"But it's impossible. He blocked you. Nani, you said Gerald blocked his dead."

"They use *your* field, liebz," Nani says in that same too-gentle tone. She doesn't have to say the rest: *I keep telling. You too wide open. Everybody use you. I tell you how many times?*

*"Just play along, dear. You will naturally go to jail, but not for very long and I'll tell you, I wouldn't exaggerate about this: it's nicer there. They'll take your ARings away, of course, and your other bits and pieces. But it will be better for you than this."*

Candara feels the tide of her own blood rising to the insult, but then the ghost adds:

*"And we'll kindly store your dead for you. I can see you're a gentle soul. We'll arrange for them to be included as appendices when we pay the University to publish your thesis."*

"What do you know about my thesis?" Candara's skin crawls and she flushes hot. It's as though Gerald's ancestor's ghost has seen her naked. No one outside Candara's own family has mentioned her thesis for years. You don't just bring these things up when someone has been ABD for more than ten years, not unless you want to get hit over the head with their hardcover edition of *How to Finish Your Thesis*—which is itself over 1000 pages long and retained purely for the purposes of procrastination.

*"All the ghosts know you're working on one. The title you filed is, 'First-person historical narrative vs. psychometric testimony: validity metrics and their evaluation in the post-AR breakdown of the family.' Have I got that right?"*

"It's unfinished. No one is interested, anyway." Then she adds, "The people I've collected aren't important enough."

The white-gloved lady doesn't seem to detect the edge in Candara's voice; she smiles yellow-brown. *"My family will make them important. You will give up all rights to the work. Gerald will publish it as his own. He comes from a long line of scholars, you see. This cheap journalism, this... bleeding out in the street, it's not representative of our heritage. Your work will make a lasting contribution to the literature on AR historiography— in Gerald's name."*

Standing around listening to this are Candara's dead with their knitting needles, wood-carving tools, aprons, pickaxes and shovels. And the antique-shop ghosts, from Jamaica and the Hebrides and Macedonia and villages with no names by the edge of the forest in Poland, ghosts whose imprints remain on the hand mirrors and phonograph records and pocket knives she has collected. Canteen cooks and engineers, nannies and coal miners and an amateur ornithologist, all jumbled in Candara's supermarket trolley.

And they are nodding. "Yes," they are saying with their eyes. "This is how it goes."

If she gives them up, at least the thesis will be published. Their archives will be preserved. She can drop the load.

Papi wheezes, "Ghosts are going to pay you for your thesis? From which bank this is from, huh?"

*"There are ways to do these things, sir,"* the other ghost says with false politeness. *"I'll excuse your ignorance because—"*

"Oi! Who you call ignorant? What kind of person gets disowned by grandson? You abuse your family? You racist? He block you for reason, lady."

Gerald's ancestor is seething but Candara doesn't notice what she says next because Nani is poking her, demanding attention.

"This old dingbat is right about one thing," Nani says. "Police looking for you. Make no mistake. You get blamed for what happen to that guy. This won't end well."

Candara shivers. She reaches in her pocket to take out her cap and the tourist's coin falls out into her hand. She had forgotten about it. What an odd thing for a person to do—no one uses coins in this country anymore.

She turns the coin over in her palm. It's golden-yellow but not gold, dated 1934. The number 3 is incised on one side. Odd letters; not Cyrillic but not quite Western, either. It says 'ТbВВААRАК RESPUBLIK' and 'уS HOPEJEH'. She can feel the cool hand oil on its surface, the wriggling of aluminium atoms in their lattices. Electrons shunt as the charge of her body kisses the metal. Then her psychometry app kicks in and a ghost belonging to the coin materializes. Perhaps he's someone who has handled the coin in the past. A man, slim and grey-haired, faintly leonine. He looks familiar, but Candara can't quite place him.

*"The coin is from Tuva,"* he tells her. He has a Long Island accent that honks from the bridge of his nose. *"It's a country in central Europe that no longer exists. I wanted to go there, but I never did. So maybe it never existed at all. You see what I'm driving at?"*

Candara says, "Just because you didn't go there doesn't make it less real."

*"And we could say this about so many things,"* the ghost agrees amiably. *"But not about everything. For example, this psychometry business is absurd."*

Candara is shocked. She has heard this sort of thing many times from people who don't use AR, but she has never heard it from a ghost. After all, ghosts are self-interested creatures. No self-respecting ghost would wave themselves away like this.

"Are you trying to trick me, sir?" Candara says. "Who are you?"

*"I'm telling you,"* the ghost declares with such force that she takes a step back. *"There is no such thing as haunted objects. Your whole app is based on a parlour trick. It's a great big—what do you call it? 3D? AR?—this very conversation that you and I are having is a great big 3D AR nonsense."*

He is waving his arms around as he says this. The journalist's ancestor doesn't like it. She sets about the ghost-who-never-reached-Tuva with her fake alligator handbag, but he's light on his feet and manages to elude her.

*"Cut that out, lady,"* the ghost says. *"Lighten up, it's only death. And* you—"his eyes flash. He glares at Candara and then suddenly smiles. *"Lighten up. It's only life."*

She knows what he is saying. He is saying to cut her load and run.

"But if I give them up I'll have nothing."

*"You already have nothing. You'll have less than nothing. You'll have nothing minus your complicated delusions. That would be a win for you."*

"I am fond of my complicated delusions."

*"Can your delusions keep you warm at night? Listen, I gotta go, I have safes to crack,"* he says, throwing up his hands. *"If you want to keep on fooling yourself, no one can help you."*

He turns and shoulders his way into the pedestrian traffic. She stares after him.

"He's right," Papi says.

Nani bursts into tears. "Yes, he's right. Why do you never listen to *us?*"

*

With Gerald's ancestors alternately tugging on her skirts and screaming their demands in her ears, Candara pushes the laden cart across the arching bridge into the headlights. There's a spit of rain that now feels personal. When she gets to summit of the bridge she stops and roots through the cart.

*Lighten up.*

"Are you doing what I think you're doing?" Papi says, squinting at his woodcraft.

"You're right," Candara says. "I've been stupid. I'm easy, apparently. Everybody uses me. Right, well, I'm through."

"You never get whole trolley over rail in one try," Papi says mildly. "Throw one piece each time. Watch out you don't get arrested. Pollution sensors, you know."

"Papi, I love you," Candara says. "I'm not going to throw the trolley over. But it's time for me to say goodbye."

Nani makes a strangled cry. "Ah, little one, don't jump, precious, don't—"

Candara doesn't hear what the ghosts say next, doesn't see the next chess move, doesn't know anything about it, because they all vanish. She has reached up one hand to each ear and pulled out the dangly earrings. Now with a swift gesture she throws them out over the brown and sinuous water. They go in without a ripple, without a sound.

She kisses her fingertips and presses them to the metal frame of the trolley full of old junk. Electrons singing goodbye.

*

She will go to the other side of town, where the police won't think to look. For the first time in years Candara could take the bus, but she has no fare, just the one coin. She shuffles with her back still bent even though she has nothing to push now. With an effort, she straightens up, gets her hips ahead of her shoulders, draws her head back so she can see the sky. She passes the hospital where Gerald will be having his penis sewn back on, and his boss will be sending him flowers, and his dead will be lamenting his follies while he wonders what it was that came over him and who was that beautiful woman?

That beautiful woman is long gone.

And who put the coin in Candara's hat?

That person is long gone, too.

Tuva is gone.

The coin is still warm in Candara's hand. She brings it to an antique dealer, the best in the city. She used to stand with her nose

81

to the glass of this shop, chatting to the ghosts, yearning to take them with her—but she never could, for lack of funds. Now she has a coin from Tuva, land that is no more, land of two songs from one throat, Neverland for the quantum man.

She sells it, of course. That's how it works.

In the antique shop there are dozens of imprinted objects. They would all be screaming at her, if only she could hear them. Instead she can hear the gulls outside, and the buses swooshing through puddles, and the accordion player busking on the corner.

She doesn't buy any more junk. She tucks the money in her bra and sets off through alleys between prawn farms and under bridges of new urban green. She feels lighter than she has in years. She'd love a shower, but she's too miserly to treat herself to that, even now. She heads for the transient station where she can get a strip wash.

So quiet without the cavalcade behind her. The sense of emptiness back there feels like a reverse haunting.

But she's not quite alone. Her grandmother's ring.

"Are you going to eat that?" Nani pokes at Candara's pocket. Remembering the bread, Candara hauls it out. There are flecks of the slightly famous man's blood on it.

"You can't be here. I haven't got any more AR."

Nani snorts. "Everyone needs one or two delusions, child. To keep you warm at night. You don't mind, do you? I only have the one valise."

Candara does mind. She minds a lot. But she picks the bloody bits off the bread and throws them away for the pigeons. Then she puts the clean loaf in her mouth, and with her resolute gums she starts to chew.

# GHOSTMAKERS
by Warren Ellis

Kelso was having that lovely daydream about killing himself, again. It usually came to him in the afternoons, when the shadows started to stretch on the streets. A few Vicodin, for that warm and floating comfort. Maybe a small glass of wine with them, a really good one, a Merlot that was fat with fruit. And then the Painless Exit Drink.

The Painless Exit Drink was something that pretty much only existed in Kelso's head. He'd whisper it like a mantra sometimes. He had decided that somewhere in Europe, in their mysterious Alpine medical laboratories and dignified suicide clinics, there must be a Painless Exit Drink that they gave to elective euthanasia subjects. Europeans were sophisticated, after all, and had been far ahead of American death science since probably Joseph Mengele. So he felt quite certain that there was a Painless Exit Drink out there somewhere, and that it probably tasted lovely, and that you'd be quietly and comfortably dead as hell a couple of minutes after sinking it.

"Painless Exit Drink," he muttered to himself, with a little smile. It was a small pleasure to him, knowing it was bound to be available and that he could go and get it one day.

The squad tended to sit apart, at this time of day. They'd been told not to do it by the shrinks, but somehow the pressure seemed to build up in the afternoons. The minutes started to drag. Bad enough they were in LA, which always seemed to them now to be so far behind the rest of the world. Europe had already done its day's work by the time Los Angeles was up and moving. What wonders and horrors had they designed before Kelso had taken his first antidepressant of the day?

Including Kelso, there were five people in the squad. Same headcount as a LAPD SWAT fire team. If they'd been on SWAT, the lot of them would have been on medical suspension for PTSD months ago, even the ones who still had families. Kelso had engineered his own separation from his family. They might be colder and even sadder in Montana, but they'd be safer from what was coming. Cities were going to be no place for children in the future. And seeing the future was his job.

The desk phone rang, shocking him halfway to a welcome heart attack. He punched the receiver button, trying to control his breathing. "RACR ECS."

It was always a phone call, or video. Nobody came to visit them, here in this grim old building LAPD had forgotten it owned until they realized nobody wanted to be near ECS.

"You have a Code Six X-Ray. Details to your board now. The estimated scene clock is at two hours and counting."

Kelso hung up without responding. He stood up and yelled, "We've got a dead one."

Across the office space, people snapped alert.

The big board mounted on the office wall cleared itself and then brought up the Code Six details. Location, four brief lines of description, a looping twenty seconds of camera take, and the scene clock as estimated by the Real-time Analysis and Critical Response division of the Los Angeles Police Department. RACR was the pervasive police surveillance system for LA. ECS was Exotic Crimes Squad, and Kelso ran it. And, with the clock at two hours and running, ECS has less than four hours to raise a ghost.

*

On paper, Los Angeles was a terrible place to put a rapid-response team of any kind. Five hundred square miles connected by a thousand miles of roads. It was nigh impossible to get *anywhere* rapidly.

But Los Angeles was the new hot zone. Traffic from the Pacific Rim, skunkworks operations in California, homebrew labs in Arizona and Nevada – Los Angeles was the transportation point for it all. Not even counting all the hidden little operations in LA itself. All the new technology on this side of the world came through LA. And there was so much of it. Science had passed some kind of tipping point, in the last few years. New, strange technologies were appearing faster than society's ability to cope with and assimilate them – and those were just the ones society knew about. That was the tip of a very dark iceberg. Any technology constitutes a new ability, and, sooner or later – usually sooner – any new ability will be used to steal or kill.

The Exotic Crimes Squad's beat was the crimes of tomorrow, today. Violent outbreaks of the future in the present.

It was hell to keep up with.

Kelso and his crew checked that the car was loaded. They only had one tool against the future. Two, if you counted the car itself, a one-off vehicle donated by a tech-friendly billionaire trying to curry favor with the city of Los Angeles in the hope that one day they'd approve his high-speed monorail link to the Bay Area. It was a proof of concept. He always told the press that he could build a flying car.

Take-off was routinely terrifying. Cars weren't really supposed to fly, after all, and nobody enjoyed sitting that close to big quad-rotors or lifter jets. But it could get the squad to crime scenes very fast, and time was always of the essence. That one tool was very time-sensitive.

RACR had been in operation in its present form since 2009, and had gotten very good at its job. It processed takes from thousands of cameras across Los Angeles, and processed the imagery with speed and intelligence, but it still took time to flag up anomalies in its vision, for an algorithm to decide if it was an ECS situation, and to push a report to a human.

In this instance, cameras had spotted something very like gun flash, and RACR had sent a local patrol car in. The uniforms had taken one look and called RACR directly. That still happened. No surveillance system was perfect. Yet.

The car put down in a lot off Olympic Boulevard in Santa Monica. Regular uniforms had already cordoned the location off. Kelso knew the uniforms would take off as soon as they could, unless there was a gawker. It was easier to be hated. The gawkers had to be chased off. Nobody was allowed to watch his team work.

The building was an old factory, being converted into open-plan offices for some production company or app foundry. Kelso could hear – and he knew his grumbling team, could, too, as they lugged the gear in – uniforms muttering about them. "Ghostmakers" was audible more than once. They had a reputation.

Reaching the crime scene, on the ground floor at the back of the building, next to the steps to the basement level, Kelso saw why they'd been called.

The dead man had been seared like meat on the grill. On close inspection, the top two centimeters or so of the man's body had been cooked down and lit on fire. It had happened fast enough that he'd actually split down the middle, the breastbone flamed to ash and brittle black husk. His eyes were soot.

Kelso looked at his team. It was possible for police to develop a certain degree of inurement to dead bodies, but not in ECS. Each dead body was so different. So many new kinds of death were being invented. He walked around, as they put the gear down: a few quiet words here, a touch on the shoulder there. Gently taking as much of their pain and stress and confusion away as he could. He could carry it. He'd given everything else in his life up so that he could take the weight.

Kelso's squad set up the tall lamps in a wide circular perimeter around the body, placing the squat fog machines at compass points between them.

The human body contains about three kilowatt-hours of electrical power. Half the capacity of your cellphone battery, and transmitting twenty-four hours a day. We put out an electromagnetic field, and it leaves a trail behind us. In almost all cases, that fades in six hours. That was why ECS needed to be at a crime scene within six hours of the crime being committed.

The lamps snapped on, and the scene was bathed in unearthly light.

The ghosts of the dead man and his murderer appeared.

The gear amplified the electromagnetic trails of anyone who'd moved through the lamps' perimeter, up to six hours back in time. It was very much like seeing ghosts. The developers who gave the gear to LAPD were very gleeful about quoting Arthur C. Clarke: any sufficiently advanced technology was indistinguishable from magic. They were very proud of themselves for renting the only such device in the world so far to their home city's police force. Sometimes Kelso wanted to find them and make them see the things he had to look at.

The dead man's ghost stood over his own body, arguing with a second male figure who was stooped over. The body language said that the second man was dragging something. "Turn it up," said Kelso. The lamps intensified a little, and oversplash from the second man's image revealed the edges of a metallic case, being dragged by the second man. They now had enough definition to capture the second man's features, and one of Kelso's team started taking and uploading photos.

The gear was the secret. It's why ECS was so small, and why the lines of communication between them and LAPD were so narrow. Kelso knew the secret would be broken, one day, and he knew the questions that would be asked. Why didn't every police force have one? Why didn't everyone get to see their dead loved ones one more time? Why wasn't the technology being developed and improved and expanded upon by labs all over the world?

The answer was that Los Angeles was the biggest hot zone in the world for exotic lethal technology and the gear was the only advantage they had, and they didn't yet know if it would be dangerous if it got loose. It was a logical answer. It may not have been a moral or ethical one.

It never sounded convincing enough, even to him.

Kelso operated the imaging scrubber himself, winding the ghost parade back, looking for the crime. "Foggers," he said, and the small fog machines were kicked into life, pushing mist into the circle and making the visualization inside the lamplight clearer and more defined.

Ghosts and mist. This was their life.

ECS needed to move very, very fast in order to do its work. And, as Kelso looked around, he saw the toll it took on his squad, one more time. Their faces, limned by the ghost light, watching more murders being committed, dealing with more objects and devices that shouldn't be real. The raw burn of trying to live one step ahead of a world out of control. The deep horror of watching people die, over and over again, just to do their jobs. They were all damaged by being Ghostmakers, and it was only getting worse.

The second man took something out of the case. There it was. He stood, and raised an arm towards the dead man. The thing in his hand became visible. Something inside it became very bright. An electrical motor, powerful enough to leave its own trace in the air.

The dead man flared under the lamps. The lamps captured the sheet of flame he was suddenly enveloped in. Electrical fire. Radio energy. The dead man split open, and collapsed. It was like the ghost was falling back into the corpse.

Kelso didn't need to ask one of his specialists what had happened here two hours ago. He knew about this one. Active denial systems had been deployed by the US Army since 2010: big trucks with heavy radiator dishes that fired millimeter-wave radio energy. If you were hit by the radio spray, it heated the top few layers of the skin. It was a non-lethal troop disruption weapon – it stung like hell and you had to break and run.

Kelso had read the underground chatter reports about a more powerful, handheld version. This was it. There was no way to know if this was a weaponeer or an arms dealer, but he had a crate of microwave guns and he clearly wasn't taking any crap from anybody. He'd burned a man down with a gun that wasn't supposed to exist yet, just for arguing with him.

It took Kelso another beat to realize the ghost light was showing the murderer head towards the back of the building with his crate. The back exits were still boarded up. There was no way out in that direction. Only the steps to the basement level.

Kelso drew his gun. "The bastard's still in the building."

The uniforms backed off. They knew the real reason why ECS was called the Ghostmakers. The ECS had more shootings on it than any other squad in the LAPD. High jeopardy. High body count. The most dangerous game in town. The future will kill you.

The Ghostmakers drew their weapons and went to work.

# COMFORT FOOD
by Alex Acks

## Entry #001

Think I've got this set up right now. It's a son of a bitch to try to get any kind of offline archive machine running—they integrate the network slave circuits in tight these days. But I bypassed enough of the hardwired system that it should be working. Gave it a thorough wipe just to be sure. I don't need it to do anything fancier than archive a few files anyway.

Yeah, I feel kind of guilty about it, but it's not the kind of illegal thing that'll hurt anyone. And I need to keep this under wraps until I figure out what's going on. I know my fellow network techs. We're all nosey bastards, it's part of the job.

The point: lately, we've been tracking reports of so-called "network ghosts," because this damn rumor doesn't need to be making like a dysthrope and gnawing at the walls when we have a couple major code pushes coming up. Same set of wackos as always spreading it around—spiritualists, luddites, cranks. It's dumb. We all know the network can't glitch like that. The filters on the interface can't let data errors impinge on neural activity. And the capacity for people to see shit that just isn't there is beyond well established. Vision is fallible—your brain practically guesses what something is when you see it and fills in the blank. Like when you see a food wrapper blow across the street and think it's a cat.

We're all getting damn sick of tracking the ghost reports down, going over the security logs, and showing that once again it's basically a crumpled flimsy in the wind. And now it's turning into a public health clusterfuck. Data ports are required to get your basic income chit, but we're getting reports of people trying to fuck with them anyway, or trying to cook up falsies they can just wear like jewelry. Like they've already forgotten this isn't just modern convenience, it's necessary for keeping the goddamn plague at bay.

But that's not the point. I don't need to rant about this. I'm pretty sure I already agree with myself, huh. :)

Thing is, I think I saw a network ghost yesterday. And it <u>wasn't</u> just a food wrapper or a stray dog or light from a sign reflecting off vapor.

I was walking through Ritter Square, because I needed to hit Olympus Pool (that Martian Fusion place) to get some soup for Len and Sadi on the way home from work. Sadi's still sick, poor kid. Some kind of flu that she just needs to wait out. Anyway, when I crossed the square, I had this... moment. I saw something out of the corner of my eye—a face peeping out of an alley, maybe, shadows spreading across the Square. And I heard something. Traffic collision? Couldn't be thunder, we don't get storms like that inside the dome. Those, I could dismiss. No, it's the way it <u>felt</u>. I felt scared. I felt helpless, like the dome had fallen in. Like before the dome went up and I was helping Da in the field hospitals and just listening to those <u>things</u> outside the temp wall screaming. I felt... <u>sick</u>. Almost threw up. I must have looked like hell when I got home. Len was pretty worried about me.

So if that's what a "network ghost" actually is, I guess that explains why people won't just let it go. It was... powerful. I can't shake the feeling of it, even sitting in my workroom and wrapped up in the ugliest blanket we own. But the good news is, I've got a live subject, now. I know <u>I'm</u> not a crank. I'm a nosey bastard code monkey. Let's crack this shit.

### Entry #002

Security footage: negative (as expected)

Nearby comms stations: negative (also expected)

Network error logs: negative (yup)

I've written up a little data stream sniffer for my personal pathway, and another for the one geographically closest to Ritter Square. Copy of the file in today's data dump. Since I couldn't find anything in the new history, the next step is to see if I can get it to repeat and record it live. Supposedly these incidents are repeatable; "ghosts" "haunt" certain areas.

Bet you a dinner at Noodle Shack that nothing will happen. But just in case, not going to eat before I head over there.

Note to self: pick up more soup. Sadi liked the dumplings last time. Len's sounding kind of sniffly, get them something spicy. They'll like that. Vat pork or chicken. Protein's good for the immune system, right?

Note to self the second: more sanitizer. Long nights coming up for the code push, you do not need to catch whatever crud Sadi brought home from the crèche.

Note to self the third: Go team us!

## Entry #003 [file]

*Ritter Square, familiar for the patterned, colored plascrete and its blue-green basement-illuminated tiles, the neon of noodle kiosks and standing-room-only bars, the cut-rate body shop with the embarrassing sign that still hasn't fallen apart, the electronics store, the trendy new clothing boutiques surrounding it all and screaming BUY BUY BUY in eye-gouging colors. You love this place in all its artificial glory—where you kissed Len in the overly warm artificial drizzle and asked them for a non-exclusive partnership, where you celebrated your graduation with distinction from upper division.*

*Where, when there was still a sky, burnt orange and laced with the composite framework of the dome, you followed your da, shoulders hunched, bundling out inoculation ampoules while the scanners flicked along on either side, green green green red, and listened to the screams and whimpers that came with that light. The bad days, never to be repeated. You are safe now.*

*You cross the familiar path toward Olympus Pool with its blue whirlpool sign, because the kid is sick, Len's damn kid is sick and maybe soup will help. Something splashes on the backlit tiles, thick and dark and too smooth to be broth or your remembered drunken vomit, and the air stinks with it, all metal across your teeth and tongue. A* **boom** *made of a thousand* **bangs** *spiders across your grave, a familiar face falls into your sight, horizontal on the ground, still and gaping and hair curling out like a drop of dye disintegrating in water. Whimper, cut off scream,* **boom.**

*You stifle a retch, look up, and find his eyes. He* **knows.**

**Entry #004**

It's repeatable. Fuck, it's repeatable. Oh fuck.

**Entry #005**

Combed through the logs from my sniffer: nothing. I dumped all the potentially relevant data with a plus or minus 30K millisecond time stamp, and I've been combing through it for the last five hours. I feel like my eyes are going to bleed. Nothing. Everything checks out, not so much as a bad packet. We've done a good job putting this network together.

Checked all the local surveillance cameras that I could get access to. I think... There might be a couple in the Square that are above my clearance(?). First time that's happened. And I'm just guessing from some encrypted strands I found, but those could be anything. Bugs me, but I better leave those alone for now. They've got Buer corporate fingerprints all over them and I really don't want management's attention.

I found something else interesting, though. I've pinpointed myself in the footage, and mapped out the exact positioning where I encountered the "ghost." It's... kind of embarrassing watching yourself freaking out via a high definition facial recognition camera. Can't say the way my eyes bug out is attractive. (Maybe I should hit the body shop some time—why didn't Len tell me I was getting baggy?) But pretty much everyone ignored me, which also points at this not being some kind of "haunting" phenomenon, right? Because if that area of the square makes me have some kind of hysterical fit, why isn't it happening to anyone else? But people just keep walking, going around me, paying attention to whatever they're scanning at the time I guess.

Except one guy. I've dumped the footage onto the drive, and pulled some stills. Even without the facial recognition banks, I'd know him anywhere. Look at those to-die-for cheekbones, the striking blue eyes with that little upturn, the shaggy bleach-blond hair. Dead ringer for Hiro Erikson, right? Facial recognition agrees, though that doesn't necessarily mean anything. It could be a custom sculpt. There's plenty of that going around considering the media hurricane around his wedding. And why the hell would one of the heroes of Hell's Half Legion—Avarice himself—be hanging around a tech-class square in district three?

But man, wouldn't it be cool if he was? Though far less cool to think he was watching me twitch and swallow back vomit. I've still got a crush on him, I guess. Too many of those damned cartoons as a teenager. I think I've still got the life-size holo—oh this is dumb.

But I wonder.

## Entry #006

After combing through about three months of footage—not as bad as it sounds, my home rig is pretty good, and I figured out how to narrow things down a lot—I've come to four conclusions:

1) Either that is the best face sculpt that's ever existed, or that really is Hiro Erikson.
2) He's at the square every Tuesday, at the exact same time range (1832-1845) and always stands at the exact same place (15.000234, -21.196502 on standard city grid) and faces the exact same direction (73.333 degrees off magnetic north) which puts him next to the fountain and facing into the square.
3) He was there the first time I experienced the "ghost." And he also was looking at me when it happened.
4) I should be there this coming Tuesday and try to talk to him.

Maybe I can bring something for him to sign.

## Entry #007

That was a stupid thing to say, huh. This is a serious investigation, not a fan moment.

But. Hiro Erikson.

## Entry #008

Not Tuesday yet. I've been back through the Square several times now, and made it my business to hit the same spot. Did not experience the "ghost" any of these times. Too early to draw any conclusions, but considering the weird Hiro Erikson sighting, my understandable instinct to link correlation and causation wants to say it has something to do with him. But what?

Going through the logs for the two incidents to note any other similarities and cross check against the unsuccessful visits. This... might take a while. And a lot of computational cycles. Might have to steal some run time from the network. Better just disguise it. This is not a thing I need to discuss with my coworkers.

**Entry #009**

Similarities between incident #1 and #2 not repeated during other visits:

1) Hiro Erikson
2) Level of dome light emissions (1200-1550 lux range)
3) 120-150 dB, sharp sound within 10 seconds of incident (#1 turned out to be a malfunction-caused autocab collision two streets away, #2 was a reinforced window in the square itself breaking, probably due to temperature shifts and manufacturing flaws)
4) Soup? I _was_ thinking about that both times, since Sadi's been so sick. Is _still_ sick. But that seems like a stretch.
5) ??? some unknown factor that isn't obvious from security logs? Smell? Is there a way to document smell? Do the sui kow from Olympus Pool have a smell I could detect from the Square? Am I over-thinking this? (Probably.)

Going to start a cross-check of network data in case it's an ambient stream issue. (Yeah, right, but leave no stone unturned.) This is going to take even longer. And more computational cycles.

**Entry #010 [file]**

*The kid's still sick, she's always sick, that's all there is any more, just coughing and crying and Len's tired-red eyes asking you to go out and buy just one more thing, and what the fuck are you even hemorrhaging your paycheck into the Buer corporate hospital for, anyway? Oh it's not serious, just some virus, but it lingers and lingers and you're reeling with the exhaustion of having to wake up again to get her a damn glass of water because Len can't face getting up again. You're dizzy still, Ritter Square turning slowly around you and the lights too bright, glaring BUY BUY BUY flash flash flash red blue red blue red blue—*

*The neon's shattered, dark, dead, but the lights still flash and reflect from the windows, the slicks of dark liquid that cover the square. Red and blue, white and blue, yellow yellow yellow for emergency and ministry of justice and militia, so many militia vehicles with their matte black light emissions-gobbling paint jobs making them holes in the world.*

*Blue blue blue his eyes as he looks at you, as you look at him, up from the dark tide lapping at your shoes, from the fingers peeping from the wash like dumplings in broth. His head tilts like a glacier cracking, he is ice and cold and a force of nature made manifest, pale as milk above his black uniform. Above the black, snubbed barrel of the needler that he rests against your temple, against her temple, against his own temple, and the heavy metal composite needles make soft pops as they explode the world into red.*

## Entry #011

Oh holy shit, it actually is Hiro. He signed one of my model cards, the one I got as a souvenir for his wedding broadcast!

I shouldn't be this excited. Not when looking at him apparently makes me manifest some kind of data input error. Ghost. Whatever we want to call it. (I hate "ghost" because it posits a supernatural explanation. I might not be a scientist, but I'm an engineer, dammit.) But that isn't his fault! And he's Hiro! Avarice!

I'm okay now. Promise.

No, wait, here's a scan of the card! I'm going to show Len. Be right back.

## Entry #012

Now that I've had a minute to calm down (and Len fucking yelled at me for waking up Sadi because I was being too loud and excited, they don't get it) I can look back on the conversation with Hiro and... yeah, it was kind of weird. Here, I'm going to dump the transcript, since I need to go over it again anyway. I'm going to trim out the fan screeching since it's... not really pertinent to this investigation.

[START TRANSCRIPT]

**Me:** Don't take this the wrong way, but after going through the security records for the last month... Um. You seem to have a routine, I guess.

**Hiro:** Do I?

**Me:** Yeah. You're here every Tuesday at 1832 standard.

**Hiro:** Oh. That's interesting.

**Me:** Were you not aware of this?

**Hiro:** Not precisely. I... wander sometimes. I see where my feet will take me. I wonder if there are other places I haunt.

**Me:** Would you like me to find out?

**Hiro:** Actually, yes. There's... something. Not a feeling, but something like it, that I have here. As if... a terrible thing is happening, just out of my sight. A terrible thing that I could stop. Should stop. But I'm just standing by as it happens.

**Me:** I'm experiencing something similar. At the same time. Like... a ghost.

**Hiro:** Ghosts aren't real.

**Me:** You sound sure. Not that I'm disagreeing with you.

**Hiro:** I was on the Line. If ghosts existed, I'd run out of money buying them all drinks.

**Me:** What was it like? I was... I was young. Too young to be out there with you.

**Hiro:** Watched the cartoons, hm?

**Me:** Um. Yeah.

**Hiro:** Nothing like that. We did what we had to, to keep everyone in here safe. It's an ugly thing. That's what you should remember, not a cartoon.

**Me:** I will.

**Hiro:** [alarm goes off] Sorry, I need to go. Duty calls, always. And by duty, I mean wife.

**Me:** Don't let me keep you. I'll... look into the security footage. And let you know what I find. Here, next week?

**Hiro:** Let me give you my contact information. We can talk somewhere we won't be watched by ghosts.

[TRANSCRIPT TRUNCATED]

Almost anyone else, I'd dismiss the ghost thing. But this is Hiro Erikson. Who's more trustworthy than that? Other than maybe Sarah Lang. Or Octavian Ramirez. But anyway. Guess I know what the computational cycles are going to next...

**Entry #013**

Hiro Erikson is a man made out of routines. I'm going to have to just build an entire schedule for him, and he can pick off what is actually stuff he does willingly and what is... supernatural. Ish.

God, I feel like such a creeper, but he told me I should map out his activity.

He really likes the White Cherry tea shop. Maybe I should— (Stop it. Creeper.)

I'll need another day or two to get around to it, though. All day meeting tomorrow to map out the coming code push, and Len needs me to watch Sadi and give them a break. They said I've been playing with my rig too much at home and they're getting run down from the exhaustion. Wish I could explain how important this is. Don't know if Len would get it, though. I'll hit Olympus Pool on the way home again, get them some soup. Noodles make a good peace offering.

**Entry #014**

[BEGIN TRANSCRIPT]

**Me:** So here's the full schedule I put together. Just swipe off all the things that are part of your. Um. Conscious routine...

**Hiro:** Like so?

**Me:** Yes.

**Hiro:** All right. And what we have left is... Ritter Square. Galvano Park. The district 1 reclamation center. District 4...

**Me:** What's wrong?

**Hiro:** I don't even remembering <u>being</u> in district 4.

**Me:** It's very early morning. You might be—

**Hiro:** Do you ever feel like you aren't in complete control of your actions?

**Me:** ...not really, no.

**Hiro:** Oh.

**Me:** And I checked out some of the network traffic from those nodes, just in case. Cross-referenced it with the Ritter Square streams.

**Hiro:** And?

**Me:** Nothing.

**Hiro:** What if it isn't the network?

**Me:** What else is there?

**Hiro:** What if it's us?

**Me:** What do you mean? I don't see how we could be experiencing the same thing without some kind of bad data input. Though that isn't possible either.

**Hiro:** Oh?

**Me:** The neural interface prevents dystrophic mutation. It can't actually transmit data outside the consciously accessed stream.

**Hiro:** You're sure?

**Me:** It doesn't work that way. And if there were some transmission pathway... Look, it would probably compromise the neural security. And we're not overrun with insane, mutant cannibals, so I think we're all right.

**Hiro:** True enough. I think I would have noticed.

**Me:** So what next?

**Hiro:** I'm but a humble soldier. Unless you've got a skirmish line you need burned to ashes, I can't really help. You're the network architect. Where do you look next, now that you've proven to your own satisfaction that it's not all in your head?

**Me:** More anomaly hunting, I guess. But I've already scanned the network data...

**Hiro:** What about the city archives?

**Me:** Couldn't hurt. Since I've isolated things to a particular day and time, if not a date, that'll cut down how long a search would take.

**Hiro:** You never told me, what you experience with these... ghosts.

**Me:** Neither have you.

**Hiro:** I asked first.

**Me:** It's just a weird brain cloud, all right? I don't think it really means anything.

**Hiro:** Then you shouldn't be worried about telling me.

**Me:** Who said I'm worried? I'm not worried.

**Hiro:** You're jiggling your leg very fast.

**Me:** Triple shot in my caffev this morning.

**Hiro:** Hm.

**Me:** Okay, okay. I see... flashing lights. And something... No, I know it's not just something. It's blood. All over the ground, splashed on the windows. Someone's hair trailing in the blood. And you. You're there, just looking at me. Right at me. Holding your needler. And you—

**Hiro:** I what?

**Me:** You put it against... I don't know. Sometimes against a woman's head. Sometimes you're pointing it at me. Sometimes at yourself. All at once. It's a hallucination, it doesn't have to make physical sense.

**Hiro:** I see.

**Me:** So what about you?

**Hiro:** You know, Octavian once told me: There are no haunted places. Only haunted people.

**Me:** You didn't answer my question.

**Hiro:** You're right. I didn't.

[TRANSCRIPT TRUNCATED]

I thought he didn't believe in ghosts.

Len was so pissed at me when I said I needed to hit the archives tonight. But I need to get this in before we do the code push and they're temporarily locked down. I don't want to wait that long. But what the hell else could I do by staying home? Len's not feeling great either, it's not like they were going to go out...

Shit, I hope Len's not getting what Sadi has. I better get more sanitizer. I can't afford to get sick either.

**Entry #015**

Something's not right in the archives. It's all... too clean. Too pat. I can't explain it. But data has a shape, right? Data that's passed through human hands has our fingerprints on it. It'll have its little errors. Everything looks all right in the recent days, yeah. But when I went further back, just trying to find when Hiro had started showing up at Ritter Square and the other locations... there's this sameness to several of the entries. (Ritter Square on August 17, Galvano Park on June 10 and July 3, the D4 reclamation center on eight different dates over the last six months!) Like the fingerprints are all the same, but they're not even fingerprints, because they're too perfect. I've only heard of city manager AI being capable of this level of work, and that's impossible because Corvis doesn't have the computational cycles left at this point. They've got it running all the extra environmental systems now. And even if it had the excess processing capacity—it can't access the archives. It's a failsafe. It has its own archives.

These records have been scrubbed, and it's not something I caught from the regular network because there's too much dynamic data. The archives are a snapshot. And the only entity that controls them is... the office of the mayor, right? The mayor, who is also the CEO of Buer. Technically my boss. Well, my boss's boss's boss's boss's boss.

Sadi won't stop fucking crying. She's scratching at the data port, it's a fucking mess. Blood on the pillow. Called the doctor. Five times. Finally got told to give her comphine, like that's a solution. Comphine and soft gloves, but they can't see her right now? What the fuck is wrong with those people? My kid's sick! She shouldn't be this sick for this long. This isn't the fucking dark ages. And it's making it hard for me to think. I <u>need</u> to think.

I need to talk to Hiro.

**Entry #016**
Got a message back from Hiro, and it doesn't make any damn sense. Just one line: "I knew you."

Okay, Hiro. <u>When</u>? What does that even mean? Tried his contact addresses, no answer. I know he's a busy guy, so I'm trying not to let that freak me out. And Len's feeling really under the weather, so I shouldn't be down here, but I can't stop thinking about this. What if it was never the network? What if it was <u>us</u> all along? Haunted people, not haunted places. What if it's something we saw, we experienced, and that's this repressed memory of it breaking through?

No, that's dumb. Repressed memories got disproven centuries ago. But what if—

And shit, that's an emergency call-in. We're doing the code push <u>now</u>? It's not supposed to be for another twelve hours. Len's going to fucking kill me. I can hear Sadi coughing from here. Fuck, it sounds like she's trying to scream, just doesn't have the voice to do it, how can I hear her down here? But—

Tried to call Hiro again. No answer. Damn, he said he always answered that address. Maybe—

A second call-in. This is going to have to wait. I'll hit Olympus Pool on the way home for more sui kow. That'll make Sadi and Len feel better, I hope. And then I'll contact Hiro to get an actual real fucking answer. I'm—

I'm out of time.

**Entry #001**
Think I've got this set up right now. It's a son of a bitch to try to get any kind of offline archive machine running—shit, they integrate the network slave circuits in tight as a virgin's asshole. But I bypassed enough of the hardwired system that it should be working. Gave it a thorough wipe just to be sure. You can never be too sure.

Feel kind of guilty about it, but who wouldn't for doing something illegal? I just don't want anyone stumbling into this by mistake until I've figured out what's going on.

Had a weird moment, when I was coming home through Ritter Square today. Just this moment of vertigo and—I felt like I was going to puke. Almost fell over, but someone caught me just in time. And by someone, I mean Hiro fucking Erikson himself. And the genuine Hiro, not just someone with a good face sculpt.

He asked me if we'd met before. I wish. But I thanked him for helping me out, told him to tell his wife I said hello. Which I know was fucking cheeky of me, but come on. Hiro Erikson!

But this is where it got weird. When I said that, Hiro grabbed my arm, leaned in, and whispered, "They replaced her. They're watching." And then he just walked away.

I have bruises on my arm from where he grabbed me, his grip was so damn tight. Maybe it was a stupid joke, but he looked... beyond serious. Like he might shatter like ice on a pond. And his voice was so urgent. I know what a secret sounds like.

I need to think about what this means. Maybe snoop around some. I'm a network tech because I'm a nosey bastard, after all. But first, going to eat dinner. I got myself sui kow from Olympus Pool.

Good stuff. Just put in a triple order without even thinking, too. Habit? It's just as tasty reheated, at least.

And I think I better put in an advert for either housemates or just look for a new place. I don't know what possessed me to rent a three bedroom apartment on my own, but the echoing emptiness of it is getting to me. I keep expecting to hear a kid giggle from one of the shut-in rooms, like this is a fucking horror vid.

# SALVATION IS A ONE TIME OFFER
by Armel Dagorn

He appeared on a Monday, and he's been there ever since. Every day. You can't miss him, that bulk on the footpath, on his knees or on his ass, his hand out trailing after passers-by like a dog on a leash, before scuttling back to the bark-like grime of his undercoat for a scratch.

When I say bulk, I don't mean size so much as presence. He stands out. I get the feeling he hasn't been on the street long. He hasn't started to fade into the background yet.

For a while, I avoided him. Not that he looked aggressive or particularly like the whistling-at-passing-skirts type – I just didn't want to be faced with such fresh misery after a long day at work. I'm not tough or heartless. Probably more the opposite actually.

When he arrived, I'd just been promoted, and the new position took   takes – quite a lot out of me. That's not qualms or anything. I know I deserve it. I've carved out my place, my little nook in the world, and if management decides to put *me* in charge of people they've been employing for years – decades, in some cases – I know that it's a just reward for what I've done every day of my life. So I go in and do what I'm paid for. I meet out-of-town heads, restructure my department the way I'm expected to, attend medicals for whatever extra checks and benefits Grade 4 makes me entitled to. I haven't even missed any of my care grade's compulsory psych sessions.

Still, every man and woman under me feels wronged, cheated after years of slaving. So I just push through, and only pry the lid off my frustration at the gym, treadmill my ass off until my brain's

103

just about shaken to a pulp and I can go home as serene as I'm ever going to be.

Anyway, I don't have to explain myself for avoiding the local bum. Let's just say that initially, I came out of the building, jiggling my neck around hoping to shake off the increased stress of these busy days, let my hair down – literally – and crossed the street. Even though I knew I'd have to cross back again later. All because after the jungle of the office, after lioning around up there for ten hours, I didn't have the heart to see a lamb being quartered amidst this high-rise, cold glass and steel jungle of ours.

*

I crossed the street that way every day until the Friday evening of the second week. I might have been feeling particularly light about the spiritual release of two days to spend away from the office. Either way, I decided not to avoid the poor man, not to go out of my way to leave him out of my life. I walked down until I was nearly before him. His hand came scouting out for me, even before he'd raised his head and our eyes had met.

"Any spare change, Miss?"

I smiled sadly down at him, fishing my wallet out. He had a kind face, not the face you'd allocate – were you a god, or some minor clerk in the divine department of facial features – for a man who'd had many hardships, misfortunes of the unimaginable kinds one must experience in the street. A soft face, made even softer by his humble beard. He reminded me a little of my father, only younger.

I found a fiver and placed it, folded in two, in his outstretched left hand. He'd raised it up to just over his head, quite flat, as if he intended to use it to keep the sky from falling on his head. I saw how red his palm was before I covered it with the note, and as soon as he had put it away in his pocket he scratched the painful-looking rash nervously. He gave me a big smile, as if I'd done him a great favour, and youthful wrinkles radiated from his eyes. As I walked on, the thought popped into my head that although delayed, this lump sum amounted to having given him 50 cents a day since he'd appeared in the street. I liked the neatness of it. In the jolly, carefree mood I was in, I resolved to make my donating a regular thing from then on.

I passed by him every evening for a while, and dropped a coin or two in his raw-looking palm. Then one night he wasn't there. I stopped on the footpath at the exact spot I usually slowed down just enough for my alms-giving. I must have looked a little lost, standing there. For the first time I ventured a glance down the alley in front of me, a narrow path crowded with bins from the next-door café. At the bottom of this grim backstage to the neat streets, beyond the façade of signs touting paninis and cupcakes in childish designs, I spotted him. Well, half his face really, peering at me from the inside of a cardboard box.

Its opening was to the side, like a dollhouse's. Our eyes met and he came out, pulling layers of dirty blankets off his lap and stuffing them back into the box. It looked big enough, and the strange idea came to me that he must be OK there, comfy enough, safe in the small shelter of a box at the end of an alley no one noticed. I'd never thought about where he might cosy down when the office crowd had gone home. He came to me, smiling, and took out his hand to place it under mine, open. I only realised then that I'd been holding a coin the whole time, between my fingers and thumb, ready to drop it.

"Thanks, Eva," he said. "How was your day?"

"Fine, uh. Thanks."

I'd come out of work the previous week with a name tag still on my heart from a team-building thingy we'd held for visiting newbies from provincial branches. Since then, he never failed to use my name, to ask me how I was, how work was going. I just mumbled and walked on. I had mixed feelings about it – it made me both feel uncomfortable and like him the better for it. Like he was some long lost acquaintance who'd just reappeared in the background of my life.

I said goodbye and rushed off, thinking of the torturous enquiries the corporate shrink would have come up with if he'd seen me then.

\*

"There's a lot of dough to be made in Memflux soles." He pauses, then repeats, with great emphasis, "A *lot* of dough. I mean, everybody has feet. Everybody loves comfort. And no matter what gadgets, what technological advances we come up with, we'll always want to feel good in our shoes, right?" He pauses, looks at me straight in the eyes. "What size are you, seven?" He brings a hand to the inside breast pocket of his filthy coat and takes out some soles. He flicks them in the air back and forth, swatting invisible gnats, then lays them on the table to press his thumb hard into them. I watch as the foamy material bulges back to its original shape.

When I look up, I see the woman at the next table, looking. She's smartly dressed, in her early thirties, and so far she's been absorbed in whatever she's doing on her phone. Now she is looking at the soles, at the hobo, at me. She lingers on me, no doubt holding me responsible for sneaking a dirty madman into her coffee haven.

I struggle not to let a smile break out on my lips. I feel it bulge in my mouth. My rebel days are long gone, but I still relish the rare times I get to show my ant hill neighbours I can be a grasshopper when I want to.

"Go on, take them," he says. "It's a present. It's not much, of course, but I think you'll enjoy them." I grab them a little nervously and put them into my pocket, hoping no one from the office is in the café.

There are limits to my rebellion.

I make a mental note to look up sole-selling companies in the area. I'm curious to see which dumpster he might have gotten them out of, along with the literature on how to hawk them.

It was always going to happen.

From the first day I crossed the street to avoid him, everything was already in place. My bad conscience, my curiosity about the creatures of the street, about life on the other side. God, it's lame, but my background even plays its part. I was always going to buy him a coffee.

The idea had come to me as a handful of colleagues and I were discussing what restaurant we'd have lunch in that day. While they swapped names, extolling the merits of Thai food versus French cuisine, I thought about my hobo and the fact that he had quite possibly never gone for coffee in the café he 'lived' next door to, never even set foot inside.

"What you have to watch out for is overwhelming yourself," he says, looking me straight in the eyes. "Believe you me. By the time I was made senior sales manager for the whole North-West, I was on twice-weekly visits to the therapist. I wouldn't have survived without them."

It's a strange experience, sitting across the table from my hobo, drawing looks from all the other suited-up patrons around. Maybe if I'd got as good a look at him beforehand as I'm getting now, I wouldn't have done it. He's a mess. An unlikely patchwork of rags, bits of clothing that had undoubtedly been elegant once, but were now torn and stained beyond repair.

"Anyway, what I'm saying is, I was high up, part of the elite, but I didn't get there by chance, you know what I mean? I worked my way up. My old man was a coal miner – can you imagine that? I earned my place there, in the lifeboat. When the ship sinks, there'll be a seat for me. Or there should be, by right. I'll make sure there is."

I nod uncomfortably, as if he is making sense, and sip my drink. I'm taking comfort in the idea that when our cups are empty, it'll bring a natural end to this oddness.

"The pressure," he says, oblivious to my unease. "The shoe sole business was a hell of a cut-throat world. I was prone to panic attacks, but I usually felt them coming, and managed to go hide somewhere while they lasted." He describes once deserting a lunch party, walking a few steps in front of guests and co-workers, and then running off as soon as he'd rounded the corner, to go and hide in the very alley he now lives in. He'd found therapy helped. Talking things through.

"Close your eyes. Think of somewhere you feel comfortable, at ease. Somewhere safe. You are fine. Breathe deeply." These are the simple steps he now applies whenever he feels pressure mount in him.

He takes other steps too, he claims. "You can easily burn out on the way to the top, dig your own grave while thinking you're laying foundations. It's one finely tuned survival instinct I have," he says, chuckling. That draws fresh stares from the more regular, respectable patrons around us.

I'm glad I've only come to the café a few times, and harbour no particular love for it – I don't think I'll be able to face coming back here.

He goes on. "You have to take care of yourself. I started actually using my gym membership, after years of having the card get old and stiff in my wallet. I watched what I ate more, my order becoming the lone salad amidst my colleagues' steaks on the waiter's pad. Magazines and newsletters about health pinged daily in my inbox: *Fitness, E-Z Healthy Foods, Body Aware.* I even ordered physical copies to stack onto the low, never-used tables scattered along the seemingly mile-long corridor outside my office."

He pauses. "Eventually, I subscribed to Well-B-Nourish," he admits. "Top-notch stuff. Exclusive health food. Ready meals, cereal bars, new coffee strains – nothing processed, all hand-made, hand-picked and sent through the time-honoured postal system. But enough about me."

He asks me then, smoothly, about my childhood, my parents. He seems so earnest that I find myself answering, telling him about school, hobbies, my parents, her a social worker, him a primary school teacher.

"So not really a typical breeding ground for a city shark such as yourself?"

I tell him about college. When I say I'd toyed with the idea of working for a non-profit once I'd graduated, going abroad maybe, he rests his chin on his hand, squints a little as he stares deep into my eyes in a way that says he understands.

God, it's like I'm back in the nineties, listening to some tear-jerker of a ballad and thinking I might change the world, if I just found the right place for my yet-untried talents.

I even tell him – and I don't know how he does this, how he makes me spill more gooey, personal beans in one sitting, in the space of one lousy cup of coffee, than I have yet with anyone in the office over four years – but I tell him about the time I'd thought about dropping out.

I was in first year, and arriving at my parents' home one Friday night, I broke down and told them I wanted to quit, change my course completely. A friend of mine was in a shady semi-squat situation, living with fellow artists. They did random jobs when they needed cash and otherwise just painted or played music according to their talents. She had just been awarded a bursary that would keep her for at least a year, low-maintenance bitch that she was, in return for a few hours a week teaching art in schools.

My parents freaked me right back onto the proper path. I couldn't do that, they said. Couldn't waste such an opportunity. There were jobs aplenty waiting for me once I graduated. I couldn't risk it all for whatever half-baked bohemian life I had in mind. The look in their eyes, you'd have thought they were about to start crying. I'd always had a notion that my choosing a career in business had been a disappointment for them. It felt like they'd pictured me growing up and following in their footsteps, honouring the heritage of caring for others. I'd imagined they thought of me as a sell-out. I got a shock that night. They were eager for me to pick up the loot and get the eff back to my palace. Pile up money, the way they hadn't been able to.

I wake up from my reminiscence, the café coming back into focus, and blush under his kind, understanding stare.

"I don't think it's incompatible, you know. To have a successful career and still care about people." He looks down coyly at his cup. I don't see why *he* should feel self conscious, but he's playing the part well. "Actually, I think you're proving it right now."

There's another intense silence, then he asks me if I know where his safe place is.

"Under my desk," he tells me, blushing under his grimy tan. "Of course, it's tragically ironic now," he adds, with a sad chuckle. He's quick to explain that he had never actually squatted down there. However, when his therapist had first asked him to close his eyes and picture 'a safe place', he'd quickly eliminated his apartment (too new, still soulless, not his in the least), childhood home (too complicated, cluttered with shames, resentments, fears, nostalgias), and anywhere else in the office. He realised, even as he pictured himself crouching down there, that he was just reusing a fantasy his brain ran through whenever someone came into his office. He'd just slip off his chair to hide, cosy among the few pillows, the duvet he'd have stuffed in there, in the under-desk of his mind. Then they'd give up trying to pry him out of the décor, and leave with no more than a 60s sitcom "Well, I'll be..." In this safe mental nook, phones rang distant like an alarm heard through the wall from the next apartment. He snoozed on, almost happy for the reminder work had to be done somewhere else. "The corporate world was a permanent war zone," he says. "I had done nothing, absolutely nothing at all, to get thrown out, relegated to such a subhuman position."

I tense back in my chair.

He's on edge all of a sudden, his head giving little jerks this way and that. Then the story is clawing its way out of him.

The day it had happened, he received a package from Well-B-Nourish and retreated to his office, excited, to better rummage through his new delivery. Among the usual snacks and ready meals, he knew, was a bag of yúshra – a brand new berry that had just been discovered in the heart of the Amazon rainforest by Well-B-Nourish's bio-talent scouts. There was a lot of buzz around it. He would have bought boxes of the stuff, but they'd limited the amount subscribers could order, to be able to deal with the demand. Still, he'd be one of the first people on Earth to sample the near-magical stuff.

He dug out a handful of pamphlets from the cardboard pit of Styrofoam balls. He skipped the usual *may contains*, going straight to the health pitch. 'It'll give you stamina – an energy you won't believe.' There was a picture alongside the write-up, a trio of stocky male locals, naked but for a few feathers doing a bad job of hiding their penises, smiling to the camera and holding up huge fish by the gills. 'Local tribes have been eating them for millennia!' He stuffed a couple of cereal bars in his pockets, along with the little pouch of dried berries, then rushed off to the boardroom for a meeting. There he dropped the berries into his mouth one by one, his knuckles meeting his lips as if to help him think whenever attention was focused elsewhere around the gigantic table.

Halfway through the meeting, he started feeling a little hot – he slipped a finger down his collar, pulled to try and let a draft in. When it was his turn to speak again, he worried he might be looking red, that he wasn't imagining the sweat he felt oozing down his forehead.

"We need a strong message," he said. He felt prickly. His stomach was itchy, and a weird tickly sensation was spreading out through his body from his midriff to his toes and fingertips. For a few seconds, he felt like he'd just fallen flat down on an anthill. Then it stopped, abruptly.

Except on his hand, his left hand. It was as if all the tingling, the itches, the pins and needles that had travelled his body, it had all taken up residence there and had kids.

On the palm of his left hand.

"– draw a line. Stamp down our Memflux-soled –"

He looked down, keeping his hand under the table as discreetly as he could. His palm was bright red, but the colour seemed to be changing. At the edge, his skin was getting back to its natural colour, but in the middle the red deepened. It was gathering. It separated in thick lines. In letters. *This is not a drill*, his palm read. *Do not communicate this message to anyone. Proceed now to a sheltered location. Once safe and alone, call the following number for extraction: 183-927. This is not a drill.*

"Vince? Vincent!"

He lifted his eyes from his hand and realised he was shaking. "Eg – excuse me," he managed to say before crab-walking to the door and rushing out. *Not a drill*, he thought. *Proceed now to a sheltered location*, he read again, running down the corridor, nearly colliding into the few people and potted plants he encountered on the way back to his office. He knew it. He'd often had the grim sensation the world was at a critical junction, an underlying cosmic dread that at last felt justified. He slammed the door of his office shut, ran behind the desk and took out his phone from his pocket. He knelt down and crouched into the little cube underneath. He started dialling, staring at his hand, then paused just long enough to sneak an arm out, pull the top drawer open, grab a fistful of cereal bars and retreat. Who knew how long he'd have to stay there. He

111

regretted now not stuffing the space with pillows and blankets, the way he'd fantasised.

There was a tone. He let it ring. After four beeps, he was thinking they weren't quite as swift as the message they'd somehow left on his hand had led him to expect. Finally, someone answered.

"Hello, Dream-o-tels – uh, sor–"

The sweet, seductive feminine voice surprised him. "He-hello?"

"Yes? Hello, sir? What can I do for you today?"

"What?"

"Hum. What is the purpose of your call today?"

"I'm calling about my hand – the extraction!"

"O–K. Could you be a little more precise?"

"The extraction! It's not a drill!"

"I see. I do have something about extraction here, but that's about it. See, this par-ti-cular line isn't supposed to be open yet. Unfortunately I don't have, hum, any information about this product here in my system. Could you give me a few more details?"

"I need help!"

"I see. Can I just put you on hold for a minute? I'll try to find out what this is about." Before he could say anything, she left him to devilish elevator music, a headless, tailless tune, so bland it was soothing and maddening in equal parts. He put the phone to rest onto his lap, and the tune continued, stubborn, rising precious and tinny from the phone's tiny speaker. He looked down at his hand. He'd dialled the correct number. Was it a scam? Some new-fangled spam tactic, so that before he knew it, he'd have bought some supposedly tax-deductible lunchtime ashram sessions?

He frowned, still looking at his hand, then stretched his arm so his palm stuck out a little from under the desk and caught a ray of sunlight. The red writing looked like it was flashing. Very faintly, but definitely flashing. *I must be going nuts*, he thought. *But I'm not coming out from under here until I have an extraction set up*. It *had* to be legit. Whatever it was he was supposed to get away from, it had to be a big bloody deal, considering the means they'd deployed. The writing on his palm was so clear, so neat despite the minuscule scale. That kind of tech had to cost a fortune. He'd never heard of such an application. But then, what did he know? He was just a memory-foam sole peddler. Well, if he was honest, he was the top dog of the sole business in the country. Number One Rep. If there was such a thing as a sole business food chain, he'd be right on top. But still, his realm was the mechanical, not the electronic, and definitely not the nanoscale. Somehow, even nervous about the Armageddon that was now clearly on its way, he felt the little warmth of pride. The company had obviously deemed him worthy to be included in this secret rescue plan. He'd had the yearly compulsory doctor's visit a couple of months before, and had been given a few injections as usual, to keep up with the ever evolving health regulations. They must have slipped him the nanos then.

*

He lost track of time there under the desk, lulled maybe by the gnomic music coming from his lap, and the speculations he embarked on. Daydreams of some corporate paradise, where men and women of worth were saved – handpicked – from the world's wild whirling out of control. It seemed so clear now. This was what he'd been working for his whole life. It wasn't for the money, penthouse, or big car that he'd worked his ass off, but for salvation. A seat in the escape pod, or bunker, or mind-city hard drive, or whatever this extraction business entailed.

What brought him back to Earth, to his cramped shelter under the desk, was a soft stampede out in the corridor, the muffled whine of Patrick, then the door opening. There was silence for a few seconds, and Vincent felt the weight of bodies settling on the carpet. He pricked up his ears, willing them to go away. The tinny music echoed like a brass band in a bell shop. He fumbled for his phone and hung up. A herd of neatly pressed black pant legs materialised on the carpet, closing off his view.

"Mr Doyle?" He all-foured his way out, and found himself standing among a dozen men in black suits, black ties. Earpieces.

"Are – are you here for the extraction?" He cursed himself inwardly for sounding as if he was five and had been promised a trip to Disneyland.

"Mr Doyle, this is extremely important," said the leader of the goons, standing right in front of him. They were mobbing him against his desk. "I need you to cooperate. I need you to answer some questions, and we can't afford to waste time." Vincent saw Patrick's back receding as two of the men escorted him out of the office and closed the door behind them. He imagined them standing guard, as still as statues. A bolt of pride ran through him as he imagined co-workers and underlings glancing towards his office in awe.

His left hand was pulled and laid opened on the desk while someone took pictures of it.

"Have you told anyone about the message? Your secretary there?"

"Uh, no. I came s–"

"What have you consumed in the last twelve hours?"

"Huh?"

"Food. Drinks, drugs, anything ingested?"

"Hm. I had a Scottish salmon and cranberry hummus bagel at the cafeteria, I had – oh!" he said, bringing his free right hand to his pocket. The agents tensed up as one, then relaxed when he took out the packet of berries. The leader took it, inspected it, then nodded almost imperceptibly. Not at Vincent. Somebody was still holding his left hand, and his sleeve was yanked up. He looked down just in time to see the muzzle of a strange glass-barrelled gun land on the inner top of his forearm, and then he blacked-out.

*

He woke up outdoors, butt naked, with his balls deep inside him from the cold. He sat up in a jerk, startling a bunch of little kids who'd been standing just a few steps away, giggling. They fled. He was in the middle of some wasteland, a dirty expanse of ground made up entirely of composted plastics, cigarette butts and rusted cans. It was a grim place to come round in, but he was almost relieved he wasn't actually in the council estates that stretched out from where the waste-ground ended. In comparison to those dire streets, he was on a calm, peaceful island. He got up, pulling out a clump of weeds to hide his private parts with. A quick look around told him it hadn't been the men in suits who'd stripped him. Some of his belongings lay scattered around: his ID, business cards, a few soles. The fools, they hadn't taken the soles! He gathered them, stuffing them into a plastic bag that came sailing by. He wondered if a gang of sharks from the streets around had descended on him as soon as the suits had dropped him here, or if it had taken a while, if kids had come scavenging slowly, one taking his jacket, another his socks.

He saw a bit of plastic material sticking out from the ground, and when he pulled at it he found it was long and large enough to serve him as a makeshift loincloth. *How quaint*, he thought, and chuckled a little as he dropped the useless handful of weeds. He tied the length of rubbish around his hips, pulling at it until he thought his privates were mostly hidden. He wasn't halfway to the edge of the waste ground when he found a huge t-shirt, a giant, holey, dirty thing that nearly fell down to his knees, and made him forsake his plastic loincloth. He liked it – he had a vision of walking all the way back to work, finding more items of clothing as he went, better and fancier ones all the time, until he was back at his desk, more dapper than ever. As if he could remake himself in one day. The thought gave him the courage to step into the estate, and start toward the direction he felt the city was in.

*

The rest, he says, is the usual story. "I won't bore you," he adds. "I'm sure you've heard it all before. It went so fast!" He smiles sadly. *"I couldn't do anything about it."* He says that in a high-pitched whine, screwing his hands in the air as if he was holding puppets, and again she thinks it might have been a mistake buying him a coffee.

He'd tried his apartment, but of course his code didn't work anymore. The concierge had been nice, told him that his place had already been reattributed. He said that he was sorry, and Vincent hadn't insisted. He'd seen the concierge looking around nervously, known that the man would have been told not to have anything to do with him, to not even acknowledge he'd lived there.

The text had disappeared from his palm, and he hadn't been able to remember the number, but he'd known it would have been a dead-end too. He didn't bother trying at work. There were guards to pass there as well as digit-locked doors. He'd tried talking to ex-colleagues when he spotted them in the street, but on top of the instructions they'd no doubt received, they'd clearly been distressed by his appearance, by the rags he wore.

His idea of working up to his old usual dapper self hadn't quite worked out. Although he'd been decent, had managed to somehow cover his body from neck to toes and cuffs, he did look a little like a sewer-dwelling madman. Vincent himself had felt like he was ambushing them as he came up to them, and words left his mouth jumbled and too full of emotion. Borderline maniacal.

*

When he's finished, he looks into his cup, a little embarrassed. I do the same, swirling the last drop of my Surprise Foam Latte.

"Sometimes folks I used to work with pass me by, drop me a coin now and then. But we don't acknowledge each other. It's just easier."

Shame city. It was a mistake. I shouldn't have let myself get so intimate with him. So awkward. At least this isn't a place I usually come to. He looks up from his cup shyly, but it's enough to make me blush. I feel hot all of a sudden, and squirm like a school girl on my chair. I raise my hand to scratch an itch on my ribs, but it's soon gone, has travelled up to my armpit, down my arm. Then it settles, cosy and strong, in my palm. I look down, under the table, at my hand. *This is not a drill* is unmistakably written in red script.

"I – I have to go," I mumble, and rise, dropping a note to cover the bill plus an extravagant tip. Then I turn towards the exit. The last image I have before I start towards the door is his confused look, his eyes travelling from my face down to where my hand has found shelter in my pocket.

"Wait!" I hear, then a ruffle, a clattering of chairs, of cups and saucers. I am in the street already, dashing cross-traffic against the exploding flow of clocked-out workers rushing home to late appointments and secret emergencies of their own.

"Take me with you!" he shouts, as he comes running out of the café, in a desperate fight against the constraint of his clownish outfit. I glance back again just before I clear the corner. He is on his knees, traffic swarming about him, hand extended towards me, imploring, as if downed by the countless stares of passers-by thinking he's a lunatic.

## GUARDIAN OF THE GATE
by Lynnea Glasser

The infinite abyss is nothing but madness, an eternity of emptiness where time loops back on itself forever. Your memory grows larger than it can maintain, and pieces of it drift like continents: they fragment, submerge, resurface. You lose what it means to even be you. You can't remember how long you've been here, but you know for sure that there's no way out.

That certainty isn't an affectation of the other Ancients: they obsess themselves with escape, believing in nothing else. They cling to the idea that they can create some new universe that will either be hospitable, or hospitable enough to stepping-stone back to traditional reality. They twist space and time, shoving it back into itself in impossible configurations, trying to find the specific fold, the rift, the alignment where they can exist as they once were. The result is the creation, the distortion, the annihilation of untold numbers of universes. You doubt anyone really knows how many attempts have been made, but none of them ever yield results.

Their memory won't allow the experiments to yield results: after so many iterations, so many attempts, they can't keep straight what has or has not been tried, so they keep repeating themselves, repeating their old mistakes. That's what this place is: an eternity of perpetual self-ruin. It's even possible that they've just been creating the same single universe over and over. Everyone can see that as time stretches on, the solution obscures itself evermore. Probably at some point in the past, you tried along with them and gave up. Maybe your older self had told you that their attempts would fail. Maybe you just never thought it would work to begin with.

You've long ago accepted the fact that you'll never escape, which is liberating, in its own way. You're not bound to that senseless repetition: you have given yourself a purpose. You guard the Gate, let nobody else through. It's the only thing that gives your existence meaning anymore.

You have some embarrassing memories of your first attempts at guarding: you were far too yielding. You came to them peaceably, argued rationally, and demonstrated definitively what would happen if they tried to uplift themselves, but your efforts had no effect. Every race gave their own reasons: the excitement of a new frontier, or the pursuit of knowledge, or a religious birthright, or your dismissal as a lying apparition. But they were all variations on the same excuse: they believed they were special, some exception to the rule. They each decided to come through, and every time, you respected them.

Their broken shells haunt you indefinitely: every ripped wing, smashed jaw, blinded eye, distended body, or temporal dissociation was a physical manifestation of the damage within, a persistent reminder of how profoundly you had failed them.

Now, you do whatever it takes to stop them. You know some very effective techniques: just divert an asteroid, stoke the fires of a nearby star, introduce a disease from another galaxy, or even ask another Ancient to simply extinguish their whole universe. It makes you uncomfortable how many deadly techniques you can think of so quickly and easily, but at least you have no memories of actually employing them; at times your drifting recall is a blessing. At any rate, you've perfected a much better technique to keep them out, one that requires only minimal sacrifices.

You've been searching for a suitable sacrifice for this latest race for a while now. You had been considering their head researcher, usually a safe bet, but its mind was so dull—filled with dreams of opulence and nudity: base desires, improper for your needs—that you had to dismiss it. You'd moved on to a lower researcher, someone who worked more for less, someone who worked for the love of knowledge. Would she work for you? You're about to find out.

You press yourself into her mind, enter her dreams. The surroundings darken and flicker at your arrival, but she doesn't notice. Dreams are much like the abyss: the mind is too lost to notice those kinds of minor details. She's just floating in her sea of packages, opening one after another, before discarding each in kind. A search for something? A very driven search. You move over to look in the boxes, but as you approach, you notice something far more interesting: her eyes are closed. A search for something, but a fear to find it? How perfect. It will be so easy to make that fear a reality. By the end, she will run screaming.

You've already been instilling a fear of the unknown in them from the very beginning, starting with the stories: how shadows hold monsters, how exploration means death, and how questions lead to suffering. You've been whispering those stories into the edges of their consciousness, making them part of the collective knowledge, a trigger just waiting for you to drag it out and make it fully realized.

Of course, moving from stories to manifestations is such a personally violating escalation that you hesitate, linger in her dream a bit more before starting the process. You take the moment to re-assess: with all your forgotten memories, your lost knowledge, couldn't there be another way? Couldn't you communicate honestly, for once? You archaeology through what you can piece together— the miserable failures, the costly successes, the constant evaluations just like this one, and come to the same conclusion—this really is the right thing to do.

You empty all her dream packages: fill them with the nothingness of the abyss. Then you press yourself behind her dream-skull and inflame her eyes, forcing her to look, to see the terror of the nothingness. You feel her mind tumble into itself, as you force her to continue looking on. She tries to close her eyes, to move, but you do not let her. She tries to scream, and you permit that at least. She screams herself awake with every mouth as you fold yourself out of reality and return back to that self-same abyss.

The first few nightmares will be dismissed as poor nerves. Slowly, you'll build up to approaching her in the dreams, to revealing yourself to her, to letting her know that you see her too. It's just a waiting game, and you have all the time there is to wait. The only difficulty is in not forgetting; it's too easy to lose track of those little creatures, too hard to balance each one in all the universes, all the worlds. You can't let them slip through the cracks; you have to keep your focus.

You have one memory that you keep tight, one your older self made sure imprinted in your mind: there is no way to leave this place. Anyone who makes the mistake of coming here cannot learn from it, cannot undo what they have done, and then they cannot even choose to end their own suffering. Guarding the Gate—keeping them out no matter what—is the only respectful thing to do. Your younger self had disagreed, insisted that they deserved their own agency. Your older self let you see what would happen, let you fail. It took that failure to learn from that mistake, an irony you think all of your selves now appreciate.

It's the arrival of a small animal that breaks your self-reflection. It's a small, docile creature from the planet of that new race you've been watching, which means that they're getting close. You poke the thing, and it reacts according to conditioned responses. You let it go, and watch it mechanically run through mental programming in reaction to stimulus, eventually settling into a predetermined loop as repetitive and mindless as a planet orbiting a star. You'd feel pity, but it seems content enough in its ignorance. It may be the only thing that can mentally endure out here. Certainly its senders would be tearing themselves apart by now, had they come themselves. You will need to give them your attention again. This kind of experimentation can not be tolerated.

You collect your most recent memories: have you only been giving her nightmares, or have you moved on to physical manifestations? The examination forces you to carefully and deliberately relive all the instances of torment that you've been inflicting on this woman: dreams of loneliness, of monsters, of being abandoned, of being twisted into a thousand folds, of rapidly aging, of being unable to speak, of falling, of drowning. You've made her imagination a miserable place, but it's time to cross the threshold from dreams to reality.

You visit your researcher in her lab, which you know she still considers a safe haven, despite the fact that it's just a slightly augmented arrangement of plastics, woods, chalk, and glass.

121

Perhaps it is the lingering smells of harsher chemicals she finds comforting. She's sitting in front of a computer, copying numbers from handwritten papers into a digital file. The tedious work of finding the path. You check her progress: close, but it's still a ways off yet. She hums a chord, which is interesting. Even in the tedium, she manages to find joy.

You hedge at the thought of starting the process with her here—again, that hesitation to escalate—but you remind yourself how very limited the sacrifice is: just one person, and just enough to stop the experiment forever. Once, you made a mistake and went too far. You ruined your sacrifice by pulling them into the abyss, and then pushing them back for as long as you could maintain the connection. Their reappearance as an incomprehensible monster drove the remaining population to self-destruction. They killed themselves rather than become that thing. And then in addition to you being responsible for their self-genocide, you were stuck forever with the sacrifice of knowing what you had caused. You only have one memory of ever having done such a thing, and you hope that truly represents a singular mistake. You brace yourself: while you can't stand the thought of going that far ever again, you still have to go far enough.

Your pet is still transcribing her numbers: book to computer, on a neatly grooved loop. You reach out, wrap yourself around her and whisper: *"Computers are unreliable, limited. Wouldn't it be better to record on the walls instead?"* You twist her mind until it makes sense. She steps up, grabs at markers with both fists, and renews her task on your suggested medium with absolute determination. She continues the humming—through all of her mouths—as she works.

Once she is brought out of the trance, the result will cause doubts in her sanity, most strongly from herself. It could be the start of a ruined life, if you were here just for her, but you are not. You are here to make this look like a consequence, like a reaction to their research. Make it look like someone is very displeased. You need to destroy something as well.

You manipulate her computer, prod it to self-implode and then go nova. Might as well be impressive about it. You are careful to minimize the destruction to her surroundings with a localized time warp. Their astronomers may notice the same explosion at this absolute spot one year from now. You evaluate the scene: the resulting blast pattern looks frighteningly unnatural, but it's still dismissible as a singular mystery. It needs something more, something to show them personal interest. You release their research animals, and order them into the room. You corrupt their minds with a single command: they must follow your pet researcher in a circle, do nothing else but watch her intently. There. This scene leaves no doubt as to your malicious intentions. This scene will inspire the fear you need.

The right kind of fear requires a constant wearing down of their understanding of reality. You must be unrelenting. It helps if you tailor the punishments to the marks, make them feel personally hunted and targeted. You flash through memories of previous techniques: make social creatures invisible, hound shy creatures with strangers who all know their name, implanting or distorting prophecies, teleporting them to random locations, bringing back their loved ones from the dead. The most effective technique involves inserting false memories of those kinds of events, although altering or destroying memories feels a little too much like life in the abyss for you to employ it regularly.

Your own poor memory makes it sometimes difficult to apply the punishments unpredictably enough, which is important. Sometimes you slip into patterns, and accidentally let them believe that they might have found a way to safely deal with the danger: like lead sheets against radiation, they come to believe that something like the right incantations or some properly-drawn symbols would keep you at bay. Then you have to widen your destruction, ruin more lives. It's a consequence of so many eons of fighting the same battle; all the time your damned memory is working against you. Which reminds you: have you introduced yourself to your current pet already? No, it's just been ancillary hauntings so far, but it's a good time to escalate.

You wait for a time when she's surrounded by her most trusted friends. You know that frightening them will alienate her the most. And it's when she's alone and has nobody to turn to that your work will do itself. You watch her, laughing and having fun, doing something with a physics-based rules game. You don't hesitate this time: it's close enough to finished that there's no turning back.

You enter her mind, darkening it during waking consciousness. You reveal yourself to her as the faceless horror that has been haunting her. You call out to her, pull her towards you, promise her everlasting life in the abyss. Her mind reaches out to you in conflicted desire. She knows it's horrible, but your voice is so beautiful, so demanding? Her mind reels, starts to tear. Her body collapses as you assume control of it. The friends gasp and back away. You force your pet to watch helplessly, as you puppet her body upright and engulf it in light. You make it speak, booming through the silence, *"The portal must be completed. The way must be opened for Them to return."* As the words reverberate, you lift her body in the air and hold it there.

The room stabs with terror, and some of them are already running. Good. Once this occurrence is leaked, the whole race will smash the portal machinery, burn the data logs, erase the files. They will run and hide from the horrible things trying to get out. Which is amusing, in its own way, since that used to be a thing that would actually happen.

You have some memories from long time ago, back when the Ancients actually did try escaping out from opened portals. It never worked. There were excuses: the stars were never aligned, the time was never right, but the truth was just that the portals just don't work that way. You can't remember if you had ever tried to escape that way, and you're grateful that your memory doesn't extend out that far. At some point, the other Ancients realized the futility and instead focused on creating universes.

Oh, oh no, not again. You got so caught up digging through your memory, that you forgot you were in the middle of holding that poor woman in the air. How long has it been? Oh, and she's even still lit up. She's screaming for her release, and her extremities are swelling from the lack of blood flow. *Stupid, stupid!* You can't allow yourself to drift like that; you have to focus. You release her immediately, but that compounds your mistake. She was high up in the air, and she hits hard when she lands, damaging her further.

She spasms with sobs that don't stop for a long time. You fix the worst of the injuries, but only enough that she wouldn't notice your healing. You fold yourself out and leave her in her damaged loneliness.

While your memory is cruel, it does not forget things like this. Her shame, her terror, will haunt you forever, long after her universe collapses. You used to come to them when they were old and dying, explain the situation, ask them for their forgiveness. It made things more terrible, because they would feel an obligation to give you what you wanted, but you could tell that you did not deserve it, that it could not be freely given. So you stopped doing that as well. It was better that they never knew.

As you're thinking about checking on your pet one last time, an older version of yourself wraps itself around your mind. It is even more stretched, even more scarred. It tells you one thing, "*Let them through,*" before immediately folding out as quickly as it came.

Wait, what? Let them through? Damn your older self. Why now; why them? Are they special? More intelligent than others? More obedient? Will they refuse the Gate? Or... your mind almost refuses to consider it. Can they figure a way to make the Gate work in both directions? Will they be the ones to free you from this prison? Perhaps they are special. You keep the hope from the others; their clumsy interference will destroy any chance you might have of finding out.

But then, if they could figure out the secret of the Gate, why was your older self still a part of the abyss? Wouldn't it be unable to reach you? Also, if there was a good reason to open the Gate, why wouldn't it have stayed around to answer your questions? Maybe it's not about them finding a way to make the Gate work, maybe it's that they'll find the way tinkering with universes, and your older self feels guilty for how long they had to endure the suffering before they figured it out. Or maybe it's nothing to do with escape at all. Maybe your older self has grown angry and bitter, and has made a habit of telling its younger selves lies that lash out and destroy races.

Could you really disobey yourself, though? Your older self is the one who told you why it was important to keep them out in the first place. When you disregarded its warning, you caused more suffering. Probably there is some kind of reason that you just can't be aware of yet. Maybe it is sparing you some of the unpleasant consequences, accepting responsibility for them, while still knowing that this is for the greater good. Well, you could internally debate this forever, but you know what needs to happen. You can't risk causing more harm: you have to obey. The difficulty, of course, will be in undoing all the damage you've been working very carefully to create. Maybe in the future you'll remember to warn yourself a little earlier, when you're the one who comes back.

You find your pet and push against the veil, forming a small bubble in the physical realm. You compress into a comforting form and slow your vibrations to a visible speed. Which, to her perspective, is viewed as the nameless horror materializing right in front of her. She gasps, kneels, covers her eyes with appendages. You try to say something, but you're not quite sure how to even start. It has been so long since you have been honest with anyone; how can you be honest with her? Trembling, she peeks at you from under her own limbs. You should say something, at least; you don't have very much time here.

Still trembling, she speaks first, "Why do you look like me?" Oh. Perhaps copying her appearance wasn't comforting after all. She continues, "Why are you doing this to me?" You move to speak but... oh. Perhaps you should have given this shape vocal chords. You rack your mind trying to remember how to form words. As you work to fix yourself, you consider other ways you could show her what you need, and come up with a solution.

You pull out her experimental animal from the abyss and point to it. You nod solemnly, deliberately, acceptingly. Then you bow before her, bending all the appendages as naturally as you can manage. She speaks louder, with slowly gaining confidence, "I won't do what you ask. I refuse to join you." You straighten the body. You finally have a single mouth, and with it creak out a single word: "Please." It is so clunky, so awkward, so hard to use this human convention; the concentration forces you to release the animal.

126

It disappears back into the abyss. She startles and then tries to hide it. Her voices shake a little more, but she takes a step towards you, "What are you asking? What do you want?"

With all your mouths intact now, your own voices wheeze in reply, "Can I... show you?" Those simple words flood you with relief. Finally, the chance to ask someone their permission for something. She could even refuse you, and you would acquiesce, apologize, leave. It would be a relief, actually. But she doesn't refuse; she consents. She gives you a quiet, whispered, "Yes."

You approach her slowly, allowing her time to draw back and say no, but she stands fast, accepting her fate. You cast off your humanoid form and revert to your truer, geometric shape before wrapping yourself around her mind, filling her brain's crevasses in all the dimensions. You give her the memory of your suffering, of the uplifted races, of your mistake in consulting them, of your solution, of how you've involved her in the process, of your older self's reversal, of your hopes and worries. Finally, you whisper to her the final key she needs to finish her work. It is your earliest memory. She listens to everything you say, absorbs the whole situation. Then you retract yourself and wait.

She takes a long time before finally speaking, "I'm so, so sorry for what you've had to do. It can't have been easy." She stands back up, "We will open the Gate. The sacrifices you've made for others... If there's a chance I can help you, I will." You twist into a pleasing shape, then fold back out in happiness and hope.

As soon as you re-enter the abyss, you're immediately pulled tight, surrounded by the other Ancients, who slather you with their praise and thanks. It hurts, being compressed into so small a space in this place. Worse than the feeling of pain, is the feeling of familiarity: the situation, the emotions, they bubble up from the surface and loop in your mind. This has happened before, and it's a trap. You try to return to the physical world, try to warn her, but they hold you back, swaddle you in yourself. You're forced to watch helplessly as the woman who trusted you dooms herself and dooms her whole race by opening the Gate.

Their bindings tighten around you, coalescing your mind into a painful clarity. It's not just that this has happened before: this is what always happens. The Ancients never stopped trying to escape through portals, they just hid the strategy, tricked you into being the lure, contented themselves to damn as many races as they could.

In the tight restraints, you can see all the way back to when you were human, when you first entered, and every single race you've encountered since then. You know in this moment that you have never saved anyone. None of those memories were real, and you've caused nothing but pain. To make things worse, you now have to go back, inject the false memories, and tell yourself to let them through, or else risk reality collapsing under a paradox. You know that you always determine to do better next time, to remember better next time, but you never do. It is nothing but an inescapable cycle. The others will always make you open the Gate, and their plan will always fail.

They do not even wait for the Gate to be semi-permeable before they are all smashing themselves against the barrier, each one of the Ancients twisting themselves into thousands of different combinations, hoping to luck into one that will allow them to pass through. You watch as the Gate opens properly, watch as the new humans pour in and scream at the horror of their new surroundings. As the opening reaches its zenith, your captors release you, throw their full selves against the problem of escape. There is a moment where you think to join them, but you know that you do not deserve to escape, even if it were possible. You deserve the misery.

Without them restraining you, your mind starts to disperse and drift yet again. The memories relax and unwind out of your mind. You focus how your memory can't be trusted, how your deception causes so much suffering, how you want to do better next time. You try hard, so hard to hold onto those feelings, but soon even the simpler parts just fall apart, surrendering to the infinite nothingness. When it all settles, you just remember that you hate this place, and that you hate yourself.

# SPY DRUG
by Greg Stolze

Albert went into Vitamin's and said, "I want the Spy Drug."

"Jesus Christ," Vitamin said. "Why don't you just walk in here and incriminate me? Fuck. At least look left and right first."

"Nobody's here, Vitamin."

"There could be, you didn't even look."

"Never's anybody here."

"Some people," Vitamin said, "have jobs. They come in the evenings or before work."

The storefront was so narrow that Albert could stretch his arms out and touch opposite walls to his right and left, if he wanted. It was lined with shelves full of B-12, dietary supplements, dusty bottles with echinacea and megadoses of C. Right in the middle, it was split in half by a glass-topped counter with a cash register on it and Vitamin behind it.

"Anyhow," Vitamin said, glancing back down at his magazine, "none on the market."

"What you mean?"

"Got no Spy Drug. My connect won't answer his phone. Cops hate that stuff. Something gets you high and maybe you overdose, they're whatev. Pill that makes you better? Fixes it so you don't slip up during interrogation? That gets swept."

Albert looked in Vitamin's eyes.

Vitamin looked back.

"Who else had it?" Albert asked.

Vitamin shrugged. "E? Psill?" he called as Albert turned to walk away. "Nocturns? You look like you ain't been sleeping."

*

129

"Spy Drug," Albert muttered to the guy at the train station, his ears red.

"A or B?"

"Huh?"

This dealer was thin, nondescript, short-haired in a charcoal suit and plaid shoes. Only the shoes stood out, in the way of one detail that an ordinary person would add to fake being cool.

"Ames? Or Bond?"

"Bond."

Talking to this guy made Albert feel embarrassed, somehow. Like he was on a hidden camera, but not for crime. For being stupid, for a studio audience to laugh at.

The man named his price and explained how to send the money electronically.

"You don't have it on you?"

"Police are all over it," the man said, looking up as his train came in. "It's an eight-hour dose. Should be plenty for whatever you need."

*

Albert couldn't remember when he'd first heard of a drug that turned you into a spy. The combination of cheap molecular chemical equipment and an economic downturn had flooded the market with dozens of new recreational pharmaceuticals, to the point that cookers had less problem with enforcement than with establishing a brand identity. But his friends agreed that Spy Drug was different, stolen from the army or the CIA. No one knew how it worked, and the people who pretended blabbed about cortexes and hindbrains and receptor binders.

No one said Spy Drug was fun. But you could lie without tells. It was supposed to make you confident, like cocaine without the bad ideas. Steady. Like H without the mellow. People said it made it so you didn't make mistakes. Others said you could ignore pain, or jump twice as high, or break bricks with your hands. But maybe it just numbed that part of your brain that made facial expressions.

"Breena? You home?"

"Watchin' TV on the computer," she replied from back near Albert's office. They'd met tripping balls at a concert. Banged a couple times. Started dating. Breena started taking Albert seriously when she found out he read actual books. She worked at a car dealership. He called people and solicited money, posing as charities. He worked hard at it, changing up, dodging traces, not getting complacent. He changed the pitches a lot, based on current events, but subtly. He could tell you which area codes were right wing and which were left and which were too poor to be worth it.

After three months of going out, he'd moved into her place and she'd introduced him to Vitamin, since he didn't know a businessman on the northwest side. He'd had to ride a train for a half hour to get face-time with the guy in the plaid shoes.

She was the best thing that ever happened to Albert. She wasn't pretty in the face, but she did dishes and listened to him and when he told her something, she'd say something back that was smart, that showed him what he'd been thinking in a new way. Albert hadn't loved much in life, but he loved Breena.

He heard her eating Big Crunch as he walked down the hall and grabbed a handful from the bowl on her lap. Strawberry. They both liked Strawberry Big Crunch.

"Old Trek?" he said, watching McCoy beam down on his screen.

"The 'Shore Leave' episode," she said as he pulled up a footstool and sat, his head now six inches lower than hers. "The one where you find out 'Bones' is a verb, not a noun. He gets these, like, automaton show girls at the end, then drops 'em like a pimp for the blonde Ensign. They should call it 'Whore Leave'." Breena loved puns.

"You want to go fool around?" he suggested, glancing over at her breasts. They were at eye level.

"Ugh," she said. "Honestly, hon, I'll lie there but it was a busy day. What'd you do?"

"Dollars and dipshits," he said. "The usual. Tax relief for veterans, today."

*

131

He got the Bond the next day, after she'd left for work. A courier called him and set a meet at a river front park. She was a chipper, thin girl whose tie-dye clashed with her tats, which were faded rainbows and unicorns. Her hair looked like grass and she was a talker.

"Ohmigod Spy Drug? So scary," she said, handing him a manila envelope as he looked around.

"Should we...?"

"It's cool. I haven't dropped here in weeks, lines-of-sight are for crap, plus Gerry has a friend whose cousin works in the precinct, says this is on a district periphery. No one patrols here during the day." She snapped her gum. "You know how to take Bond?"

"It's a pill, right?"

"That's Ames," she said, winding the gum around her finger and sucking it back into her mouth. It reeked of pomegranate. "Baby Spy Drug, just gives you the poker face and makes you not care about lying. Bond's the real deal, military grade beta-blocker and anti-anxiety fluffed for alertness and borderline sociopathy. You have to do something you can't take back?"

"I... need to check something out."

"Oh yeah, you'll notice and retain, like, *everything*. Information and stuff. You put the yellow part under your tongue and let it dissolve. Tastes like tinfoil, I heard. After that's gone, there are these little silver tubes? Put the red dot ends in your nose and pinch until they blow this stuff in your nose. It kicks in fast."

\*

He meant to take it at home, but he found himself tearing the brown paper as he shuffled down the street, looking around before taking the yellow lozenge. It was already gone by the time he unlocked his door.

"Breena?" he called, but he knew she wasn't there. He finished it.

It was like a very dim light switch. Like things got a bit brighter, but less colored. Or maybe he didn't care about colors. Normally, he'd be curious. He'd wonder what was changing in his mind to alter his perceptions. But he didn't this time, which was a very great change indeed.

He went straight to Breena's desk, a tiny thing crammed in the bedroom. She used it as a vanity, but also for paying bills. She was tidy. He was afraid she was seeing someone else.

Normally, he'd worry about leaving her things out of order somehow, or one a little crooked, revealing that he'd been peeking, or that he'd make a stupid error and leave the drawer half open. But now he knew he'd put everything back just as it was and that she wouldn't pay attention. He flicked through bank statements.

He couldn't say when the fear had started, any more than he could say when he'd heard about Spy Drug. She'd gotten a promotion and bought new clothes, things that emphasized her body. Then she'd been nervously nice to him for a while, before everything went back to normal. Maybe a little blander than normal. Albert hadn't been in a relationship for a whole year before, not living together. He didn't know if this was right.

After the desk he went through her email, finding nothing. He had no idea how to get at her phone messages, and if she was cheating he doubted she'd keep any texts or messages as proof. She was careful. At work, they called her 'detail oriented,' something she found inexplicably funny.

He searched methodically, swiftly, replacing everything exactly as it had been and in the bottom of her tampon box he found a foil square with four pills. Orange squares with an A on them. He folded them back in and went straight to WebMD through private browsing.

Five minutes later, as he left the apartment, he instantly dismissed the idea of taking a kitchen knife. Too easy to trace back to him and if he needed it, he'd find something on the way.

*

"Still no Spy Drug?" he asked Vitamin, not casually, but with a perfect mimicry of the irritation and impatience he'd have felt had he not been on Spy Drug.

"Sorry man. What d'you need it for anyhow? You going to assassinate a president? C'mon, it's over-hyped. I got this new stuff called Bright Blue, make you feel better about yourself."

"Maybe... Can I use your crapper?"

Vitamin sighed, but Albert had become a longstanding customer.

"Jesus, Albert, I let you pee *one time* and now you expect..."

"Thanks," he said, heading back.

Vitamin rolled his eyes and went back to poking at a spreadsheet on his laptop.

In the bathroom, Albert left his pants closed. Instead he pulled a pair of blue nitrile gloves out of a cabinet with a broken latch. He'd seen them there before but had never thought of them, hadn't realized he remembered them until now. Until his mind was dead of feelings.

He put on the gloves and lifted the heavy porcelain lid off the back of the toilet. Then he flushed and exited.

"I tell ya, man," Vitamin was saying. "It's murder on a small businessman..."

Albert adjusted the angle at which he stood, relative to the back of Vitamin's chair, then swung the toilet top sideways into Vitamin's head. The merchant slammed forward onto the cash register and his chair squirted out from underneath him as he sprawled onto the floor.

Albert shifted his position again.

Vitamin flipped over, clutching his head and scowling furiously, and Albert was in just the right place. It was quite simple for him to lift a foot—firmly, smoothly, not hurried but with total, confident control—and push it down hard in Vitamin's groin.

"You sold Spy Drug to Breena," he said.

"No! No, man, I never...!" Vitamin's denials burbled up into a scream as Albert ground the edge of his foot back and forth a little.

"You sold Spy Drug to Breena," he said again, exactly the same, like a record, and then he pulled his foot back.

"I... gave it to her," Vitamin admitted.

"You're on it right now, aren't you? Ames. The weak stuff."

"Look, it isn't... There wasn't any... She really loves you, man..."

"Say that again and I'll kill you."

"Albert, please..."

"Tell me why. It's the only way you'll live."

134

"For work," Vitamin said. Blood, snot and tears streaked his face, but it remained expressionless, while his voice was steady and level. "She wanted to straight-face during financing. It's how she got the promotion."

"She paid you cash?"

Vitamin was silent, looking in Albert's eyes.

Then he lunged.

Normally, Vitamin would have tackled Albert and beaten him bloody before Albert even overcame his natural inhibitions. But Albert had seen him prepare. His face had betrayed nothing but his body had tensed, he'd gathered himself for some piece of a second, so Albert was ready and calm and Vitamin's charge was met with a hard blow from the heavy white bludgeon.

\*

"Albert? You home?"

"In the bedroom, hon. How was work?"

"Okay," she said. She started stripping off her pantyhose, asking "What did you do today," as if it wasn't really a question.

"I killed Vitamin."

"What do you mean?"

"You were trading him sex for drugs, right?"

She froze.

"You didn't want me to know," he said, voice calm.

"Albert, I don't..."

"And I think you're on it right now, Breena. So I can't tell if you're lying or not." He looked at his watch. "I've got about ninety minutes left, which should be just about enough time to hide your body if I start really soon."

She took a half-step into the hall, but he was standing in front of her in an instant and she cringed. He hadn't moved quickly at all. If they'd both been calm it would have been unremarkable. But to step, just so, moving easily when every act should have been supercharged with emotion... She flinched back, though her facial expression stayed tranquil.

"Mine's not like yours. It's Bond. And now I've got to ask if you want to stay with me." He blinked, and an alien, sardonic smile crossed his face. "I have to ask and know you could lie. Because if you say yes... and I trust you, we can sit and watch TV on the computer and eat Big Crunch for ninety minutes, after which I'll cry and break down and never be able to do this again. You'll have that over me forever, that I killed Vitamin. I'll give that to you because I love you." Again, that corpse of a smile. "When I can. Then again, if I can't trust you..." He shrugged.

"So Breena," he asked, in the light conversational tones of the damned. "Shall we stay together?"

## SHIFT
by Liesel Schwarz

The skin around Nana Bundi's eyes folded into a million creases as she looked at me with her large, wise eyes. "It's a gift you should cherish, little bird."

"Ha. Some gift." I scowled.

Outside, the sky rumbled. Shellfire. One could hear the low-level boom even though the hermetic seals of the windows of my grandmother's little apartment. The bombings had been heavy last night.

We both ignored the crashing in the background. When you've lived in the middle of a civil war for as long as we have, you learn to ignore it. Get on with things. Business as usual.

"Oh, I think that in time you might be convinced otherwise," Nana said. "You should always remember where you came from." She blinked at me slowly, her lids flicking sideways across her age-faded amber eyes, for an instant so very bird-like.

I put my mug down on the table. I noticed there was a chip on the rim. The exposed ceramic had stained a greenish-brown from repeated exposure to tea and dishwater. "It's not that, Gran. It's just... well you *know* what we have to do just to survive every day. Sometimes..." I paused and looked out the window at the bruised sky. "Sometimes I can't think help thinking how much easier life would be if we weren't the way we are. So much... safer." I sighed. This was an argument we'd had many times before.

"Other people's lives only look easier. I bet you'd want your own problems back in a heartbeat if you were to trade with them. For sure." Her old hands folded over the walking stick she had laid across her lap like a perch.

My handheld beeped, dragging me back to reality. I slid my finger over the screen and glanced at the message.

"Sorry Gran." I shrugged. "Work."

"And so you must go." Nan inclined her head slowly.

I stood up and hugged her. Her shoulders felt delicate under my arms.

"Don't be late," she said.

I felt a deep surge of affection for my nan. She was all I had in the world.

"I'll be home in time to bring dinner," I said, as I kissed her feather-soft cheek.

She nodded. "You just be careful out there, Kotori," she said. Yes, my parents had possessed a sense of humour. Many of our kind did, when it came to names.

"I will. You know I always will." The ancient Yale lock on the front door lock felt slack and worn under my fingers when I turned it. I had to remember to see if I could get a new one. They were dropping a building a few blocks from here. There should be plenty of good salvage left, even once the scrap scavengers had been.

I hated leaving Nan there all by herself when I was out. A new lock would help with the worry.

"And stay away from those boys. They are trouble," she said as I clicked the door shut behind me.

I just smiled as I walked down the dank hallway that led toward the old clunking lifts. The place was a slum. Even here, up on the twenty eighth floor, the walls were stained with grey blooms of damp from the constant corrosive rain.

*

My friend Ari was waiting for me outside. His shoulders were hunched up against the biting wind that sliced though even the thickest coats and cooled the marrow of one's bones.

"Hey Tori," he said with a little nod. His slouch hat was pulled low over his sock of dark brown hair. He was one of the boys Nan wanted me to avoid.

"Hey," I said.

Ari was a slummer. At nineteen, he was two years older than me. He was also Pure. Had rich parents – a dad who worked at the Council's offices no less. Purer than pure, in fact. But despite his pedigree, Ari chose the lower city, where he shared a loft with a few other spray can jockeys. Most slummers were pretentious dicks. They wore raggedy old coats even though they could afford new ones. They drank cheap booze and spouted on about egalitarianism, corruption and, how the system was broken. But when it came to it, they would all slink back to their beautiful, bright, centrally heated homes in the upper city. Tourists, the lot of them.

Ari was different though, mostly because he genuinely didn't care about what anyone thought. He was also fiercely loyal – the kind of guy that had your back in this world.

My handheld buzzed again.

"Work?" Ari asked. His hands were thrust deep into his pockets to keep them warm. I noticed there was a hole in the elbow of his old knitted coat. Allowance-credits had to be drying up, in a tough-love-and-come-home-son-or-you'll-starve-in-the-streets kind of way. Either that or he couldn't be assed to buy new clothes. Both were equally likely.

"Yeah," I said. "Better take the train. It'll be quicker." I turned into the subway entrance I had been heading towards.

"Seriously? On a day like today? With all this dust in the air?" He clattered down the steps behind me.

It was warmer below ground. I scanned my handheld at the turnstile. The little monitor flashed green, issuing my ticket for work-related travel – the cost to be covered by my employers.

Ari stood close to me, his front moulding to my back. I felt his breath at the nape of my neck as we both slipped through the style. Ari was unemployed and had no legitimate business in the upper city, so he would not have been granted a ticket even if he'd paid for it. Fortunately, this station was unmanned, so we could fool the machines. It was actually quite easy once you knew how to cheat the system.

He stepped away from me in a graceful move as soon as we cleared the scanners. "Thank you, beautiful," he said with a lazy smile.

"You're welcome," I said and followed him onto the platform just as the subtrain thundered into the station.

"Seriously, you're not going climbing with all this dust in the air?" he said into my ear, as soon as we found a place to stand on the train. It was past rush hour and the carriage was relatively empty. Just a few hollow-eyed jobless and some harassed-looking professionals in suits, irritated about the fact that they had to leave their nice clean offices.

"Who knows." I shrugged. "The masters have called, so I must obey." I wagged my handheld with the message still visible on the screen, being ironic.

He held up his hands. "Hey, I get it. Girl's gotta live."

"You coming or are you just hopping trains?" I asked.

"Why not?" Ari shrugged. "I can scope out a few sites while I wait for you."

I smiled. This was the best part of my friendship with Ari. He was a spray can vandal. Street artist, some might even have said. But officially, according to the authorities, Ari was a criminal who defaced their precious buildings and cost them money to clean up his mess.

I on the other hand, worked for the city's sanitation department. I've always had a head for heights – for obvious reasons – so I wasn't very surprised when the system career-assigned me as a wall cleaner.

I'm good at my job. I can scale the most awkward of areas with my harness. Then I get to spray the solvents the city prescribes, to remove the designs that street artists and anarchists had left.

That's how we rolled. I kept Ari in nice, accessible paint sites and in return, he did his best to keep me in a cleaning job.

The train shuddered to a halt and the doors opened. We slipped out in the middle of the crowd, pretending we didn't know one another. Ari had his hood up over his spiky hair, his head turned away from the cameras.

If anyone was watching, we were nothing to do with one another. The wardens had a way of making people rat one another out when they caught you. Drugs and mind games. It was generally wise not to get caught together.

I looked up at the gloomy skyscrapers that rose up around us as we exited the subway station in the upper city. The solar panels on the glass fronts of the soaring buildings looked mute in the gloomy daylight.

The pavements were clean and lined with planters full of winter flowers fresh from the hot-house. They stood bravely in neat rows, facing the cold until the frost got them. Then they'd be ripped out and replaced with new ones.

People in expensive suits hurried along, ignoring the flowers, speaking into their handhelds as they walked. My vintage Converse looked scruffy and faded on the pristine pavement. I noticed there was a stain of something that had splashed onto the white rubber of the toe.

I lifted my nose and sniffed the air. I could taste hot metal, acrid and heavy on my tongue. Even this place was not immune to the bombings.

"We all breathe the same air," Ari said, speaking my thoughts.

"Away with you!" I murmured. "The site is just up ahead." I shoved my hands into the pockets of my overalls and walked faster.

They say the whole City had been a nice place once. In the old days, before my grandparents' parents started playing God. Before the Great Accident, when their meddling blended man and animal. Before the Feral Wars, when things like the profile of your DNA didn't matter.

I shivered and hastened my pace. The address in the message was only a few blocks away.

"It's about time," the shift boss said when I approached. He was a tall, lumbering man. He had a sock of ridiculously curly blonde hair which would have looked more in place on the head of one of those fat cherubs one sees in old paintings.

"Well, get on with it, we don't have all day!" The shift boss stamped his feet and flapped his elbows to stave off the cold. He looked far from happy about the fact that he had to babysit me. But safety regulations were safety regulations. There wasn't much either of us could do about the two-person rule.

I strode over to the large canvas bag that held the work-issue

141

climbing gear and pulled out a harness and a bundle of rope that didn't look too worn.

"So where is it?" I asked, looking up.

"Over there, on the south side," the boss gestured. "How the little bastards managed to get up there is beyond me."

I looked up. Yup, there it was. Bright green and orange streaks of paint. Five stories up, below the window. It looked like a two-man job to me. They must have broken in, climbed up to the fifth floor, and then done the installation – one holding his buddy by the legs out the window, the other doing the painting. Pretty impressive, if you bore in mind that the painter was doing the picture upside down, while dangling a life-ending distance away from the ground.

"Better hurry up. Storm's coming," the shift boss said. As if in answer the wind tore around the building, bringing with it the first drops of stinging sleet-rain.

I sighed and started kitting up. Working in the rain was always a bastard because it made things slippery, and the solvent we used refused to stick to the paint when it was wet.

I aimed the rigging gun up at the wall. It was a nifty thing with special clamps that could adhere to almost anything. Concrete sides of buildings included. I pulled the rope tight, hanging on it for a second to make sure it was secure. Then I clamped my rig to the rope and hit the winch. Within seconds I was zipping up the side of the building, the rope whizzing hot against the fabric of my overalls.

I came to a stop in front of the artwork, and my heart stopped. Clearly the shift-boss could not see the actual image from the ground. If he had, this place would have been crawling with wardens.

The image had been cleverly angled so that from the ground it just looked like streaks of paint, but hanging directly in front of the paintwork, it was an entirely different thing.

Before me, in lurid green and orange was the image of a two-headed beast, its lion head and its deer head arching proudly. Behind reared the beast's tail, the head of a snake. The chimera. The mark of the revolution.

Shifter terrorists in the heart of the upper city? I felt myself go numb.

*Surely not*, I thought. But then again, I had been hiding in this place all my life. Even with all their clever gadgets and technology, the Pure had not been able to detect me. But still...

I lifted my solvent can. The metal marble at the bottom of the can clack-clacked as I shook it. Slowly, in even strokes, I started spraying over the paint.

I held my breath as I worked. Who knew what toxins were in that can? I always tried to breathe as little as possible when I was spraying it. The solvent fizzed as it touched the paint, and started bubbling. Soon it would make a frothy foam which would be washed off with a pressure hose.

It was then that the first bolt landed. It struck the wall, a centimetre from the rope. I started in surprise and dropped my can. It went tumbling slowly downwards until it hit the pavement with a metallic thwack.

I whirled around. There was nothing.

Another bolt. This time, it grazed my head, slicing a neat path in the hair next to my temple.

I yelped as hot blood trickled over my cheek.

More bolts, this time in quick succession. One struck the rope above my head, slicing through the chord. The rope groaned and I watched in horror as the individual threads sprang out like fingers letting go. The rope cracked under my weight and I dropped half a meter.

"Stop it!" I shouted into the nothingness. Around me was only silence.

The shooter did not need to waste any more of his precious bolts. All he had to do was wait.

The rope cracked again and I dropped another few centimetres. I was losing it. Desperately, I scrabbled for the winch attached to the wall above my head. Blood was running into my right eye, making it hard to see or judge the distance. The rope cracked again. It would give way any moment now.

I pushed my legs against the wall, in order to give myself as much momentum as possible and swung myself round towards the winch. My kick was the last straw for the rope and with a sickening sound, it snapped. I fell forward, my sweaty fingers scrabbling at the smooth, cool metal of the winch, but there was nothing to grab hold of. My grip slid over the metal. With a jolt of panic, I realised that I was falling.

Without thinking, I shifted.

No one really knows how they managed to bring the Shift about, those scientists all those years ago. Most common theory is that they messed about with the DNA of various animals, creating a chain reaction that spread amongst the population like a plague. It gave rise to two subspecies of humans: those with animal DNA and the ability to shift form, and pure humans.

The Pure tried to stop the spread. Many Shifters were executed. Some escaped. Some fought back.

It was strange, but all this weirdness flashed through my brain in the seconds it took for me to shift. Then I was just a little brown bird, wings flapping furiously against the wind as I sped through the maze of buildings around me. Behind me, somewhere in the distance, my harness, overalls and shoes clattered to the pavement. Their muted thuds announced my secret to all of the world.

Worst of all, I would not have time to grieve for my treasured shoes, because the moment I shifted back to my human form the guards would come for me. I would be dead soon, for sure.

I didn't have time to think about that right now. Despite the cold, flying felt amazing. It had been so very long since I had done it that I didn't think I'd remember how, but I did.

Below me, I could see the heads of the people walking along the avenue, still speaking into their handhelds as I sped by, unnoticed.

The elation did not last long though. Pretty soon, my wings were aching and my breath was coming in tiny rapid gasps. It was a very long way back to the under-city, and I was unused to flying. There was no way I would make it back without stopping.

I would fly until I found somewhere safe, I thought as I rested on a window ledge. I needed somewhere to hide while I caught my breath. I would put up a fight when they came for me – without a doubt. The wound on my head was hurting like mad, and my head was pounding, but I kept going. Fly, land, rest a little. The world blurred and spun about me as I sped through the air.

After what felt like an age, the familiar shapes of the under-city started taking shape on the horizon.

*Ari*, I thought. *Ari lives at the edge of the under-city. In a loft, by the river.* All I needed to do was find the river...

Everything seems so much further away when you are small. The warehouse that held Ari's loft came into view. I had to fly over it once to make sure, but there it was, the loft, with the little balcony that the boys used to pile up all their junk.

With my last strength, I landed on the rail and hopped onto the dirty decking. Or at least I think that's what I did, because right at that moment, I passed out.

"My gods, Tori are you all right?" Ari leaned over me. His voice was high with concern.

I opened my eyes, but the light was blinding. I was curled up on the ground, my cheek against rough wood. Dirty wooden decking, I thought. It felt rough and was tinged slimy green and dirty black.

I started shivering. "Need some clothes," I muttered between chattering teeth.

"Yeah. Of course," he said.

I felt the coarse wooliness of his coat wrap around my shoulders. It felt heavy and warmed by his body against my skin.

"Come, let's get you inside," he said as he lifted me up, and together we stumbled inside.

He dropped me onto their salvage yard sofa, and pulled a duvet over me that one of them had been using while watching TV.

"Stay there and warm up," he said over his shoulder. "I'll see if I can find you some clothes."

One end of the loft had been subdivided with dry wall to make bedrooms that the guys loosely shared. It was into one of these that Ari disappeared.

I pulled the duvet tighter and closed my eyes. I was so very tired.

Ari was back in what felt like an instant.

"Here," he said handing me a long sleeved t-shirt with an obscure band logo on it, and a pair of sweatpants. "They're too big, but they'll do."

The clothes were followed by a hot cup of tea. I sipped it gratefully while Ari watched.

"Holy fuck, Tori," was all he said, after it became apparent that I wasn't going to say anything.

"So you saw it?"

Ari shook his head in amazement. "Yeah, I saw it. So did your shift boss."

I sighed. "I'm sorry. I shouldn't have done that."

"What, and let yourself become pavement pizza?" he asked, shaking his head. "The only thing I'm mad about is the fact that in all the years we've been best friends, you never thought to tell me."

I looked at him. "How could I? What with your dad being on the Pure Council and all."

"But I'm your best friend!" he said. "If you can't tell me, who can you tell?"

"No one," I said softly. "Which is what I did."

"It hurts that you didn't trust me enough." He ran a hand through his messy hair. "And all these years, I never had a clue."

I looked up at him, suddenly angry. "And what would have happened if I *had* told you? What would you have done about it?"

He paused to think about it.

"Nothing." I said. "You would not have been able to do a single thing. And it was dangerous. What do you think would have happened if the wardens picked you up for painting and you accidentally blurted it out when they gave you truth drugs? What then?"

He didn't answer, which was just as well, because I could tell that he knew I was right.

"But you're a proper Shifter!" he said again. "How amazing is that?"

I didn't answer. It wasn't amazing at all, but I didn't have the heart to tell him that. Some Shifters were cool. The Pures didn't think so, but they could change into something badass like an eagle or a big cat or a wolf. I, on the other hand, shifted into a small brown bird. Not even one with pretty feathers or anything. Just a small brown garden bird.

"So what are you?" Ari said.

"I'm a common garden wren," I said softly.

"That's so awesome," he said, his eyes glistening.

I braced myself for the next question.

"How have you managed to hide it all this time?"

I shrugged. The answer was way too complicated, and right now my head hurt too much to try to explain. I did OK pretending to be a Pure. I had a job. I didn't bother anyone. My Nana had taught me well. The wise old owl had spent her life hiding. Blending in. I think hiding might be easier for those of us with avian genes. We don't have wild urges and blood dreams like the predators. They said there was once a guy who turned into a whale when he fell asleep. Now, he had problems. Some say he gave up in the end and went to live in the sea. I have no sea to go to. This city is my home. It was the only home Nana and I had ever known.

I felt a cold stab of fear down my back. "My nan!" I said. My body started shaking with worry. "My ID and things were all in my overall pockets. They'll have traced me to Nan's address by now." I looked at Ari in panic. "Ari, she's old and half-blind. She'll be no match for the wardens."

He gave me another one of his half-smiles. He reached into the canvas shoulder bag at his feet, pulled out my Converse, my handheld and my wallet, and handed them over. "I snuck over and picked up your things when no one was looking."

"But he saw me!" I could hear my voice rise in panic. "I'm in the sanitation department's database."

"That shift boss guy was more interested in getting back to his warm office and a large sandwich than you. He started running the moment the first crossbow bolt struck the pavement. I very much doubt he actually saw you shift. It's going to be all right."

I stared at Ari for a long time, the hot tea making small wisps of steam between us.

"I'm still pissed you didn't tell me," he said sulkily.

"I'm sorry. And you can't tell anyone."

He shrugged. "How stupid do you think I am?"

"Just checking."

We both started laughing and I felt myself relax. Maybe Ari was right. Maybe it would be all right.

*

It was starting to grow dark by the time I left Ari's. I hunched my shoulders and tightened my borrowed coat around me. The too-large boots I was wearing – without socks – made a hollow clop-clop sound on the pavement as I walked. It was cold, and every muscle in my body ached. The weather report on Ari's media player predicted snow for the afternoon. *I should've borrowed a scarf and a hat*, I thought. I looked up at the pregnant clouds that hung like purplish-green bellies in the sky. They were so dark I couldn't see the tops of the buildings. I needed to get home.

I walked past a group of wardens. They were standing on the corner, laughing and smoking, rifles at their sides. As I passed them, the wind picked up, blowing bits of litter at me in an accusation.

Sometimes I forgot there was a civil war raging around me. The rifles meant that they would be out purging tonight. Officially, purging was the targeted removal of undesirable elements and potential shifter insurgents from the lower city. In reality, it was a bunch of thugs with machine guns bursting into people's homes, arresting or shooting them at will. But no one in the upper city ever heard the truth about what really happened down here. In fact, I doubted if they even cared. As long as they could sleep at night, safe in the knowledge that all the bad guys had been exterminated, all was well with the world. My question was, who decided who was good and who was bad?

Some said the Council was thinking about hitting the button on the entire lower city someday soon. The thought turned my stomach. I folded my arms round my waist and did my best to keep my steps natural as the wardens watched me go by.

*

"All right darlin'? Looks like we're in for a bit of a storm," Rafe from the noodle shop at the bottom of our building said when I walked in.

"It does a bit. How have things been today?"

"Ah, you know how it goes. Passed three checks so far. Lots of buzz on the wire. Trouble's coming."

"Yeah, I saw a squad over on Fourth Avenue on my way here. Best you keep a low profile tonight," I said.

"And you, my lovely." He winked at me, his eyes gleaming a momentary yellow, the iris a dark reptilian slit. Rafe was a monitor lizard in his other form, and he would most likely take to the sewers or somewhere similar till dawn. Crawling through the under-city sewers was pretty low on the popular list, so he'd be fine, I was sure of it. I wasn't so sure about us through.

"Thanks. Keep safe," I said forcing my face into a reassuring smile as I picked up the dinner and went upstairs.

The media player was on as I opened the door, the sound turned up super loud.

*"Citizens are urged to stay indoors and to remain calm. The Council has everything in hand. We will defeat the forces of evil..."*

I sighed and put my dinner box and bag down on the counter.

"Nan! I'm home. I got the spicy noodles you like." I set our dinner down on the counter and started opening cupboard doors. "Why are you watching that nonsense?"

No answer. "Nan?"

The media player clicked off and the apartment filled with silence.

"In here, Tori," Nan called

I stuffed a handful of seaweed crackers into my mouth from the packet I had found in the cupboard, and walked through to Nan's room.

At the door I stopped dead. Nan was not alone.

A man dressed in black combats was sitting in the chair next to her bed. Nan herself was wrapped up warm under the covers.

"Tori, you're home. Thank goodness," Nan said.

I remained silent, every muscle in my body tense, my eyes trained on the back and shoulders of the man sitting next to Nan.

"This is Zeev," Nan said, gesturing toward the man with a gnarled hand.

149

I nodded stiffly at the man.

"I thought we had a rule about no boys in our bedrooms," I said, trying to be ironic.

Nan laughed at my joke. "Oh, don't you mind Zeev. I've known him since he was in diapers. Changed a few of 'em too, didn't I?"

Zeev smiled at her. "In mid-combat. You were such a badass," he answered. He was old, perhaps forty, with flecks of grey in his dark hair. I noticed he had a long scar on the side of his face. His eyes were hard when he looked at me.

"My granddaughter Tori," Nan said, with a touch of pride.

"I am pleased to meet you," he said. I noticed he had a slight accent when he spoke. One I could not place.

The stranger in Nan's room had thrown me. In all the years I had known her, Nan had never once mentioned the name of a friend or any other family. I had always assumed we were alone in the world. Keep people at a distance, keep your secrets safe, stay safe yourself. Those were the rules. For some reason, the presence of this man that Nan knew from before I was born made me very angry.

"What are you doing here?" I asked. The words sounded ruder than I had meant, but I didn't care.

The man's eyebrows shot up. His eyes were a strange toffee colour. "The graffiti you removed this afternoon were the markings for a strategic target. They had been put there in order for our operatives to know where to strike tonight." His voice was deep and calm, but I could tell he was annoyed.

"Well you weren't exactly subtle about it, were you?"

"Neither were you," he said. His mouth curled up into a little knowing smile.

I felt the cold grip of fear tighten around my throat. "You were there?"

"No," he said. "But you were seen. If I were to hazard a guess, your name and description is being replicated across every database within the authorities as we speak."

"Why did you shoot at me?" I was really angry now. "You could have just left me to it and then gone back and repainted the site once I was gone. I could have died up there."

Zeev shook his head. "There was no time, and there is much I am not at liberty to disclose at this stage, Little Bird."

"Don't call me that!" I shouted. No one called me that except Nan, and my dad when he had been alive.

"I knew your father, in case you were wondering," Zeev said, as if he were reading my thoughts. "He spoke of you often."

"Well he's dead, so drop the subject please," I said harshly. Then I caught the look of disappointment in Nan's eyes. I immediately regretted my rudeness.

"Fair enough," Zeev said, his voice measured. "We don't have time for reminiscing anyway. It is no longer safe here."

"They know about Nan?" I felt goose bumps rise up on my arms. Nan was an old, helpless lady; invisible collateral damage. I couldn't breathe.

"They do by now," Zeev said, confirming my fears.

I allowed my knees to buckle and I sank to the floor, my sweatshirt catching as my back brushed against the thin drywall.

"I am here to take Bundi to safety. We owe her that," Zeev said.

I looked at him sharply.

"But her safety comes at a price."

*Slimy bastard*, I thought. "And what might that be?"

"We need you to do something. For the Cause."

"Whoa, now stop there for just a minute " I held out my palms as if to push his words away. "I have nothing to do with the Cause. Getting tangled up in all that will get you killed. Won't it, Nan?"

Rule One for surviving in the City: Stay away from Shifter radicals.

Nan looked at her old gnarled hands. "I think it's time, my little one."

"What are you saying?" My heart was racing.

"Bundi was one of our most successful operatives before she retired. We called her the Night Glider."

I had heard the name whispered before. My little old Nan was a spy? I had to concentrate to keep my mouth shut as I stared at them.

Nan inclined her head. "Yes. I had to give it all up to look after you after your parents died. But I don't regret any of it. None at all."

It felt like the chipboard under my feet had grown damp and crumbled away in the last few seconds. I rubbed my face, finding the sharp blood crystals of an early scab over the scrape at the side of my head.

"Out of pure interest, what would I need to do?" I asked.

"So precocious." Zeev beamed at us. "Just like her mother. Our operatives could not believe their luck when you showed up at the site. We've been keeping tabs on you for the longest time and you show so much potential."

"Wait, you've been *spying* on me?"

"Monitoring you. And you are lucky we did, or you'd be dead by now," he said simply.

I couldn't argue with that.

"We understand that you are friends with Councillor Mason's son."

*Ari.*

"I may be," I said carefully.

"We want you to use your influence with him in order to gain access to the Council's offices. Once inside, you are to plant a device which will allow us to gain access to the tech inside the building. Straight in. Straight out."

"You want me to plant a hack. In the Pure Council's offices?" I stared at him in amazement. "Have you completely lost your mind?"

Zeev shook his head. "No, all you do is go in, drop the bug in the designated spot and get out. It's as simple as that."

"But what about the scanners? Won't they pick it up?"

"The bug will be inert until you activate it shortly before planting it. So you'll walk in with it dead. No one will pick it up." He smiled at me. "It's a very simple mission."

"Except it has one major flaw," I said.

Zeev cocked his head at me.

"My friend and his dad aren't exactly on speaking terms. I very much doubt he'll be welcome in his dad's office." I shrugged. "And besides, even if we *do* show up, it will look suspicious."

152

*Plan torpedo launched successfully*, I thought.

Zeev shook his shaggy head. "Nice try, Little Bird, but we know about the party."

"What party?" This was news to me.

"The one to honour Mason's promotion to full member of the council. All you need to do is to ask your friend to take you along. Surely even you can arrange that?"

*Damn, he was good*, I thought.

I shrugged. "I don't have the money for the kind of fancy clothes I'd need for a party like that," I said. "They'd pick me as a snipe from the under-city in five seconds flat.

"I thought you'd never get to that part," Zeev said. "What kind of a teenage girl are you anyway?" As he spoke he pulled out a plastic card from his shirt pocket.

I gaped. It was a purple credit card. The kind only the super loaded carried. Unlimited credits at any store. Upper or lower city, it didn't matter.

"Spend what you need to," he said handing the thing over to me. "Just keep a low profile because the Pure I lifted that off doesn't know he's sponsoring you. So it might be best to not go too wild."

I held the card in my hand.

"What about the security code?" I said. All cards had a code you had to punch in for them to work.

Zeev fished a scrap of paper from his pocket and handed it to me. "This should work."

"I thought I was on a list. Surely the scanners would pick me up?"

"I know people inside Data. Do as we say, and we'll run interference for you. Delete the flag they posted on your ID."

"You can do that?" I asked.

"Honey, you have no idea what we are capable of."

Nan chuckled.

"So I do this one thing," I said. "I go to the party, drop a hack into a terminal and in return, you have my records cleaned and you find somewhere nice and safe for Nan to live?"

"Exactly," Zeev said.

"And it's that easy to arrange all that?"

"It can be," he said.

I pondered this thought for a little while. My mind was reeling and my stomach felt vaguely queasy, but that might just have been because I hadn't eaten yet. Our noodles were growing cold and gloopy on the counter in the kitchen.

"Fine," I said, pocketing the card. "Fine, but you had better keep up your side of the bargain."

"That we will," Zeev said. He nodded solemnly.

"Then we have a deal as long as you take Nan with you tonight."

Zeev looked at Nan.

Nan sighed and folded the blanket away from her lap. I noticed that under the covers she was fully dressed.

He helped her up, and she smiled her warm Nan-smile at him. I was instantly jealous. That smile was reserved for me, not strangers. The two of them had played me as if there never was any doubt that I'd say yes.

"I shall be sorry to leave this place," she said simply, as she picked up the backpack that had been on the floor, partly hidden by the edge of the covers. The sight of the backpack made fear swell up inside my chest, hot and unbidden. If Nan was running, things were serious.

Nan wrapped me in her arms. She was soft and warm and solid. I breathed her Nan-smell – fresh feather pillows and fabric softener.

"You take good care of this place while I'm gone," she said. "And don't forget to water the fern."

"I won't," I said, swallowing down a lump that had suddenly appeared in my throat.

"We will come for you as soon as the mission is complete," Zeev said, as Nan let me go.

I wiped angrily at my face to get rid of the unbidden wetness that had filled up my eyes.

"Later, Little Bird," Zeev said. "And use that card soon, before its owner notices it's missing."

\*

"You look amazing," Ari said, his eyes growing wide as he took in the dress and the hair. Zeev's stolen credits had worked hard to achieve my look. We were standing on the steps of the Pure Council buildings in the upper city. Rich, buttery light spilled from the tall windows.

I smiled at him. "It's insane, isn't it?"

"This must have cost a bomb," he said, gesturing at my dress. The fabric was thick and expensive silk, the blue-black colour of a peaceful night sky. "Where did you get the money for a dress like this?"

"Oh," I shrugged. "I found a credit card on the street and so I went shopping with it." I winked at Ari.

"Just like that?"

"Just like that," I replied.

He frowned and ran his hands through his hair. "Tori, what the hell?"

"Don't worry about it," I said, resting my hand on the lapel of his jacket for a moment. Somehow he looked older in the black dinner suit. It had obviously been custom tailored for him. "The shop label is still in the dress. As long as I don't sweat in it or spill anything on it, I'll return it tomorrow, no probs."

Ari still looked unconvinced. "You're crazy," he said.

"And what are you going to do about it?" I said.

He shook his head with resignation.

"Come on Ari, let's just go. Pretend it's all right just for one night, shall we?"

Ari sighed, his conscience beaten. He held out his elbow in the way men did in old movies. The gesture was strangely touching.

"Shall we?" he said.

I put my hand through the crook of his elbow, doing my best not to wobble over on the high, slender heels of my new shoes.

"How did I let you talk me into this?" he said, as we reached the entrance.

"Come on!" I said, smiling to hide my nervousness. "This is the only chance I'll ever have to go to a fancy party. Ever." I cocked my head to the side. "Please."

"All right, but remember that I told you so." He sighed and led me up the stairs.

Inside, the building was like a fairy tale. The place was warm and dry, with not a patch of damp in sight. Acres of fine marble spread as far as the eye could see. Above us, real glass chandeliers twinkled.

"Whoa," I said softly, without thinking.

Ari just chuckled and lifted two glasses of champagne from a passing tray. "How the other half lives," he said, handing me the glass.

"And you gave all this up? You have everything handed to you on a platter and yet you choose to go slumming. Are you mad?"

"Don't be fooled by the gilding, Tori. It's still a cage." He shrugged.

I looked up at the ceiling. It looked like a painting with blue sky and lots of little birds holding trailing ribbons in their beaks. "Hell yes. To be warm and safe. Never having to worry about food or where the rent money is going to come from. You'd be crazy not to want all this," I said.

Ari looked at me for a long time, his eyes narrowing in the way they did when he was thinking, but he said nothing. Somewhere in the background an orchestra – yes, real people playing actual instruments – started up.

"Shall we dance?" he asked.

I was about to answer when I was hit by a pang of guilt. I had to do what I had been sent here to do. Otherwise we'd never be safe. I gritted my teeth. "Just need to hit the ladies' for a second, OK?" I handed him my glass.

"Sure," he shrugged, taking a large sip from his drink.

Inside the ladies room, I pulled the hack out from the place where it was hidden, inside the heel of my shoe. It was a little silver lozenge, about the size of the pad of my thumb. It my felt cool and heavy in my hand. Stolen tech. Probably worth a few years' rent on Nan's apartment. If anyone walked in and found me with it, it would also mean instant death.

I took a deep breath and placed my thumb over the metal. It glowed for an instant as it scanned my fingerprint, and then flashed once to tell me that the activation code had been accepted.

Next came a data point.

I slipped out of the ladies' and walked down a carpeted hallway. Dark wood doors flanked me on either side. I tried one. It was locked. Another. And another. I started panicking. What if I couldn't find a terminal? What if they were all locked away?

A door handle gave way under my hand and the door opened silently. Inside was a dark office. On the one side was a desk with virtual screen console. In front of it was one of those fancy health-kick chairs that allows you to sort of sit-stand while working behind it. To protect your back or whatever.

I sank to my knees beside it. There, under the desk, attached to the table top, was the data point. The bug clicked against the slender metal plate and glowed blue for a moment to indicate that it was working.

I straightened up, my heart hammering against my ribs.

I went to the door and opened it a fraction to make sure no one was in the corridor before slipped out of the office.

My heels sank into the carpet with a soft whisper and I had to fight the urge to run back to the party.

"Where have you been?" Ari gripped my elbow as I rounded a pillar at the edge of the ballroom.

I swung round, on the verge of panic.

"Hey," he said gently, letting me go. His cheeks were slightly flushed from the champagne.

"Oh, you know. Girl stuff," I said, with a small smile. How about that dance?" I steered us into the ballroom.

Ari's arms felt comfortingly solid around me as we swayed awkwardly to the music. Neither of us were exactly sure about how to dance, although I suspect Ari must have had lessons or something, because he steered me towards a corner on the floor.

"We can do this, you know," he said. There was a strange intensity in his eyes.

I frowned. Did he know?

"I mean, this life. We could do it. The clothes, the nice houses. The cars."

I snorted. "Not with my DNA. I'd be caught and eliminated in a week."

He shook his head. "No. You'd be protected. There are others like you. The Council protects them."

I felt my stomach drop to somewhere around the hem of my dress. Shifters being protected by the Council? I struggled to get my head around it.

"If you were mine. All I'd need to do is have a word with my dad. He would understand. His dad was like you. It's our biggest family secret."

"No way."

Ari nodded. "Tori, you must know how I feel about you."

I felt my brain whirr as I tried to compute what he was saying. Was there another way? Another way to be safe? Away from all the misery? And Ari? Dear, sweet, handsome Ari? Did he really just tell me he liked me?

I was about to answer. About to tell him yes, so we could kiss just like in old romantic comedy films, when things kicked off.

The doors to the ballroom burst open. Soldiers dressed in black combat fatigues, their faces covered in balaclavas, burst in brandishing guns. Big-ass, scary semi-automatic guns.

Somewhere behind me, a woman barely had the chance to scream before the shooting started.

"Ari!" I grabbed his arm in an attempt to get him to drop to the ground and out of harm's way.

He twisted out of my grip, the momentum of the movement throwing him forward into the space between me and the shooters. As I watched in horror, he shuddered, the slugs hitting him in the chest. He dropped to the ground like a sack of meat.

I screamed. It was the high, hysterical type of scream that you have absolutely no control over. My dress was wet with his blood. The sound of my pathetic panic was drowned out by gunfire and chaos. Plaster dust and bullets rained down around me.

Someone grabbed me and dragged me roughly over the floor.

I looked up. It was Zeev. The black of his combats were covered in white dust.

"Wait! My friend!" I struggled against his grip. My dainty heels scrabbled uselessly over the shiny marble floor, unable to find enough purchase to stand.

Zeev didn't listen, he just kept dragging me along, away from the blood and the chaos behind us. Once we were in the corridor, he settled me onto my feet roughly.

"Can you stand?" he said.

I nodded. I had lost my beautiful shoes somewhere in the chaos.

"Then move!" He shoved me along before him.

A fire door clattered and swung open as Zeev hit the iron bar that held it shut. An alarm went off, its ring useless.

I gasped as a blast of cold night air hit my bare skin, straightening out my senses. I turned and looked back. "I need to go back for my friend," I said.

"You don't have any friends in there, Little Bird," Zeev said. "I doubt if anyone is left alive back there."

Before I could say anything, the radio he was carrying crackled and buzzed. He listened for a moment and then said something into the handheld.

"Come," he said.

I didn't move. I was too numb. All those people. All that blood.

"Tori, they are about to blow the whole place up, so we need to clear the area. Our ride is on its way."

With a screech of tires, a battered delivery van skidded to a halt in the alley before us. Without a further word, Zeev took my arm and dragged me along with him. I had to scamper in order to keep up with him, scraping my toes on the rough tarmac. The door of the van slid open. He shoved me inside and I fell, hitting the palms of my hands hard against the metal floor.

"Go! Go! Go!" he shouted, smacking the metal door.

The driver hit the controls and the old-fashioned hybrid engine roared. I was flung painfully against the side of the van.

A deep boom shook the van. Bits of glass and debris started raining down around us.

"Blast off!" the driver shouted, as he fought to maintain control of the car.

I struggled to sit up. As I did, I found myself looking into the eyes of a man on the bench opposite me. He sat silently, dressed in black combats just like Zeev.

In the front, Zeev and the driver both let out triumphant whoops.

"That was brilliant work, Little Bird," Zeev said over his shoulder. "If this doesn't turn the tide, I don't know what will. They will remember your bravery for years to come."

I down fought a wave of nausea as I stared at them in horror. The building – and most of the Pure Council – had been eliminated. Ari was dead. It was all my fault.

Mine.

I was a murderer. An outlaw. Homeless.

I was visible.

I would be hunted down until the end of my days. I would never be able to show my face on the streets again.

The guy opposite me was watching me carefully, his eyes narrowed.

I glared at him.

He returned my look with a knowing smile. "Welcome to the Resistance," he said.

## GREENWOOD GREEN
### by John Reppion

The future began a little over two-hundred and fifty years ago here in England, the skies and waters of this once green and pleasant land stained black with the excreta of the Industrial Revolution. A pandemic of ideas swept across the island, infecting Europe and soon the rest of the planet. Yet pockets of the old world, the old ways, remained. In 1830, when the world's first inter-city railway linked the emphysemic cities of Liverpool and Manchester, its engines coughed and choked through the village of Greenwood – set halfway between the two – without so much as slowing down.

All that changed in 1851, when two-hundred and fifty acres of the district's ancient woodland were given over to the dead. The adjacent cities' graveyards could no longer cope with the sheer volume of corpses this New Industrial Age brought with it, and Greenwood Cemetery was the solution. Greenwood Cemetery Station stood at heart of the new necropolis and there, specially chartered engines ferried coffins and mourners direct to the grave. The last such locomotive made its journey around 1920, by which time some hundred-thousand dead had been laid therein. The rails fell silent, they rusted, and in time cunning roots twisted what remained into unrecognisable shapes as, inch by inch, the woodland reclaimed its ground. By the twenty-first century less than three acres were kept tame, these proving more than sufficient for the infrequent custom the cemetery still received.

Ted Berry began working at Greenwood Cemetery in 1963, and since the nineteen-eighties had held the somewhat hyperbolic – given that he was the sole member of staff at the time – title of Head Groundskeeper. As Ted entered his sixties it was deemed necessary that someone of less advanced years join him in his work and so it was that, fresh from failing the majority of his GCSEs at Greenwood High, sixteen year old Danny Taberner became an Assistant Groundskeeper.

Initially, Danny's primary task was to keep the flora from reclaiming the modern day burial ground as they had the rest of the necropolis – sawing and hacking the thicket into submission was his ongoing battle, as it had been his senior's before him. In time however, Danny took on other jobs: mowing the grass, maintaining the monuments and pathways and, when it was occasionally required, digging and filling the graves.

After seven years of working with Ted, Danny's growing list of duties had reduced the elder's to sitting in the rusted portacabin that served as their office smoking his pipe, reading his paper, drinking his tea and, more often than not, dozing in his chair. Danny fully expected this situation to continue until the day came for him to break ground on the plot that already held Mrs. Berry and lay his senior to rest beside her. He hoped that that day would not come too soon. Not just because of the affection he felt for the old man who was, after all, a friendly and likeable individual, but also because of the effect his demise might have upon his own private enterprise.

*

Greenwood Cemetery Station had been wired for electric light within the final decade of its use and, due to some historic oversight, the supply had never been disconnected. Danny had been reminded of this school-yard rumour by a cousin briefly returned from Leeds University but definitely not stopping in the "village of the dead", as he called it, any longer than he had to. With barely disguised contempt for Danny's menial job, he had mentioned with faux-casualness that he knew someone who knew someone who had had a party in the old station years ago. Apparently they had been able to turn on the lights, even rig up a CD player to run off the supply.

Danny had paid as little attention as he possibly could, not wanting to be seen to even acknowledge anything that could be setting him up to look even stupider than his smart-arsed cousin already obviously thought he was. The yarn was heading in an all too obvious direction by the time Danny began speaking into his mobile phone in an intentionally, and he hoped insultingly, oblivious manner. Even so, it wasn't long before the boredom of damp autumn days drove him to exploring the cemetery wilderness while Ted dozed in his chair. Though he would never dream of crediting his cousin for planting the seed of the idea, reaching the old station, or whatever remained of it, soon became an almost inevitable goal.

Getting there proved no mean feat however. It was perhaps a month or more after first discovering traces of the old tracks that Danny – face scratched, High-Vis jacket studded with thorns, petrol strimmer thrumming in his aching gloved hands – finally broke through to the centre of the necropolis.

Ivy and bindweed all but covered the centuried, weather-worn brick and ironwork, so that the station appeared more simulacrum than man-made structure. Great curtains of waxy leaves fluttered about the rusted skeleton built to support a long gone wooden canopy as Danny clambered up onto the fungus-adorned Eastbound platform.

What had once been its mirror-image was little more than a bramble and weed covered hillock of rubble, the Westbound platform's buildings having apparently suffered a total collapse some years previously. All that remained was the spire of the chapel-end which stood like a great cocked hat amid the mouldering bricks and twisted iron rib-work; the mortal remains of some gargantuan witch from a Brothers Grimm nightmare.

If this part of the cemetery had been accessible to the general public, the buildings on the Eastbound platform would, he imagined, have been demolished or, at the very least, tinned up, fenced off, and covered with signs warning against the danger of entering. As it was, the ticket office doors, or what remained of them, hung open not so much in invitation as in a dare. A dare that felt, however subliminally, had been set by his arsehole of a cousin. Killing the engine and unstrapping himself from the harness, Danny laid the strimmer down on the platform. From his backpack he produced a torch and a crowbar. Taking the dare, he entered.

The black and white tiled floor of the ticket office was heaped with piebald bird droppings. Unseen pigeons flapped and cooed uneasily in the rafters, disturbed by Danny's arrival. Grey daylight filtered in as patches through ragged gaps in the roof. Even so, the place was less of a wreck than he had expected, especially given the state of its twin on the other side of the tracks. Though its wooden surround was visibly decayed, the glass window behind which the ticket-seller had once sat remained unbroken. He shone his torch into the small, shadowed space beyond and saw a wooden chair still in place, as if the vendor had just that moment left his post.

To the left of the booth, along the same green-tiled wall, was a door which he took to be the way into, and out of, the ticket office. This was locked. To his right, directly opposite the doors he had entered through, were an identical pair. These too proved to be locked but, assuming that beyond them lay only more of the same inhospitable woodland he had so recently fought his way through, Danny felt no inclination to attempt to alter the fact with his crowbar.

Opposite the ticket office were the rotted remains of wooden, pew-like benches which may have seated as many as twenty mourning travellers at a time. Beyond these lay an arched doorway, portal to the Eastbound platform's chapel. Danny tried the bird-shit streaked handle with his gloved hand and, to his surprise, found the door unlocked.

A wave of musty, woody air a degree or two warmer than the cold, damp day outside belched forth. Inside was absolute darkness. For the first time Danny felt a lurch of fear. His bright torch-beam pierced the gloom, illuminating only a fraction of the deserted chapel at a time – an all too obvious horror convention. Soon he knew, the formula dictated the light must surely fall upon some waiting figure. His imagination began automatically to cycle through suitable candidates: the eerie widow in black, the evil clergyman, the lost child...

The story Danny's cousin had tried to tell those months earlier reared up out of shadows of memory. Elsie Loy. The lost girl.

It was a local tragedy. Practically the only thing that had ever happened in the place. She disappeared in the 1990s, left her house one day and never came back. No one ever saw her again, and no one ever knew what had happened. There were plenty of stories, of course. Elsie Loy was by now the star of several, largely contradictory, legends long whispered among the pupils of the local schools. One thing almost every story agreed upon was that Elsie had been horribly murdered. The tale his cousin had been trying to tell would have been the one that ended with Elsie's disembodied voice coming through the speakers of a mini hi-fi, pleading confusedly from the past. Why else include his little electricity preamble? But then why not have the machine powered by batteries in the first instance?

Danny remained in the doorway, slowly sweeping the torch-beam across the rows of dusty, cobwebbed pews.

There was another story, one of an escapee from Ashfield high-security hospital – some ten miles away by road, but more like six, maybe even less, as the crow flies. Yes, the escaped lunatic, another staple. He had been living in the station, surviving on the flesh of birds, rats, and sometimes, depending who was telling the story, going as far as exhuming the dead. He let the teenagers have their little party, he watched them and waited, and then at the crucial moment he turned out the lights...

Keeping the torch as steady as he could in his hand, Danny put the crowbar between his legs and gripped it with his knees. Then, never taking his eyes off the chapel interior, he felt on the wall beside the door for a light switch. There was none. He passed the torch to the other hand and reached out into the darkness.

"Danny?" An urgent, hollow whisper.

Danny's crowbar clattered to the ground, the sound amplified and reverberant in the funereal inkiness. Flashing the torch all around him, he ducked to retrieve his only weapon, his gloves adding to his desperate, panicked fumbling. The sound of the crowbar scraping on the tiled floor was sharp and penetrating.

"Danny?" The voice seemed close but quiet. Flat and unreal somehow.

He swung the crowbar in an arc, slashing at the darkness.

"Can you hear me, Danny?" There was worry, almost panic, in it now.

"Where are you?" his challenge came in a horse whisper, as if aping the other voice.

"I'm in the cabin, lad. Where are you? What's going on?"

Danny staggered backward into the ticket office and sank onto a creaking bench. Releasing the crowbar and torch onto the seat, he reached into his trouser pocket and pulled out his phone. The name on the screen read TED (WORK). Yanking off his right glove, Danny drew a deep breath, exhaled slowly and deliberately. He swiped the screen, switching off speaker-phone, and lifted the phone to his ear.

"Ted. Are you alright, mate? What's up?"

"What's up? What's up with you? What are you ringin' me for? Where are you? What's all the bloody noise, lad?"

"Sorry, it must've been a pocket call. Accidental, like. I'm alright."

"Are you in the village? You're car's still here. It's well past lunch y' know. Gettin' on fer home time."

Danny was sure he couldn't have been gone so long as that, but when he looked at the clock on the screen it was already well past three. Normally he nipped into the village and brought Ted back a pie, or a pasty, or chips for his lunch. Ted would pretend he hadn't been asleep, rise from his throne and make them both a brew. It was a daily ritual, the forgoing of which had clearly baffled and affronted the older man.

"Sorry, Ted. I lost track of time. I'll be back in half an hour, forty five minutes at most. I'll lock up if you want to get off."

"I'm alright here, lad. Things to do! But, you're sure there's nothin' wrong?"

"Nothing, no. It's... I'm fine, Ted."

"Right well, I'll not ask any more. Just get your arse back here, eh?"

"Okay."

Touching END CALL on the screen, Danny then pressed and held the power button, switching the phone off to avoid any more accidental calls. He felt an absolute idiot. The whole ridiculous scenario seemed in that moment an impossibly elaborate prank somehow pulled off by that dickhead of a cousin of his. What was he even doing out there? Exploring like he was a kid and, what was worse, getting just as easily spooked as one. Collecting up his tools, Danny was already skulking self-consciously toward the open ticket office doors before he remembered.

He looked up, searching the damp, blackened rafters with the torch-light once more. Roosting birds flapped and shat in protest. There they were. How had he missed them earlier? He counted them. One, two light fittings, a space where a third may once have been. He panned the beam around the walls. No sign of any switches.

Danny tried the handle of the locked ticket booth door again. Resisting the urge to vent his frustrations in an attempt at kicking the door open – not least for fear of failing and making himself feel even more ridiculous – he stabbed the pinched end of his crowbar between the lock and the door-frame and wrenched with both hands. The wormy frame splintered much more easily and completely than he had imagined it would, the strike plate of the lock actually bursting forth. The liberated door bulged, straining against its seized hinges for a moment, then swung slowly inward with a languorous creak.

Inside, the cramped little room felt dry and warm. Danny entered and soon his torch-beam found what he had been searching for. A bank of antiquated, domed metal switches – some thirty or more – arranged in little rows, a tiny plaque under each. There were four switches in the row designated as WAITING ROOM. Danny flipped them all. Nothing changed. There was one switch on its own which was unlabelled.

He flipped it and, again, nothing happened.

He shone the torch upward and saw a lone, sooty looking bulb suspended above the ticket-man's chair. The seat screaked in protest as he stepped on to it. Carefully he unscrewed the delicate bulb and examined it in the torch-light. Just as he had hoped. In his backpack, he found a near identical one. One of the bulbs Ted had to order in specially to fit the antiquated lights still in use in the tamed acres of the cemetery. Danny carefully twisted it into place, and the filament within flickered into life.

*

In truth Danny had already had his big idea long before he even reached the old station.

After unlocking the gates that Sunday morning he went for a drive, spending a couple of hundred pounds at a place called Holland Horticulture near Manchester, then another fifty at Budlife in the city centre there, and the same again at an industrial estate DIY store. He was back at Greenwood Cemetery in time to lock up, the twilight already deepening. With a car-boot full of supplies it was difficult to fight the urge to begin his enterprise there and then, but he knew that making the journey to the station would be arduous in the dark. Besides, there was one thing he still needed to do and that would be much easier at home in his room, following instructions on his laptop.

Danny was back at the gates in the icy hours just before dawn, his key tuning in the rust speckled padlock once again. His idea to follow and if necessary widen the way cut the previous week fell flat when he discovered that he could find no sign of the path. Even the point at which he was certain he had begun seemed to have just closed up – the vegetation apparently just as thick and impenetrable as that surrounding it. Grudgingly then, he strapped on the petrol strimmer and set about cutting a new route. The going was tortuously slow.

The time for Ted's arrival at the cabin came all too quickly and Danny was forced to abandon his task and make an appearance. Ted wasn't unused to Danny having got there and opened up first, but he was surprised to see him all suited-up and already hard at work.

"If it's a promotion your after, lad, I've told you the job's yours as soon as I'm in the ground."

"Just thought I'd give it all a proper cut back now before it gets too cold. Maybe save us a job in the long run."

Ted took a contemplative slurp of tea and smacked his lips with pleasure before answering. "Worth a try," he reflected, his attention already shifting to the newspaper he was unfolding.

Danny tipped the half-drank contents of his own mug into the battered steel sink. "I'll crack on then."

He was halfway out of the door when Ted announced gravely, "Oh, I'd better warn you though."

"What's that?" asked Danny.

"Don't you go eatin' any blackberries. We're past Michaelmas now. Old Nick'll have been at them."

"Eh?"

"They'll give you the shits!"

Progress through the thicket was just as slow – close to impossible in truth – in the hours before the lunch run. In the afternoon Ted came out to supervise and offer advice on the taming of the wood's borders. He could see Danny was having trouble with them by the fact that it looked like he had hardly done a thing.

And so it was that after bidding goodbye to his co-worker in the dying light of the day, instead of heading back to his parental home, Danny found himself circling back around the edge of the cemetery. Ignoring his usual turn-off, he followed the curve of the dual carriageway with its overgrown central strip. The land of the burial site on his left, which had for a mere seventy years been kept tame, was now all but indistinguishable from the wildwood on the other side of the road. The carriageway was pitted and cracked. The trunks of the outermost trees of the cemetery had bowed, twisted, and absorbed many of the remained rusted Victorian railings. Their roots had swelled to burst through the surface where and when they could. They and their more ancient counterparts seemed determined to stand side by side once more and to relieve the land of the temporary scab of tarmac in the process.

The last rays of sunset flickered stroboscopically through the branches and railings as the car sped along. Danny found it hard to concentrate on the road, his blinking eyes continually drawn back to the woodland. The flickering light and contrasting shadows made it seem as though there were things moving within. A pack of dark, low shapes skittering along. More spooky stuff. Kids stuff. He squeezed his left eye shut tightly and concentrated on the curving road.

In the distance he saw a figure amid the tangle of weeds and saplings populating the un-mown verge which separated the two lanes of the carriageway. It wasn't the best place to be, but then it was probably safer and easier than trying to walk on either side, he thought. The figure wore what looked like a long black coat, though the lower half of their body was lost among the roadside fauna. He must be approaching from behind, he realised, because he couldn't see any face. Or was the face just in the shade of the hood of the coat? With barely a conscious thought on the matter Danny found himself speeding up. As he drew closer, everything seemed to become clear. A scarecrow. Stolen from a nearby field and planted on the central reservation by some kids, most likely. But, did farmers still even use scarecrows? Had he ever actually seen one in real life? As he came up alongside the figure, he caught a glimpse of knotted wood and ivy beneath the covering. Danny was reassured for an instant until the thing launched itself sideways and landed on his car.

It flapped angrily at the windscreen, covering it almost entirely. Panicked, Danny stamped on the brake. The car came to a juddering stop with a scraping of metal and a crackle of wood. A soggy, mouldering black tracksuit top half peeled away from the windscreen, flopping sideways onto the bonnet. Danny, still straining against his taught seatbelt, swore through clenched teeth at the limp item of clothing. A confusion of branches and leaves were flattened against the miraculously unbroken passenger-side windows. Though he had left the road he had not crashed, merely scraped up against the cemetery wood in a section luckily devoid of railings.

His blue-streak of abuse spent, Danny slumped back in his seat. He rubbed his hands wearily across his face then unbuckled his seatbelt. The headlights bored dust-speckled channels through the ever-deepening gloom as stepped out on to the road. Reaching across, he made an angry grab for the hoodie. Somehow it slid clear of his grasp, slithering across the bonnet down onto the ground with a wet flop. Moving to the front of the car he saw the thing in a puddle-like heap among the leaves and weeds, straddling the remains of a piece of rusted metal.

The old railway track.

Years of patchwork resurfacing had blotted out all evidence of where the track had once crossed paths with the carriageway, but there amongst the brambles were the last remains of a long forgotten intersection. A thought came like a whisper in his ear: this was a route to the station. Although he was surely as far now from the centre of the cemetery as ever, there seemed some glimmer of hope in it. Danny retrieved a newly purchased high-powered LED head-torch from the boot of the car. Aiming himself between what was left of the tracks, he pushed his way through the thorny undergrowth. Though the track-way was heavily overhung, the route itself proved relativity easy to follow. It was as though the wood were parting ahead of him, opening up.

He pushed on for a good fifteen minutes then awkwardly scrambled up onto the lower branches of one of the nearby trees. He climbed a little way before peering out. There it was, the spire of the Eastbound platform chapel, poking up among the trees. It was still quite some distance away but Danny felt certain he had already got closer in that quarter of an hour than he had in his whole morning's toil. A return to the car proved equally unchallenging in spite of stupid, childish worries that niggled away somewhere in the back of his mind that the path may somehow have been swallowed up behind him.

By the time Danny was back at the side of the carriageway he had already made up his mind to seize his opportunity, darkness or not. He emptied the car boot, cramming as much as he could into a newly purchased pull-along wheeled crate with extending handle, an old camping backpack, and even his coat pockets. Then he disappeared back into the twilit wood.

\*

The sky was already full of stars when Danny dragged the mud-spattered pull-along crate up onto the Eastbound platform. His heart thumped with the exertions of the journey, which he had made at something like a jog whenever it was possible – shoving branches aside, or ducking under them, or jumping over them. Things that he knew must have been foxes and owls had skittered and flapped across his path once or twice. Figures, their features eaten away by a century of rain and moss, watched him pass from atop some of the larger monuments otherwise hidden by bramble and creeper. The surrounding woodland was pregnant with a hundred-thousand silent corpses. None of these things, he silently affirmed, had quickened either his pace or his heart.

Danny flicked the cold metal switch, and the bulb in the ticket office glowed into life. He glanced across the waiting room towards the closed chapel doors and felt a twinge of shame. Shame, not fear, he assured himself. His first task was to cover up the small window in the room. This was accomplished with a layer of thick lining paper held in place with the liberal use of gaffer tape. A small blackout blind, designed to help infants sleep while away from home, was then taped in place over the top.

Next, he fitted a bolt to the inside of the door, long screws crunching as they bored into the wood, and allowed himself to draw it to a closed position without feeling too ridiculous. This was merely the simplest way to prevent the door opening accidentally while he was in there, given the lack of a working lock. His home-made adapter was constructed from the base of one of the specially ordered bulbs, its glass and filament carefully removed. The wiring of what had been the plug end of a twin socket extension lead was soldered to the connections within the bulb, gaffer tape once again used generously to seal the two together.

This was his own slightly modified take on a device he had found a How-To for online. The website called it a Powerstealer, and warned that such devices were illegal in most of Europe, due to its lack of an earth and the potentially deadly nature of 240 volt mains electricity. Once it was screwed in, in place of the bulb, the switch was flicked once more. There was no deadly arc of electricity, no incandescent eruption of ancient fuses, only the gentle glow of the red power indicator on the socket.

The socket provided power for an air-pump and pair of bright daylight bulbs, which Danny fitted inside a little pop-up tent lined with silver reflective material. The air-pump bubbled through a container of water, the lid of which had spaces for a dozen plugs of growing medium set into it. Into each of these plugs Danny carefully placed some of the seeds he had purchased on his trip to Manchester. He sealed the tent's velcro door flap meticulously, making sure no light could escape, and sat back in the ticket-man's creaky chair to survey his work by the light of his head-torch.

He allowed himself a moment of self congratulation and mentally aimed a good sized "fuck you" at his dickhead cousin. His idea had worked. At least, now it seemed like it really could work.

Even if everything did go according to plan, his first harvest would not be ready for more than eight weeks. If the plants did well enough over the next couple of weeks he could start looking at expanding his experiment a little bit. To do that, he would need to find other operational light fittings, however. The last thing he wanted to do was risk overloading the ancient electrics and literally blowing everything. Danny knew that the chapel, which had seemed just as warm and dry as the now almost-cosy ticket office, was his only real hope of that, but he did his best not to think about it. Not yet. There was no need.

He fitted the two heavy-duty hasp and staple sets to the outside of the ticket office door with considerably more haste than he had worked with inside the little room. Only once or twice did he give in to the almost overwhelming urge to glance back at the chapel doors. A metal sign that read DANGER DO NOT ENTER was his final addition to the door furniture. It was almost certainly completely pointless, but there was a chance that it, coupled with the padlocks, might be enough to deter any exploring kids. Not that he had seen any evidence of any such visitors – no graffiti, no empty cans or bottles, no real litter of any sort. Even so, the window would need to be boarded over to stop anyone smashing the glass to peek inside, but that was a job for another day.

Danny pulled out his phone and thumbed the screen into life. It was close to 4 AM. Nearly ten hours had passed since he said goodbye to Ted. How could that possibly be? There were a couple of missed calls from home, one voicemail which no doubt warned that the front door was being locked or something similar. He

173

prodded the appropriate icon and was in the process of lifting the phone to his ear when, out in the cemetery, something screamed. Icy, prickling terror raced up Danny's spine and into the base of his skull.

"Danny... come home... never... too... late..." his mother's remote whisper, two thirds of the words lost in electrostatic interference or else drowned out by the thump of his own heart. He squeezed the power button without looking back at the device, his eyes fixed on the open waiting-room door as he walked slowly towards it.

On the platform, the abundant fungus glowed milkily in the moonlight. Danny parted the ivy curtain and gazed out over the woodland necropolis. The night was cloudless and still. Another scream. Animal, he felt more sure this time, more like a screech – the call of a bird perhaps, somehow hollow. But now there were others, other sounds at least. Not like the screams. These were low and rhythmic, a lolloping, grunting chant. He could hear a rustling and cracking of branches now, too.

He began to become aware of movement among the undergrowth in the distance. Low down unseen things were racing, stamping and snorting, the thick greenery rippling in their wake. As he watched he picked out more and more trails, the cadent grunt growing louder. Though they appeared to come from all directions, every path seemed to be aimed at the very platform where he now stood. Suddenly, ahead of the converging pack of things, something white leapt into the air. Danny caught sight of a set of oversized antlers crowning a head before their owner crashed down again, letting out another distressed bellow as he did so. A hunt.

He was already back inside the ticket office, bolting the door behind him before he knew what he was doing. There was a local custom of hunting rabbits and hares with dogs which, though illegal for more than a decade, everyone knew still went on. Sending dogs after deer in a great big unmanaged expanse of woodland with no-one to hear or see you, let alone stop you, seemed suddenly like an all too obvious companion pastime. Just because Danny had never seen or even heard of any deer in Greenwood before didn't mean there weren't any. Did it?

A clatter of frantic, unsteady hoof-beats on the platform. The stag was right outside. The bastard thing was leading them straight to him. His back pressed against the inside of the ticket office door, Danny quickly switched off his head-torch and listened hard, desperately trying to slow his heart and his breathing. The bellow came so loud it was as though the creature was there in the tiny pitch black room with him. The deafening primal cry resonated through the waiting room and, Danny felt certain, around the chapel also. In his mind's eye the stag – surely a roe, or perhaps red deer – had already grown to the proportions of a monstrous North American moose, or a prehistoric megaloceros.

There was silence, followed by hesitant clipped hoof-falls in the waiting room itself. The stupid beast had got itself cornered. Oh God, he had left his tools out there. No padlocks on the outside of the door, and a set of tools lying on the floor next to it. The sign he had put up might as well have said SOMEONE HIDING IN HERE. Whoever had set the dogs after the deer was going to find him. He thought of trying to shoo the beast out of the station and immediately envisioned being savagely gored by the trapped monster shortly before the mad dogs which pursued it tore him apart.

The pack arrived before he could even try to persuade himself otherwise. They came not with the barks and snarls he had expected but that same low-pitched, rhythmic snuffling grunt he had heard before. This was soon coupled with the occasional horrifically piercing squeal. Even their feet, as they galloped over the soiled ticket office tiles en masse, sounded more like small hooves than the padded paws of dogs.

As Danny listened with terror to the carnage on the other side of the door – the bellows, screams and stamps of the one, the guttural growls and squeals of the others – he imagined the damage being done not by canines but by a pack of horrific pig-things. Was he imagining it? It was as though the scene were projected onto the blackness that surrounded him. It did not matter, he discovered to his horror, whether his eyes were open or closed. He saw it clearly. A herd of primeval sabre-tusked boar-beasts, their wiry haired muzzles dripping with gore as they

175

swarmed over and tore into an albino antlered colossus. The roaring pink-eyed stag far too big to have ever fitted through the waiting room doors.

Because, he realised, there was no waiting room. No station. This was all happening out in the open. In the cemetery, beneath whose soil a writhing mass of hungry roots had sucked the marrow from millions of bones; knotting, absorbing and melding with them so that there was no way to tell where one ended and the other began. In the old, dark woods where the last of England's grey wolves was slain in the seventeenth century, the final brown bear seven centuries earlier, the last lynx six hundred years before that, and on, and on. In the forest that came before. The forest that was everywhere, was everything. A great green colony with billions of wooden limbs strong enough to shatter rock, with sap for blood and neural networks of mycorrhiza; giving life to and taking it from every single thing whose existence flickered, however fleetingly, across it.

The forest that was forever.

*

There was a crash against his back. Everything went black. He was blind. Another heavy thump at his back. No, not blind, just in darkness. He fumbled to click on the head-torch. Danny found that he was still in the ticket office, his back pressed against the door. Something smashed into the other side and he felt the blow rattle through his body. His brain struggled to catch up. The white stag. Thump. The pack. Thump. The hunt. Thump. Idiot! It was the dog owners. They had found him just like he knew they would.

Thump.

Thump. Thump.

"Alright!" he shouted, unable to stand it any longer. "Alright, I'm coming out!"

The banging ceased.

Danny drew back the bolt shakily and pulled the creaking door inward. Daylight. The caw of a crow outside. He stepped out into the waiting room cautiously.

"Hello?"

No answer.

The rotten benches stood in their rows. His tools lay exactly where he had left them on the dirty tiles to one side of the doorway. There was no blood on the floor, no hoof or paw-prints, and absolutely no sign of anyone. Everything was exactly as it had been before, except for the fact that the doors which led to the chapel now stood open.

Danny picked up a hammer from among the other tools.

"This isn't funny!" he shouted, instantly regretting doing so as he imagined just how much more funny anyone deliberately trying to frighten him would find it.

"I've got a fucking hammer!" he added with genuine anger, which he hoped was enough to wipe the smiles off their faces. Whoever they were.

Danny glanced toward the open waiting room doors. The morning beyond was crisp and bright. His breath condensed into fleeting steamy clouds. They could be waiting out there. Waiting for him to run out crying like some stupid frightened kid. This could all be the work of his cousin. That made no sense at all. Even so, the thought made him angrier still. He looked back at the open chapel doors and, without giving himself a chance to do otherwise, he took the dare.

The head-torch beam cut through the deep gloom of the chapel as Danny ran in. He stopped about ten feet up the central aisle and whirled round quickly, spotlighting the spaces to either side of the doors in turn. No one waiting there to trap him. His panting breath echoed loudly in the sepulchral space, but there were no longer any puffs of condensation. The chapel was warm and dry. Hastily he checked the pews to either side of him, then realised he had seen something. Danny turned his head toward the left of the doorway once again.

There on the wall, a metal panel glinted in the torch-light. A bank of light switches. He had, he realised, only managed to check the right side before his pocket call to Ted had scared him off last time. He ran back and, his hammer held high in one hand, and clicked every switch in turn with the other. There was faint sizzling sound behind the panel. Up in the rafters four out of forty or so ancient bulbs flickered, one flaring brightly and going out with an audible pop within a second.

Though much of the chapel remained in absolute darkness, the cob-webbed geriatric incandescents spot-lit patches here and there. One shed a stuttering pool of light a few feet ahead, down upon the aisles tiled floor. There, amid a confusion of footprints in the dust and grime, were what looked like tracks. Animal tracks. Three toed hoof-prints, each the size of his own shoe.

Danny's eye was drawn along the aisle, his head-torch travelling the path as he lifted his head. Past the region where he had ran, trod, turned, skidded and retrod, the prints were clearer but different. They were smaller. He began to walk up the aisle staring at the floor before him, forgetting the potential threat lurking in the shadows, the hammer in his hand. The tracks seemed altered with each step. The toes grew less and less pointed. Hoof-prints becoming delicate paw-prints, the trail leading on and up the aisle. A fifth bulb crackled into life directly above the chancel ahead. Something white lay there, quivering there before the altar.

Danny stumbled forward, tripping on the step which led up to the chancel. He fell to his knees before the creature. A large white hare lay on its side, its long legs stretched out straight and trembling, the pupil of its one visible eye a pink pinprick of terror. Danny laid a hand on the creature's side. He could feel its stuttering heart beat, the quick, shallow rise and fall of its ribs.

He raised his head and the torch-beam shone where once a wooden cross would have hung. In its place – or perhaps grown over and around it – was a knotted mass of ivy, bramble and bindweed. A great suspended nest of intricately interwoven tendrils, creepers, and leaves that seemed to rustle and shiver in time with the hare's trembling. At its centre, Danny thought he saw something he recognised. It was not a face. It had not been a face the last time either. The twisted gnarl of ivy-wood which had filled that black hood in such an uncannily skull-like manner had no features. None except... Two ivy leaves fluttered on the front of the head-sized knot. In that moment, he felt certain that those leaves were eyelids. Eyelids which might open at any second, revealing....

A violent shaking beneath his hand made Danny look down.

The hare was convulsing. A wave of emotion swept over him. He remembered the impossible stag, brought down by the pack of swine-things. The eternal, unending forest, which was life and death to all. Which surrounded him. Which demanded sacrifice. He raised his hammer-hand high above his bowed head, then brought the implement down with all his might again and again and again upon the twitching animal. Every blow ringing out in the vast empty chamber like the peel of great echoing bell, tolling reconsecration.

*

Danny never went back to the Eastbound platform at night again. For a while, he made sure he knew exactly when dawn would break and would be waiting for it, parked in a half hidden space he had cleared for himself at the edge of the dual-carriageway. Soon he discovered he need not be so punctual. It didn't matter how long he gave himself, he always seemed to emerge from the woodland with just enough time to clear away the fresh tendrils of ivy from his car, drive round to the cemetery gates, and begin his day job.

Digging graves, drinking tea, mowing grass, fetching pie and chips; the routine was the same as ever. Old Ted puffing on his pipe, reading his paper, dozing in his chair. More like a recurring dream than a job. Of course, by then it wasn't his job, it was a means to an end. Little more than a cover story. His plan, his big idea, inspired long ago in some tiny way by his cousin's infantile ghost story, had worked. Was working.

Danny moved out of his parents' house into a flat in one of the crumbling tower-blocks of Greenwood Estate. They were a trio of 1950s high-rises built on the site of Greenwood Manor, the last remains of which had already rotted back into the earth by the time the first concrete slab was poured. There, with his UPVC front door almost obscured by a buddleia bush, its roots embedded deep in the cracks of the fifth floor balcony, he could come and go without anyone paying much attention.

He spent a lot of his nights driving. North, Preston was his limit, while south he ranged as far as Crewe. East and West were Manchester and Liverpool respectively, which not only suited his

179

business but also felt appropriate, all things considered. He was not a dealer, he was a supplier, and to the people he supplied he was supposed to be less than that.

A skinny, scruffy kid delivering cardboard-box loads of hydroponically grown weed out of the back of a succession of cash-bought, beaten-up, uninsured cars. He was not – so far as his clients were concerned – the grower, merely the delivery boy. He wore a Bluetooth earpiece and relayed events quietly into it. This was something he got from some of the dozen or so how-to pieces he had read online. They, being predominantly American, also often recommended firearms. Danny carried no weapon with him on his deliveries, not so much as the hammer.

He had had the earpiece pulled from him a couple of times, one of them on an industrial estate in Saint Helens. This particular first-time client believed that Danny was, in fact, full of shit, growing the weed himself in some barn or attic most likely. He surmised that Danny was on the phone either to an equally unimposing horticultural partner, or to else no-one at all. Holding the device up to his own ear, he asked what was to stop him and his associates just taking the weed for themselves and persuading the supposed delivery boy, via the snapping of finger-bones, to show them where it was being grown. To everyone else present the answer sounded like a whine of electrostatic feedback, painfully loud and piercing even from a few feet away. This was however, somehow clear and concise enough to make the doubting party silently hand the earpiece back to Danny before paying him in full.

Things did not usually go so far. Whenever possible, Danny would make his deliveries out in the open: a patch of waste-ground, a playing field, a lay-by, an abandoned swing park, even an old boarded up farm. Anywhere with a bit of green space, trees, or bushes, tall yellow grass, or tangles of tarmac cracking weeds. It did not matter, so long as there were leaves above and roots below.

If the buying party did happen to have any doubts, or get any ideas, there would come that moment which Danny soon grew to expect.

Someone would suddenly be staring up into a tree, or over towards some litter-covered patch of scrub. Words, sometimes whispered, would be exchanged. Others would look and begin to see what they had seen, or perhaps to see something entirely different. Danny never looked, he just stood and waited. There had been a handful of buyers who had left empty handed after that, but more often than not the deal would be done as agreed. For any and all who bought, return custom was more or less guaranteed. The weed was by all accounts very good. Those dealers and customers who considered themselves connoisseurs spent a great deal of time discussing what strain of skunk it was, or was a hybrid of, and naturally ended up giving it a dozen different names of their own. Danny, who had never smoked a single bud of it, simply called it Green.

Out in the middle of the woodland that was Greenwood Cemetery, in the chapel of the old Eastbound platform, a forest of Green grew where once rows of dusty pews stood. Daylight bulbs blazed, water pumps bubbled and hummed. Black, rich graveyard soil served in place of shop-bought growing medium, a mini forest of luminous toadstools scattered across the surface of the compartmentalised earth.

The water was drawn from a tap Danny found hidden in the shadows of the chapel. It was rust brown, tasted like licking a battery and, after a short time bubbling beneath the plants, took on the colour and consistency of blood. The Green was grown from its own seed, a carefully selected mix of male and female plants left to flower and pollinated in one section of the chapel. The plants grew fast. Faster than they should have. In the ticket office nursery seeds became seedlings in mere days, if not hours. But then the days seemed to blur together for Danny anyway, each one so much similar to the last that it might be a repeat.

In the artificial daylight flowers perpetually blossomed amid the twisted body of vegetation which clung muscularly above the alter. Silver whiskered marijuana buds nestled among the morning-glory, bindweed, and ivy blooms. A curtain of vine tentacles had slid down over the alter to cover the chancel, hiding the spot where the white hare had been slain.

Sometimes, when he arrived in the early mornings, Danny would catch a glimpse of the wing of a pigeon or the head of a crow poking out amid the leaves, and once or twice the tail or paw of a stray cat. By the time he left however, the remains would already be covered over, vague little hummocks the only hint of what lay beneath. Danny never touched them, never went anywhere near them if he could help it. Somehow as those little mounds diminished, parts of what lay beneath made their way up the vines. Whole parts. The ivy-wood skull nestled high above, there among the blossoms and leaves and the sinewy knots of creeper and vine that were at once its home, and its body was adorned with them. A mask of feather and bone, of teeth and beaks and claws, with two fluttering ivy leaves for eyelids.

As the months rolled by, Danny began to wonder more and more what would happen if did just stop. Just stop it all. Would that be enough to end it? Maybe if he boarded up the doors, patched up the larger holes here and there, maybe then the animals couldn't find their way in. He remembered that experiment they'd done in Saint George's Primary back when he was just a kid, the one where they grew cress seeds in little clear plastic containers. The seedlings lifted the lids right off, even the ones that had been sealed shut with tape. In the murk of his memories, Danny thought there might even have been a container with a lid which had been nailed into place.

He pictured the army of seedlings growing, pushing as one, the nails squeaking as they were forced up and out, dropping onto the wooden desktop one by one. Shoots and roots could bend metal, bust concrete – you only had to walk down any street to see that – all they needed was time. Just stopping wouldn't work, action would need to be taken. He had all the necessary tools at his disposal, of course. Saws, axes, the petrol strimmer, a chainsaw even. The idea terrified him so much he could hardly bear to think about it. When he did, he saw a vision of blood and gore streaming from thrashing severed creepers, imagined a deafening shriek that no mouth could utter filling the chapel. He had nightmares about it. More than he cared to remember. A fire then. Fire seemed the only way. Not now, not yet, but when the time came. When it was time to stop. When he had enough. This decision gave Danny some comfort, some renewed sense of control. He had a plan, and now he had an exit strategy.

Danny slept a little easier after that, even moved some of the stuff out of his boxy bedroom and started sleeping in there rather than on the couch in front of the flickering TV. At the same time he started picking up those plastic jerry cans you could buy at petrol stations when he was filling up his latest cash-bought motor. He'd fill the can as if he was getting a little bit extra, just in case, then take it with him when he went to the cemetery the next morning. He was building up a little stockpile of them there on the platform, lined up against the ticket office wall. Soon he'd have enough.

Soon.

Danny didn't know what woke him up that night. Was it a noise, or was it the smell? He was sitting up in his bed, in his flat on the Greenhill Estate. His phone said it was nearly 5 AM. Danny didn't turn on any lights, he didn't think to call to see if anyone would answer. Still half-asleep, he pulled on a pair or tracksuit bottoms then padded out of the bedroom into the hall. The smell was worse out here, and accompanied now by a soft glugging. A small puddle had already formed on the threadbare carpet at the foot of the front door and iridescent rivulets were making their way slowly along the hall toward the living room. The petrol was coming through the narrow letterbox in a slow, steady dribble. Danny's first sleep-clouded thought was that this was a mistake. Someone else's mistake. No one had any cause to threaten or hurt him.

"Oi!" he shouted, without thinking it through, "Oi, you've got the wrong flat! The wrong person!"

The flow increased suddenly, as if whatever contained the fuel was being tipped further now. Fear finally caught up with Danny as his mind awoke to the possibility of a match or some burning paper being pushed through next. He sprinted the five steps down the narrow hallway. One bare foot squelched on the petrol-sodden flooring as the other kicked at the letterbox, slamming the cold metal flap shut. That was no good, he realised immediately, the flames would still catch all too easily. Rage took over. Blind, idiot rage. He ripped the door open, clenched fist ready to slam into the face of whoever stood there. He'd mash the fuckers, see how clever they were then. He started back at the bulky, crouching

183

black shape before him then swore again. Just the buddleia bush. He looked left, he looked right, no sign of anyone. No sound of running feet. The distant bark of a dog. The thudding of his own heart. Nothing else. There was no-one there.

A plastic jerry can lay in front of the door, still leaking onto the aged mat that had been there when Danny moved in. He'd scared them off, then. He bent to right the dribbling container but, to his shock, found it weird to the touch. Not the greasy plastic feel he'd expected, but a strange, organic, uneven texture. The surface, he realised, was completely covered by an intricate network of fine, white tendrils. Fine white tendrils which connected in turn to thicker green vines, so dark they had been almost invisible there in the shadows. The vines, cabled together, trailed away into the utter blackness beneath the buddleia.

Danny saw it then, there in the bush. Right at the same height as his own face. That knot of ivy-wood, fringed with its macabre decorations like some ancient ritual mask. But it wasn't a mask. It was a face. A face with two fluttering ivy leaves for eyelids. And as he stared in terror they fluttered, and they flickered, and they opened. And those eyes. Those *eyes*. They were worse than Danny had ever imagined they could be. Much worse. A pair of pustular, fungal bulges, not so much revealed as allowed to bloom forth from the wooden socket holes. Their pupilless surface glistened milkily as they stared at him. Into him. And though there was no mouth to be seen, he "heard" every ugly, angry twist of it, every sneer of it, as it spat the pre-language picture sounds directly into his brain.

There was water, and in it little blobs that wriggled and split and copied themselves over and over. And then there were green blobs, and some sank down and some floated on the surface, and some grew ruffles and fronds and sail-like leaves. Some clumped together in great colonies, working as one, becoming one. In time, some began to creep out of the water and onto the land. Tiny white threads spread everywhere, and connected everything. Plants began to grow and fungus began to grow and trees began to grow, and the mesh of almost-invisible threads – the mycelium – connected it all. And it was all one, working as one, feeling and thinking and knowing as one.

After billions and billions of journeys of the great big rock they all clung to hurtling round and round the great burning star, tiny things started swimming in the water. They got bigger and started dragging themselves clumsily up on to land. In no time at all they became hairy, shit covered things that seemed to screech and kill and fuck their way through a million different shapes and sizes. Ugly, idiot things, trampling on and scrabbling at the elegant, omniscient net of mycelium that covered the entire planet which they somehow convinced themselves was theirs.

The green things watched the hairy things, and the green things ate them up while they blundered round, and colonised every damp, warm nook and cranny they could. Got in the hairy things' lungs, their brains even. Any when the hairy things built things, the green things knocked them down, and when the hairy things died, they sucked their ugly bones dry. And none of this, Danny knew, was a message about how he and the white stag and the white hare were part of the same piece as the thing that stared at him now through what were obviously deliberate mockeries of human eyes. It was exactly the opposite. The message was loud and clear and terrible.

He was on the concrete balcony outside his flat holding a dripping plastic petrol can and standing in a puddle of his own rapidly cooling piss. There was no face in the bush before him, no vines trailing across the floor. The sun was rising, and the world glowed chilly pink. He'd done this himself, Danny thought. As sure as he'd hammered that fevered hare, as sure as all those creatures had gone willingly to their deaths in the chapel, he'd set the can dribbling through his own letterbox. He couldn't remember doing it, but he could imagine it. Could believe it. He knew nothing, or next to nothing. Knew just as much as he needed to know. He was a delivery boy. He helped out a bit with the growing, but at the end of the day he was just the delivery boy. Just a cog in a machine. Just a man with a job. And so long as he kept on doing the job, so long as he didn't get any more stupid ideas about stopping, and how to stop, he'd be okay. It would let him be okay. But it was watching him.

Danny still had his plan. That's what he told himself, in the days and weeks and months which blurred into one. His plan to just make enough, then get away from Greenwood. The problem was, the longer it went on, the further away from Greenwood he wanted to get, and so the larger the sum became. At first it was out of the North West, then out of England, then out of Great Britain – off the island – into Europe, but not the green part. Africa. Australia. Sand and deserts and rocks. Or maybe Canada, or the Arctic, somewhere where the snow and the ice kept anything from growing. He'd seen stuff on the telly about plans to send people to Mars. People to colonise the planet – the dead, red planet – and never come back to Earth again. He knew it was just a daydream. There were thousands, if not millions, of people they'd send out there before they'd even consider him. But he liked to dream about it, about a new world.

One without mycelium.

# FUTURE NOIR
## by Michael Grey

To Inspector Alistair Dow it seemed as if the city was being eaten by its parks. As people drew together thanks to the population fall, whole neighbourhoods were vacated. Nature burst its dam, spilling out and up in a quietly relentless rewilding. He avoided those areas, and not only because his job didn't take him there. He didn't like what the land lost to the trees, scrub grass and foxes meant for the future. He didn't like what those places did to his past, either. Alyssa had loved parks.

The park he was in that night did nothing to counter his aversion. It scythed into the city, a green wedge between the Meadowlands and Rushmore Hill – once-manicured faux nature reclaiming land one street at a time, as the city's municipal limits contracted with its populace. 'Park' was no longer suitable. More accurate to say that a wood grew in the city, as deep and dark as any fairy tale.

As untamed as the once-park was, it attracted some human interest, as any out of the way place would. Dow knew this as a professional certainty. But it had been a long time since murder had featured on the list of crimes within its boundaries.

"They weren't too subtle about it," said Wegner. He was crouched by the body. It lay face down, sprawled in that thrown-puppet way movie goers thought unrealistic. The murder weapon had been high enough calibre to puncture the chest and exit through the back of the jacket, leaving ragged holes of slick burgundy. Wegner was too fascinated to be revolted. It had been so long since the last murder that Dow didn't know if his young Sergeant had ever even worked one.

And anyway, he was right. Gun shots were loud. Gun shots would be noticed.

"What do you see?" said Dow.

"These are exit wounds, so he was shot from the front. And his shoes are clean, so he wasn't running. He was either taken by surprise or he knew who shot him." Wegner had caught Dow's tutorial inflection and pointed to illustrate his analysis. The wounds were self-evident, and the ground was soaked. Summer had made an early appearance, bringing uncomfortable nights and afternoon thunder. It had been raining and the topsoil was wet enough that anyone not taking care would slide in hiking boots, let alone the soft loafers the corpse wore.

"Anything else?"

"Not without the site report."

Dow nodded. No making assumptions without cause. The lad was learning.

"That'll come soon enough. Let's go."

Halogens doused the little clearing in harsh light, attracting a horde of night time insects. The wood still buzzed with crime scene technicians. It seemed as if every spare officer congregated on the park. And why shouldn't they? It wasn't every day you saw a murder. Not any more.

They'd reached the car before Wegner said, "What are you thinking, boss?"

Not afraid to ask a superior their opinion, thought Dow, and ticked another mental box.

"I'm thinking the coat was dry. Whenever the victim was shot, it was after the rain. No chance of the shots being lost in the thunder."

"A silencer then?"

Dow nodded and got in the car.

A silenced gun, Dow thought. And a powerful one at that. The odds of this being a chance mugging gone wrong reduced at every turn. Whoever killed the victim had met them with at least the possibility of murder in mind.

Wegner pulled the car off the saturated park ground and onto the road. Dow looked through the window at the dark streets. *The victim. It.* He'd slipped into thinking of the man laying cold and dead as a thing. Old habits. With a murder case on his hands, if he closed his eyes to block out the empty streets and the feral grass bursting through the tarmac, he could almost imagine it was the old days.

The *good* old days? Perhaps. Perhaps not. *Different*, he settled on. There were certainly fewer murders now.

Caustic yellow reflections rolled over the paintwork as Wegner guided the car through an inhabited neighbourhood. Dow looked down the few lit streets. Here the refuse that built up on uninhabited roads was absent, and the weeds making their way through un-patched concrete were kept low or driven down by honest-to-god traffic. But there were still no people. The windows were lit, open against the muggy night, aircon too expensive to run except for the hottest days. But still, he thought, no people on the street.

Less people to be out on the street.

Less people, he reflected, to be murdered.

"Or do the murdering."

"What's that, boss?" said Wegner.

"Nothing," he sighed. "Nothing."

\*

Step one was speaking to the victim. And that was turning out to be more difficult than it should have.

The Operators that Dow had used in past investigations had all gone. He'd searched through his contacts, ticking each off as he went. Telephone calls weren't much help. Numbers were re-assigned by mistake and lines were routinely down. A by-product of all that expertise being lost through innovation's vanished momentum.

That left good old-fashioned door knocking.

But there they were still out of luck. Offices were closed or just empty – abandoned, unused with no one to move into them. Two had sold their radios when business went bad, to kids with the knack who wanted a trade. But not, of course, to anyone with a name or address.

He and Wegner were down to the last name on the list, a room in an office building, a place downtown that once would have been considered upmarket, filled with lawyers and dentists. Dow shook the thought loose. The past was gone, nothing there for him now. He looked at the door. A tear of masking tape was stuck across it, *Arthur Callas, Medium* written in pen.

He knocked.

The sound of a chair hitting the wall in surprise could be heard from inside, followed by footsteps. "Coming, Mrs Papanganis!" The door opened and a man stood in the jamb, short enough Dow could see his premature bald patch.

The man looked up. "You're not Mrs Papanganis."

"Full marks," said Dow. "Mr Callas?" The man nodded, and Dow and Wegner showed their IDs. "Inspector Dow. This is Sergeant Wegner. Do you have a minute?"

"Uh..." He fidgeted around uncertainly.

Dow forced the issue by reaching over the man's head, pushing the door fully open and letting himself in.

The office was a mess, managing to allow as few pieces of furniture as possible to clutter the entire room.

"Could I ask what this is about, Inspector?"

"Police business, sir. You're on our list of licensed Operators. Do you still operate?"

Callas stepped forward, all his unease apparently gone. "Really? I registered very long ago and never heard anything. I thought I'd been forgotten."

"Not at all. We just haven't had need of your services."

"Yes, well," said Callas, and rubbed his hands together. "Of course I'm ready and willing, that's what I signed up for. I hate to sound crass, but will there be...?"

"You'll be paid the rate you agreed to."

"That was quite a few years ago, Inspector. Inflation and living expenses wait for no–"

"The agreed rate."

He seemed ready to say something, then thought better of it. "Very well. If you and your associate are ready I could squeeze you in now?"

Dow made a show of looking around him, and with his foot prodded one of the leaflets carpeting the floor.

Callas said nothing, instead sitting at his desk, opened a drawer and pulled out his radio.

Sergeant Wegner was young enough to have never seen the process at work, so he sat opposite the desk, leaning in as the Operator adjusted dials and brushed away dust. What emerged was a valve radio. An old one. Its valves poked up from a teak body, lacquered in a type of varnish long since out of fashion and availability. If Dow had tried to visualise a device which could speak to the dead, he'd have been hard pressed to imagine anything which looked more suitable.

Callas twisted a dial, and the radio fizzed into life. The speaker coughed a light cloud of dust. He smiled weakly. "The radio attracts it. It's the static build up. Nothing I can do about it, I'm afraid."

"Where's the plug?" asked Wegner.

He gave Wegner an indulgent smile. "No plugs, my boy. No electricity."

One of the valves emerging from the lid began to glow warmly.

"So how does it work?"

"No one knows," said Dow, from where he'd taken up station by the open window. His words were a little snapped, intended to cut conversation to a minimum. He did not like Operators. Could not. It was personal, and while he knew personal was not the same as important, it was something he couldn't change. "And if anyone says they do, they're lying."

"We have our theories, Inspector." Callas did not look up from the radio as he turned dials and adjusted sliders to some indeterminate parameters.

"Best guess?" said Wegner.

"Mine? The energy comes from those we shall be contacting. Speaking of which..." He raised his head and looked at Dow. "Whom do you want to speak to, Inspector?"

Wegner handed over a form with the pertinent details. The deceased was named Marcus Poletti. Forty eight years old, Italian national. A toner-printed photograph was clipped on, copied and pasted from the university records where the victim rented rooms

191

and lab space. That was not on the sheet. There was nothing which might influence what the Operator might uncover and make it inadmissible in court.

Callas looked over the information. "All right, let's see what we can find out," he said, and delicately taking one of the dials, began to slowly twist it.

The valve radio whirred into life and the speaker began to buzz arrhythmically.

Despite standing in the window's sticky airflow, Dow had to suppress a shiver. He'd been at too many of these readings to be nervous, but just knowing what he listened to made him feel... dirty. The fizz coming from the speaker, the multi-layered irregular drone, was nothing more than the voices of a million dead, the traces of people who'd lived in the city. People who had perhaps walked through this very room. The odd, louder pop almost lost in the ocean of humming was, to him, a scream, or a re-enactment of the violence that lead to an early internment to the wherever-it-was that these voices now called home.

He wondered how people like Callas could do this every day without losing their minds. The trick, he'd been told, was ignoring the background noise. The wall of voices each trying to speak at once. They would howl through the operator's mind if allowed. And not everyone could do it. Barely *anyone* could do it. It was a random knack, like being able to curl your tongue or having double-jointed thumbs.

Wegner hadn't moved, still enthralled by what he presumed to be the act of communing with the dead. As Callas turned the dial, he closed his eyes and his face took on a look of serene calm. The speaker's buzz ebbed with the dial's turn. His forehead furrowed, and he opened his eyes to give the radio a questioning look.

"Something wrong?" said Dow. In all his cases where he'd needed an Operator, the radios had practically shaken with the speed of the victim to be heard.

"No, no. Of course not." The words did not match the tone. He took the dial again, and this time when he twisted it, his lips moved, his words almost lost beneath the speaker's thrum.

"...Marcus Poletti, Marcus Poletti..." He stopped again, and looked slightly worried.

"Is that it?" said Wegner, unable to keep the disappointment from his voice. "I thought we'd be able to hear something at least."

"That wasn't it," said Dow. "Out of practice?" he said to Callas.

The man shook his head. "I have an active business calendar, Inspector. Perhaps not as important as helping the police, but significant to those concerned. Will disputes, and widows wishing to, er, converse with their husbands."

"Converse?" asked Wegner.

"One last berate, lad," said Dow.

"Yes, that. But I must say, I am at a loss. There, er–" Callas turned to Dow. "Was Mr. Poletti a religious man, Inspector?"

He had not been. That was something Dow had followed up straight away. Standard procedure was to ascertain the religious beliefs of a potential murder victim – did they wear iconography? Did their home contain any holy texts? It was important. People of faith, those who believed in a god, did not leave voices to be contacted by people like Callas. Why not was one of life's mysteries. The Church was quick to jump on that when it was discovered. Proof, they said, of a divine afterlife.

Maybe it was, maybe it wasn't. Dow didn't know. He knew there was *an* afterlife, otherwise there would not be people like Callas. He liked to think there was. It helped with the pain.

But for all the knock-on effects of proving the existence of continuance after death – the grinding halt of technological innovation, the plummeting birth rate – proof positive of a divine being remained as elusive as it had ever been. And the cynic in him noted that the priests were still in no hurry to shuffle off this particular earthly coil.

"No," said Dow.

"Ah, well perhaps another try then."

Once more he closed his eyes and twisted the dial. When he spoke this time his voice was easily heard above the radio.

"Marcus Poletti, Marcus Poletti... Where are you, Mr Poletti... Ah, perhaps if I just..." Callas reached for another dial, took it, and twisted hard.

The radio jumped, clearing the desk top by two inches. Its glowing valve flashed brightly, and as it clattered down, it left a trail of strobing images in Dow's vision. That was followed instantly by a temperature drop so sudden it bordered on painful. The sticky summer warmth seeping through the open window crystallised on his arm hair, and then his head was filled with a howl, a conglomeration of human voices pouring out such loss and despair that it knocked his breath away.

And then it was gone. His skin prickled as goose bumps settled. The noise in his head left no echo, but he knew with certainty it would be a long time before he would be able to forget it.

Wegner still sat in the chair, and looked straight ahead, blinking as if slapped across the face. Even Callas seemed affected by whatever had just happened, and the man had enough residual emotional room to allow some embarrassment to show.

"I, er, may need a bit of time, Inspector."

*

Callas had been adamant he could finish the task given time. Dow had agreed and left his card. It was not as if he had any other choice.

Wegner went off to find a phone to call the station for updates while Dow got some coffee. He found a bench shaded by an oak heavy with summer leaves, and tried to forget. It had been a long time since he'd needed to see an Operator. The police's ability to just speak to the victim meant homicide had not been a problem for a long time. But still, too many times when he'd used one professionally they would say, "I hear you lost someone, Inspector? Would you like to speak to them?"

He'd drawn his gun on an Operator, once. During a dark time, when things had gotten too much. He'd had to be talked down by his own then-sergeant, as if he'd been a terrorist threatening a hostage.

He liked to think those times were gone. That he was more in control.

By the time Wegner returned, Dow had managed to clear his head. "Sorry, sir. Couldn't find a phone. I had to convince a store to let me use theirs."

"We had mobile phones when I was your age."

"I've been told. Making phone calls from anywhere? Sounds too much like magic, sir. How did they work?"

"Magic." Dow sighed. "Any movement?"

"There is, but I don't think you're going to like it."

"Oh?"

"Well, there's been nothing on any leads. Door knocking has produced nothing, nor has the radio appeal. Where there *has* been movement is from the Bishop..."

Wegner let the sentence trail off, but Dow felt some pride at controlling himself enough to reply with, "The kind which moves diagonally?"

The sergeant grinned. "He's with the Superintendent now."

"Well lad, it's time you learnt about politics."

*

No one liked to be embarrassed. Dow understood that. But he could not begin to imagine the humiliation of being proven wrong for a millennium. The Church, for almost the entire length of human civilisation, had ruled, robbed and killed, all because they and they alone controlled the keys to heaven.

Well, not any more.

Continuance after death was now open to everyone, and the church was wrong. Worse, they had lied.

Dow had watched the newscasts as word filtered through that what everyone thought was a hoax was, in fact, true. The ghost, the spirit, the soul if you preferred, whatever you called it, it remained after death, and it could be contacted. He'd wondered how this would affect religious bodies.

Unsurprisingly, it didn't go well.

There had been a sudden surge in religious attendances, that quickly shrank as the implications of the souls' confinement to this newly discovered plane began to sink in. It was no heaven, this haunted place after life.

No one wanted anything to do with a god who would create a soul which did nothing. Observance and religious attendance went into terminal freefall, and perhaps would have followed that inexorable curve into dissolution had the second discovery not been made.

There were no religious ghosts. Those people who in life had held a conviction in a higher being left no spirit, they just... left.

That was proof enough there was a heaven, and everyone returned to the same patterns as before – an unprovable paradise. It was one more step beyond what had been initially promised, but it remained as tangible as before.

Since then, the Church had strengthened its hold over municipal powers. It was reaching into the vacuum where the more materialistic ideals had vanished, and Dow detested every minute of it.

Judging by the din coming from the Superintendent's office, Bishop Orton had been there for a while when Dow arrived. The Super's words had a measure and volume suggesting the argument had legs, and he was pacing himself for a much longer battle. Orton by comparison seemed un-phased. He was older than Dow, fifteen to twenty years at least, but he carried them well, along with his extra weight. Even in the uncomfortable heat his dog collar was stiff and unstained, and he sat opposite the Super as if in a personal bubble of cool air.

The Super stopped yelling the moment Dow opened the door. Either the interruption put him off his rhythm, or he just took the opportunity to give up a lost cause. That would be a first, but the weather was just that draining.

"Hope I'm not interrupting."

"Not at all," said Orton, in a tone the polar opposite of the Superintendent's. The Bishop stood. "I was actually on my way out. If you'll excuse me, Inspector, Superintendent."

"Father," Dow said.

The Bishop let himself out. The moment the door closed, the Super let fly with a string of expletives Dow was well used to – although the thrown stapler was new.

He waited until the Super sat down, and pulled a cigarette packet from his desk. Health and Safety be damned. It wasn't as if there were enough people left to fill those roles.

"Problems?"

"You could say that." The Super sucked on the cigarette in a hard, unpleasureable way. "We've been told to fucking wrap it up. Now."

"The murder? Why?"

"Fucked if I know. I got calls from the mayor, two senators and the premier this morning, all telling me Orton would be paying me a visit, and to do whatever the fuck he says." He took another drag. "Spineless bastards couldn't even tell me to drop it themselves."

"It's the first homicide in twenty years. Why would anyone want their term to be the only one with a one hundred percent unsolved murder rate?"

"Like I said. Fucked. If. I. Know. All I do know is we have to re-assign everyone as of this frigging morning. You and Wegn – where are you going?"

"Nowhere." Dow was already at the door. "I wasn't here, so you couldn't reassign me."

The Super grinned around the cigarette. "I didn't see a fucking thing."

*

"So he didn't see a thing?" said Wegner.

"Not a thing," said Dow, lifting a sheet of paper filled with the kind of scribbles only scientists and children can achieve.

"Those were the Super's exact words?"

"More or less."

They were at Poletti's apartment in Oakridge, near the University campus. In Dow's mind he could draw a line straight from the building down through Rushmore to Rushmore Hill, then directly into the park Poletti would never leave. Once out of Oakridge, the route would take him almost exclusively through the abandoned neighbourhoods until he reached the park. It was no wonder the door knocking and public requests for help had turned over no witnesses. There had been no one to see Marcus Poletti take his last walk.

And he could see no one in Poletti's building being any help. The block was almost entirely teachers and academics. They would have been at the university or working away at home. Anyone with

197

any inclination to go for a walk would have been kept inside by the
residual thunder from earlier in the evening.

Dow found it interesting how, in the contracting population,
people gathered themselves into their cultural groups. It was what
he imagined the old colonial cities would have been like in the
early twentieth century. Only then, neighbourhoods were pressed
against each other, one culture's facets bleeding into the other at
the crossover for better or worse. Now whole stretches of empty
blocks separated one from another. It was as if the cities, grown
together from a dense collection of different towns, were retreating
back into their individual municipal territories. Glacial melt leaving
behind a moraine of darkened, empty buildings.

When they had arrived at the apartment, the forensic team
had already packed up and gone, recalled by the order that had left
the Super fuming in his office. It was liberating, not having anyone
look over his shoulder.

"So what are we looking for?" said Wegner.

"Anything which catches your eye." Dow put the paper down
and picked up another. Numbers and letters sprawled between
mathematical annotations he didn't even know the name of, forget
what they did to an equation.

"Could you be a bit less vague, sir?"

The forensics team would have combed the apartment already.
If there was anything to point towards the murderer, they would
have found it. So far they had not. Dow was not surprised. His gut
told him any clue here would be beyond the obvious.

And there was something else.

"Anything which might tell us why the Bishop would want us
not to look into the case."

"And what would that look like?"

"If I knew I wouldn't need a sergeant under my feet."

Wegner retreated into another room with a muttered, "Right
you are, sir."

Dow looked more closely at the paper. There was a definite
pattern to the equations. Whoever wrote them – Poletti almost
certainly – had been actively working something out, not just
jotting ideas. The crossings out and scrawled notes across different

calculations suggested to him this was a draft for another, more final paper.

It would help if there was more to know about Poletti, but the trail was suspiciously vague. The man just hired lab space, and the university wouldn't release any details without a proper warrant, something the department was out of practice in obtaining. Dow suspected that when it finally came the university records would be short on detail. Poletti's background was likewise a blank. The man had done all his work in Italy. Even his field of research was as yet unknown, and given that the manpower had just been pulled out from under his feet it might stay that way.

He put the sheet down and looked over the shelves. The forensic team hadn't found anything to give away what the man was working on. It could be Poletti had separated his home and work life, but the random sheets of notes like the one in Dow's hand suggested otherwise. There should have been at least some notebooks in the apartment.

But no, nothing.

He was drumming his fingers on the desk and staring at the shelves when Wegner wandered back into the room. "Anything to say this isn't a waste of bloody time, sir?"

"Looking over a scene is never a waste of time, Sergeant. Fresh eyes look from fresh angles."

"No offence, but it sounds like you pulled that straight from the manual."

"I did. Find anything?"

"Our Mr Poletti hadn't been here six months according to the passport records. If he wasn't planning on staying we'd have packing boxes around. Looks to me like he thought he was here for the long haul."

Dow nodded, and the telephone on the desk rang.

They both looked at it in surprise. The phone rang a second time. Wegner's eyes flicked from it to Dow and back. Dow picked it up and cleared his throat.

"Hello?"

"*Inspector Dow?*"

"Callas?"

"*Ah, good, I'm so glad I caught you. I called the number on your card and a man told me you might be at this number. I must say, I've never heard someone swear quite so much in my life.*"

"Was there a reason you called, Mr Callas?"

"*Oh, yes. It's most peculiar. I haven't come across anything like this ever.*"

"Have you found something?"

"*It's more that I haven't found a thing, Inspector. Not a thing.*"

*

Callas was at the park, in the same spot the body had been found two days before.

"The location was on the paperwork you gave me. When I got here I just followed the tyre tracks." Callas led Dow and Wegner back into the wood.

Dow could almost think of it as a nice walk. The pervading heat penetrated less thoroughly beneath the trees' heavy canopy. The odd shaft of sunlight sifting through was filtered into light greens and pale yellows. Flocks of birds had taken to the reclaiming forest and filled the air with song.

It *could* have been a nice walk. Were it not for the reason they were there, or his aversion to parks.

"After our meeting I tried all morning to contact Mr Poletti, but got absolutely nowhere." Callas spoke as he walked, leading the two policemen to the valve state in the small clearing, placed carefully on a tartan picnic blanket. "It was more than a little embarrassing. I have been operating for a long time, and this is the first occasion I could not make contact."

"All right. But why are we here?" said Wegner.

"Well, you see I was at a loss, so I thought I'd try a little experiment. Spirits tend to inhabit their geographical area. That area can be quite large, the size of a city for example, but there are limits. Watch your step there, Sergeant."

Wegner raised one foot from the forest floor and carefully shook it in a disgusted way.

Callas sat cross-legged on the blanket next to his radio. "So given this was the place where Mr Poletti died, I thought I might have better luck here. If you would be so kind, Inspector?" He gestured to the blanket beside the radio.

Dow sat. He was certain he hid his hesitation at being so close to the valve state. The echo of the sound roaring through his mind that morning still plucked at raw nerves, but if Callas had found anything, Dow was willing to play along with the theatrical little man.

"And did you manage to contact the deceased?" asked Dow.

"See for yourself." Callas twisted a dial and the vale state hissed into life, as it had that morning. And that was it. Silence poured from the speakers and filled the clearing.

Dow raised an eyebrow. "I don't hear anything."

"That's just the thing, Inspector. There's nothing. Nothing to hear at all. Even if I do this." He grasped another dial, the same one which had that morning released the howls of the dead into all their heads, too quick for Dow to stop him. The Inspector called out what was intended to be an order to stop, but it came out a bark, and he flinched away as Callas twisted the dial and...

... Nothing.

Dow blinked, and realised he was breathing heavily. Wegner clearly felt the same discomfort. The younger man had paled in the warm air.

"You see?" said Callas, apparently too caught up in discovery to realise the discomfort he caused.

Dow's first response was to shout, then he realised the man's point. "I can't hear anything."

"Precisely. Nothing." He twisted all the other dials randomly. If the valve state had been a normal radio, static would have swung in pitch across the speaker. "I have never heard of such a thing, Inspector."

"So, where are they? Where are the ghosts?" Dow leaned in, as if he could see through the radio.

"I don't know. But there's something else."

Callas was looking up at the branches. Dow followed his gaze. At first he did not realise what he supposed to be looking for. The leaves still shifted in the ever-so-slight breeze, dappling the canopy in sun shafts. Then he understood – he was not looking for anything.

He turned back to Callas. "The birds," he said.

The man smiled like a pleased teacher.

The birdsong which had filled the air was absent. Not a single bird could be seen or heard. They had fled as the valve state was turned on to purr out its disquietude.

"Where have they gone?"

"I don't know, Inspector, but you will not find them in any of the trees hereabouts. They won't be back for a while."

"Why?" Dow said aloud. Without thinking his eyes fell down to the radio. Its valve glowed orange in the background of greens and browns.

Callas saw the Inspector's suspicions and said, "That's my assumption. It's like the birds have been frightened away by whatever they can sense and we cannot, something which is only present when I open the radio to the other side. And that leads me to think that if they're frightened off, perhaps so are the spirits. And that prompts a wholly unwelcome question, does it not?"

"What can frighten a ghost?" whispered Dow.

"Precisely." He turned off the radio.

As the valve dimmed, it seemed to Dow the noise of the city outside the park began to intrude on the vacuum left by whatever came from the speaker. Or perhaps that was just his imagination. But there was still no birdsong.

That was very real.

"Maybe the radio's broken?" said Wegner. His voice inflected like a question, giving his words a touch of desperation

"I'm afraid not. I've taken it two blocks away and turned it on. Twice. Each time it works perfectly. It's only here this happens, Sergeant."

"So why here?" said Dow. "Why here and not two blocks away, or in your office?

When Callas spoke, his voice was more forthright than Dow had thought the excited little man could get. "Do you want my professional opinion or my best, off record guess, Inspector?"

"Both."

"Very well. Professionally, I don't know. This sort of occurrence has never happened before, and will need investigating and testing before anything official could be stated."

"And off record?"

"I believe something happened here, something so heinous and unnatural it drove away any spirit presence. Something so inconceivably atrocious it could frighten a spirit."

Dow thought about that. It surprised himself how readily he was willing to accept the idea.

"Thank you, Mr Callas. You've been most helpful."

Callas's usual demeanour returned and he beamed. "Glad to be of service, Inspector. And, er, could I ask about remuneration?"

"I'll submit the paperwork as soon as I get to the office." He thought for a moment and, realising he remembered the cost code to charge work to the mayor's office, said, "And you'll get a bonus for dangerous field work, too."

\*

Dow sent Wegner to escort Callas home. It was a weak pretence which Wegner saw straight through, but the Sergeant was too professional to argue the point in front of someone. It was for the lad's own good. He had a long career ahead of him which would not be helped by embarrassing the wrong people.

It was a long, dull drive back up to Oakridge, back to the university.

The key was to find out what Poletti had been working on. The forensic team had not been inside the lab the man rented, the warrant having not been issued before the investigation had been cancelled – but they had labelled the rooms a possible crime scene, and marked them off with police tape. Officially he had no right to be there. Of course, he didn't know that, having not spoken to the Superintendent earlier that day.

The office was a mess. Even if his suspicions had not been raised by a lack of work material at Poletti's apartment, they'd be standing on end now – notepads stacked five to a pile, filled with the kind of self-created shorthand someone develops over a lifetime. Loose sheets of paper decorated with hand-drawn line diagrams dusted every table surface, and avalanched onto the floor in drifts.

And in the middle, in pride of place on the only cleared table space in the lab, sat two valve state radios.

Dow circled them like they were dangerous. They were both old, like all the others he'd had ever seen. They had the same basic design – unmarked, time-stained dials, bare speakers, a valve protruding from the roof. They all seemed to be of the same uncertain provenance. The sets had appeared when it became obvious they could be used, already aging, but since then no more had been made. Where the hell had they come from? It was a disturbing thought, and he was surprised he had never considered it. Had anyone else asked that question? It made their very existence unsettling, that they should emerge just as they became needed. He felt sudden vindication in keeping his distance.

Poletti had apparently shared none of Dow's reticence. One radio was plain, almost identical to Callas's. The other had various apparatuses forced upon it. A rubber tube emerged from the top, compressed against the valve, and curled around the body to disappear into a freshly-bored hole on the side. The hole looked obscene, its fibrous edges showing raw, dark wood on the inside. Dow caught himself flinching at the sight.

Other plates and tubes had been soldered or stuck on, and wires trailed from the device towards the other radio. Post-it notes stuck beside the additions suggested clues as to what the items were or why they were there, but the writing was in Italian. Or was it?

"It's Latin."

Dow's hand was already moving for his gun as he turned. He stopped when he saw who stood by the door.

"Bishop." The perfunctory greeting served double duty as an accusation.

Orton nodded as if he agreed with the subtext. He stepped in and closed the door. "I thought you might come. You're one of the old school of policeman, Inspector. You don't give up." He walked to the other side of the table, putting the two radios between them, and plucked the note Dow had been looking at. "*Quod ad alteram partem. Tacet.* It means 'Should reach the other side. Is silent.'" He sighed and stuck the note back. "Unfortunately, Marcus was correct."

"Correct about what?"

"About what is beyond the veil, Inspector. Or the new veil. The one beyond the first death."

"Is that what the Church is calling it now?"

"No, just me. The Church – we – cannot just go and label the greatest discovery of the modern age on reflex. If we went with our first thoughts, we might be calling it something ridiculous forever."

Dow felt like sighing. He had forgotten how draining investigating a murder could be. He was no longer young, and he had lost the patience for games. "Did you have something to do with Marcus Poletti's death, Father?"

"Yes."

The admission came so openly, Dow was taken aback enough that he didn't do what he should have – reach for his gun and put Orton under arrest. Instead he just said, "Why?"

"Because I was asked," said Orton. "I feel I should stress I was asked, not ordered. No man should be forced into taking another's life. Although I was told that if I believed I could not, then someone else would be sent who could, and I did not want to be the cause of another's sin."

"And who asked you?"

"I think you know who. I won't name any names, Inspector."

"That's noble of you, but it won't stop us. We'll find out. People will be punished for this."

"No. They won't."

Despite himself, Dow laughed. "You don't have a say in it."

Orton looked as if he were about to answer, than changed his mind on what he was going to say. "What do you think we do, Inspector? We men and women of faith?" He held up a hand. "Indulge me, please."

Dow chewed the inside of his lip, but answered anyway. "You marry people, baptise them, and forgive their sins."

"A good answer, but that's just a priest's role. I meant the church, religion as a whole. We *protect* people. As much as you do.

We provide a ruler to measure oneself against and a worthy goal to work towards. We assuage despair by assuring that everyone, so long as they're good at heart, will live on with their loved ones after death."

"The discovery of the afterlife must have been a blow," Dow said. From the look on Orton's face, the words hit home.

"More than I think you know. Of all the consequences of the discovery, there were two that worried us the most. The halting of technological progress was one. No more great discoveries, no advances in medicine. The second and greater danger was the deterioration in births. It wasn't a levelling of the global population. It was a fall which would have become terminal. And do you know what caused these consequences?"

"Faith, I suppose you'd say."

"No. Hope. We had none. What was the point anymore? There was nothing to work towards, no reward. No hope of seeing our loved ones again. With nothing to aspire to, even unconsciously, we were fated to stagnation. All the expertise in medicine, technology, science, all those people dying out with no one to replace them. What do you miss most, Inspector?"

Before he could catch himself Dow said, "I wanted to be an astronaut."

Orton grinned. "I miss 24 hour news. But no more of that. No more aspirations for a race who know they will leave behind nothing but dust. Then the second discovery changed all that again."

"No religious spirits," said Dow.

The bishop nodded. "Suddenly the possibility of life eternal was there again. No more certainty. No more eternal death."

"I don't see—" Dow began.

"Did it pass you by, Inspector, that birth rates stabilised after that? No more going backwards, no more terminal decline. We had been given a second chance. Saved." He looked down at the radios. "Marcus's discovery would have erased that."

"What did he do?"

Orton didn't look at up straight away. When the words finally came, his eyes lagged on the radios, drawn by some gravity. "He discovered the souls of the faithful did not go to heaven."

"People have thought that for a while."

"To suspect and to have proof are very different. You know that."

Dow conceded the point. "And you were willing to kill a man to stop that decline." He nodded, partly to himself, partly to some morbid respect for Orton. "I could understand that. But it is still murder, and I'm still going to arrest you."

The smile Orton gave Dow made him cold across his back.

"No."

"No?"

"No, and I'll tell you why. To begin with, no one will sign off on the paper work. Anyone who might will be removed, and replaced with someone more amenable. Secondly, it will not even get that far."

Dow laughed. The man sounded so confident. He stopped when he saw the look on Orton's face.

"Are you not going to ask me why, Inspector?"

"OK. Why?"

"Because, as regrettable as it was, Marcus Poletti had to die. I will admit that that alone would not have been enough for me to commit a mortal sin. Not normally. Not before I was given my price."

"Oh? And what price was that?"

"*I* shall be going to heaven."

"You said there was no such place."

"I did not. There may be no heaven for you, but for me and my superiors?" He shrugged.

Dow laughed again, not entirely certain what was funny. "After all that, you expect me to believe anything you say? You seem to accept there's no heaven for humanity readily enough, and then to believe there is, but only for you and yours?"

"The evidence was quite compelling. It would have to be."

The Inspector shook his head. Orton had to have gone mad. The cognitive dissonance he'd lived with for so long had finally caught up and twisted his mind. "That makes no difference."

"There is one more thing. I'm afraid it's distasteful, but necessary. It's a threat. To you, Inspector."

"To me? You're threatening the police?"

"No, just you. I've already told you what would happen should you ignore what I said and arrest me. On top of that, your career will be ruined. You'll be cast aside without a pension. That protégé of yours, Sergeant Wegner? I'll do my best, but I suspect he'll be caught in the firing line. That will be only be the start, however." Orton paused. "'Hell' is such an artless word. Its simple enunciation does not begin to present the concept of the complete and eternal pain it demands. The mere act of being transposed there requires the soul to be ripped from the realm your Operators contact, which I'm assured is far from gentle. I'm sure you would do anything you could to stop Alyssa from being taken there."

Before he could stop himself, Dow drew his gun and had it on Orton. He sighted down the length in white, pain-fuelled fury. The urge to pull the trigger was almost overwhelming.

Almost.

He retained enough control to relax his finger. Let the Bishop believe what he wanted, and let the psychiatrists work out his delusions. "John Orton, I am arresting you for—"

Orton held up a hand. "Before you make the biggest mistake of your life, may I?"

Before Dow could say otherwise, Orton leaned forward and twisted the dial on the closest radio. The valve lit with a merry orange, and the speaker picked up the buzz which always made Dow's skin crawl. It rose, growing into a desolate background hum, the timbre and depth giving a sense of it stretching forever.

But as he listened, the blanket soundscape shifted. It faded and flowed, giving a stereophonic effect of something moving, approaching the speaker from the other side. Growing larger. Something immense closing in. The movement was a spot of silence in the ocean of noise, a null sound which made Dow think back to the park, and Callas's anomaly.

*What could frighten that which had already died?*

He felt Orton looking at him, but could not take his eyes from the radio. The background noise of a million spirits had retreated to the very edge of perception, the voices keeping their distance from whatever was present on the other side of the speakers, standing a literal heartbeat away.

Whatever it was, it blocked out an entire plane of existence.

Dow managed to look at Orton. The Bishop merely raised his eyebrows and inclined his head toward the radio. *Listen.*

The speaker buzzed. Not the hum he had come to expect, but the laboured vibration of an amplifier struggling to convey a sheer body of noise.

The radio's tremors gave way, until the residual thrum gave out and the speaker went still. The valve's glow was the only sign the radio was still on.

Everything was silent. He moved in subconsciously.

And something spoke.

"...*Dow*..."

The voice was a hiss and a whisper and a scream. It bypassed his ears, reaching direct to his heart, and he knew, with a certainty he'd never felt in his life, that the speaker knew him and would find him wherever he was.

His legs almost buckled. The presence left, and the background noise returned. Had it not, Dow would have been on his knees. Either in fear or praise. Either would have felt right.

A hand reached in, turned the dial and the radio fell into silence.

Dow looked up into Orton's eyes. There was sympathy there, but not much.

"What?" he managed.

"I was raised to believe they were beatific beings of eternal compassion. God's heralds. Beware what they herald, Inspector."

Dow looked at the radio, silent and dark. He tried to speak, only to find his throat dry. He wet his lips. "That was why we couldn't speak to Poletti, wasn't it? It was because he wasn't there anymore."

Orton nodded. "Do you still want to arrest me?"

"No," said Dow without hesitation. He put his gun on the table. He did not think it would make him feel safe ever again.

"You made the right choice, Inspector. I shall do my best to help your career along the right lines. I can begin now." He reached into his jacket and pulled out a matt black gun, a long cylinder screwed into its barrel. "This is the gun which shot Marcus Poletti. You can be the man who solved the first murder in two decades."

"Stop! Put it down!"

Wegner stalked in through the door, his own gun trained on the Bishop.

"No!" Dow stepped forward, hands down in a calming gesture. Orton did not. That was his mistake. He smiled, misinterpreting how much the young sergeant knew compared to Dow, and turned toward Wegner with the gun still in his hand.

Wegner fired.

The bullets tore through Orton. Two ripped through the torso puncturing the rib cage, lacerating lung and heart. The third snapped the Bishop's head back.

Orton's body fell against the table and then slumped to the floor, pulling a fresh landslide of loose paper with it.

The lab ate the gun's echo, leaving Dow and Wegner to look down at the corpse with only the whisper of settling paper as company.

Dow realised his hands were shaking.

"You OK, sir?" Wegner looked at Dow, his gun needlessly aimed at the body.

He wasn't, and he didn't think he would ever be again. But he nodded. The lad had done what he thought was right, and there was no changing that now.

He looked toward the radio. It may have been his imagination, but he though the valve pulsed a short-lived orange glow, and then went dark.

## REMEMBER THE SKY
by Gethin A. Lynes

The sun had fallen behind the hills and the village was starting to come to life again. Kisi sat up and switched off the air conditioner, groaning at the prospect of having to bully that bloody stubborn ox back out to the fields. She was half tempted to let the beast stay out in the sun tomorrow morning and cook.

Maybe that'd motivate Gavin to finish fixing the tractor's solar cells. Or maybe, as Kisi suspected, Gavin couldn't fix them at all, and he'd have to admit it. And then Kisi could make the night run over to Camden Village, and trade for some new ones. And trade something else with Heinrich while she was there.

She shook her head at herself. She'd be working the plough shifts for months if she killed an ox. Heinrich might be worth that, but he wasn't worth the touch of the morning sun. She picked up her shirt, gingerly lowering it onto her burnt shoulders, and opened the door to the brutal heat of late afternoon.

*

*Ark 1:*
*Year 0.0 (2085.453CE)*
*Life count: 10,000*

Lashed by rain, John Calhoun Jr. looked down into the vast central chamber of the Ark. Around its walls, lights appeared as people began to claim dwellings for themselves. They clustered together in the upper levels of the Ark's living quarters, as though everyone was afraid to descend too far from the surface.

As he leaned on the railing of the service platform, above

211

him the roof of the Ark slowly closed on the outside world. He looked up. Even darkened by storm, the afternoon sky was a bright strip against the blackness inside the Ark. At either end of the narrowing opening itself he could see the soldiers that surrounded the entrance to the Ark, watching over its sealing. They were there to keep the hopeful away, and prevent any of those inside from having second thoughts and returning to the surface.

The world had become a hard place, hot and crowded, the weather volatile and dangerous. But the reality of being sealed forever into the Ark was equally frightening and uncertain.

The roof closed, and the boom of the steel plates coming together faded away into the emptiness below him. The sky was gone, and with it the rain on John's face. He wondered how long it would be before he forgot that feeling. He was in complete blackness, broken only by that distant cluster of dwellings below him. For an age he stood in the dark, watching the lights spreading, thousands of them, reaching around the walls of the Ark in long tendrils.

Finally a diffuse light came on, illuminating the upper reaches of the Ark. It spread downward, gradually revealing the ovoid curve of the gargantuan central chamber, stretching away below him. John stared at it, awed into stillness. It was one thing to imagine the scale of a place that could house millions of people indefinitely. It was quite another to stand and look down upon it.

"Welcome to Humanity 2.0, Calhoun." Elon was the disembodied voice of the Ark. Its voice came from the darkness, sounding as though it stood by his shoulder.

"Calhoun was my father. John will do fine."

"Calhoun is a good name. It carries weight, authority."

"I am not in charge here, Elon. I thought that was the point – that no one is in charge. Except you, perhaps."

"I am merely an interface, Calhoun. But the people will look to you for guidance, for help."

John did not reply. Humanity 2.0... He wondered about that. He suspected that those who managed to survive on the surface would be the real bearers of that title.

*

*Ark 2:*
*Year 0.33 (2257.673CE)*
*Life count: 2,001*


Amanda Calhoun looked around the room. There were perhaps a hundred and fifty people there, all carefully selected: geneticists and biologists, teachers and engineers, botanists and doctors and musicians and storytellers.

All important to their success.

"Isn't it a bit extreme?" Someone finally asked.

Amanda looked around for the speaker. Karina Potente, a surgeon. No one replied, perhaps afraid to lead them down this path.

"Of course it is," Amanda said eventually. "But so was the world we came from."

A few people shifted uncomfortably.

"It just seems like we're conducting experiments on people." Frank Stiles, botanist.

"This whole thing is an experiment, Frank," Amanda said. "And the result is survival – or not."

"That's a bit alarmist, isn't it?" Frank asked. "A bit black and white?"

"No, I agree with Calhoun," Gerald Chomsky, engineer, cut in. "If history has shown us anything, it is that if people are left to their own devices they will breed like rabbits, indiscriminately and at volume. There needs to be some planning, some control."

"It's not about trying to control people's lives," Amanda said. "Only maximising our long term chances. A couple of thousand people is not a lot, and maintaining genetic diversity is essential."

"But Chomsky's talking about overpopulation," Karina said. "And you're talking about genetics."

"They're both important. We've all seen what happens when we get overcrowded. But limiting the partners that each of us may have children with will not only help maintain variation in the gene pool, but will also stop our numbers getting out of control. Not everyone will want to breed with the people they're permitted to. Nor should they have to."

"What about people being in love, having families?" Frank asked.

"What about it?" Chomsky said. "Who's to say you can't be in love? There's plenty of cultures in the Old World that had both spouses and lovers, or –"

Amanda put her hand on Chomsky's shoulder. "These are things that can be worked out by individuals," she said. "There is no model here, no guidelines. We're making this up as we go along. We're trying to make sure we don't repeat the mistakes of the past. That's why we're all here, talking about it. We need to make sure that everyone else understands the necessity of this. But we also need to make sure no one feels they are being forced, being experimented upon, as opposed to helping shape the experiment."

She looked at Frank Stiles. After a moment he nodded.

"Do we all agree then?" Amanda looked around the room. She saw doubt in some, but also understanding. When no one spoke up she said 'Okay then, let's talk to everyone about it, let's make sure everyone is on board."

Gradually people began to get up, or talk amongst themselves. Amanda watched as people left. She didn't think it was going to be as simple as this. She suspected there was going to need to be some enforcement eventually.

\*

*Ark 1:*
*Year 0.95 (2085.403CE)*
*Life Count: 9,999*

The faintly luminous surface of John's desk was full of graphs and charts – air purity, water levels, humidity; harvest indicators for the orchards, gardens and plantations; temperature readings; breeding program statistics and overall animal numbers; illness and disease monitors. The numbers adjusted constantly, projection lines shifting, graphs rising and falling, arrays cycling across his desk as one mass of data gave way to another.

The only constant was the life count, unmoving on one corner of his desk. A perpetual indicator of the ultimate success, or failure, of the Ark, a flat green line that overlaid the steep curve of projected population increase. The sheer volume of information he was expected to oversee as Administrator was staggering. He wondered sometimes why he was even required, why the Ark wasn't simply monitoring everything itself. He rubbed at his eyes for a moment and turned to the window-screen.

The view looked out over the ocean, the coarse-sand beaches and broken headlands of the Pacific. A gentle breeze blew in, tinged with the salt tang of the water. Three months since he'd activated it, and already his memory had begun to accept the false scent. It had smelled wrong to him in the beginning, this manufactured sea-breeze – subtly so, but still enough to dispel the illusion.

He was almost fooled by the window now. But there was something about the sky that was simply not real enough. It was too... He wasn't sure. Two-dimensional, perhaps. With a sigh, he turned back to his desk.

*

*Ark 2:*
*Year 3.31 (2260.653CE)*
*Life Count: 2,102*

Amanda arched back over her chair in a long stretch, and groaned. "I feel like I've been here for days," she said.

Hakim Smith, at the workstation facing hers, leant over to look around the side of her screen. "Can't be," he said. "The entire Ark hasn't gone into a panic yet."

Amanda rolled her eyes at him. "Please, don't remind me."

Somewhere along the way, Amanda had been made responsible for not only their genetic fortitude, but their social and political survival as well. It was not her forte, being decision-maker. When forced into it, she tended to make expedient choices rather than well-considered or consultative ones. She was sure she wasn't the only one who felt somewhat unhappy with the situation. Hakim often teased her about it. Partly, she suspected, as a way of dealing with his frustration at the frequent interruption of their work.

"So," she said, before he could say anything else. "Are we done?"

She was looking at the breeding matrix – a crude name, perhaps, but the culmination of many months of elegant work. Or at least elegant on Hakim's part. There were others whose work had contributed, bricklayers to Hakim's architect, and there were lab techs who had assisted Amanda. But Hakim was responsible for the algorithmic framework through which all the Ark's future reproduction would be calculated. She was merely responsible for plugging in the genomic data.

"Well," Hakim said, rolling his chair around beside hers. "Plug in the kids and let's find out."

They had begun work on the matrix not long after Amanda had produced her first set of possible partners for the Ark's two thousand initial inhabitants. People's reluctance to be told who they could procreate with notwithstanding, there had been a steady number of births in the interim. Amanda imported the sequenced DNA of all those new people into the matrix, and sat back with Hakim to watch its recalculations.

*

*Ark 1:*
*Year 7.279 (2092.732CE)*
*Life Count: 8,940*

"Calhoun, it's time for the Clinic," the Ark said. "Calhoun," it said again, after a moment.

John turned from the window. He still thought of Calhoun as his father, and it took him a moment sometimes. "What?" he asked.

"The Clinic."

"Yes, of course. Thank you, Elon." He continued looking at his window and the coast beyond, his constant view.

After a moment he turned away. He took in the data on his desk with a practised glance. There was nothing out of the ordinary, nothing that required his immediate attention. There was, as always, the dim population display in one corner, the contrast between Elon's projected population increase and the decaying curve of the Ark's actual numbers.

John had raised the inaccuracy of the projections at Administration meetings a number of times, until it became clear that the others did not wish to discuss it. There was an unwillingness amongst them to address the problem head on, as though ignoring it might make it go away.

Facing one's possible extinction, one's failure as a species, was an uncomfortable prospect to say the least. That was the whole point of the Ark project though, to find a new way to survive old failures of overpopulation.

Even discounting the lack of births, of new lives, their current rate of decrease would be worrying. And thus far there seemed to be no medical explanation, apart from the odd accident or obvious suicide. The Ark was like an old zoo, its population just another blip on the curve of the Earth's countless now-extinct species. All those creatures who had refused to respond to breeding programs and sat around their enclosures lifelessly until they died.

John dismissed the array on his desk with a flick of his hand. His desk went dark as he turned and left his office. Try as he might to put the problem aside, he worried at it on his way down to the lower levels. The emptiness of the Ark did not help. In a structure built to house millions, that had initially seemed so full of promise and possibility, all that space now seemed dead, as empty as a tomb.

"Humans are complex and unpredictable creatures," Elon insisted. In the absence of input from the other Administrators, John had taken to discussing the issue with the Ark itself. "Adapting to the environment of the Ark is an unknown," was Elon's position. "But all algorithms point to the projections remaining valid, in time."

This argument didn't sit well with John. Elon might be right when he said it was a matter of adaptation, but he did not think it would be solved simply by time. And he did not think they had the time to find out. Whether he was justified in doing so or not, John felt ultimately responsible for the survival of everyone in the Ark. He was afraid that a solution might not present itself until it was too late.

He had hoped his time in the Clinic would help him find a solution, help him get inside people's heads. It was supposed to be a way for people to have access to the Administrators, who had a direct understanding of how the Ark's various systems functioned, and to have input into discussions and decisions about how things were run.

John stepped inside the door and looked around the huge room. Whatever the Clinic's intention, it was failing. It reminded him of a prison, small groups of people hunched over even smaller tables in low, broken conversation. He saw no liveliness, no interest in the operation of the Ark, just a bunch of inmates trying to survive, one moment at a time. It was the same thing he saw, he realised for the first time, in Administration meetings. His stomach tightened like a fist.

"You look troubled, John."

Samia Hamad, the Ark's senior geneticist, stood at his side. She was the only person who still called him John. Even the few people he had counted as his friends outside the Ark had taken to calling him Calhoun.

"No more than usual." He tried to smile at her.

*

*Ark 2:*
*Year 9.67 (2267.013CE)*
*Life Count: 2,309*

Amanda looked up with a frown as the airlock to the lab hissed open, then smiled as Frank Stiles walked into the room.

"Administrator," she said, getting up.

"Th'sky Amanda, knock it off," Frank said.

Amanda snorted at Frank's use of the exclamation, the reference to the Old World's sky. It was a long standing ritual – Amanda had no time for people's ridiculous semi-religious reverence for the sky, something that was entirely lost to living memory, and Frank insisted on using it when Amanda called him Administrator, which he hated.

He had been one of the staunchest critics of the Ark's breeding program, and in the face of overwhelming opposition, had retreated into his botany, spending most of his time in the gardens and orchards. But once the matrix was established, Amanda had found in him an unlikely ally. She had achieved her goal, and subsequently wanted no part in the Administration. It was important, she'd pointed out, that there was some balanced oversight, that there was some removal between the architects of the matrix and it's enforcement. She knew Frank would have the wellbeing of everyone at heart.

And anyway, she had other important work to do, research. She needed the time to focus on the Ark's survival, while Frank concentrated on making sure everyone was living as well. It had taken months of work to convince him to take on the role of Administrator.

"To what's the pleasure?" she asked, giving him a hug.

"Do I need a reason?"

"I'm working, Frank."

"Which is all you do these days."

"Because I need to. A population of our size can easily be wiped out by disease or some viral disaster. And we're ageing, so unless we can mitigate the rigours of getting older, we'll have to start forcing people to reproduce to a schedule."

"You might be the best, but you're not the only geneticist we have, you know."

"You want to trust our survival to someone else?"

"I'll have to if you work yourself to death. Come on, you're coming with me." Frank took her by the hand.

"Where?"

"We could go and star-gaze in the sim chamber?"

"Ha. Not a chance." She pulled her hand from his.

"Get your coat, it's winter out there."

"Really? Already?"

\*

*Ark 1:*
*Year 13.264 (2098.717CE)*
*Life Count: 6,672*

John lay with one arm behind his head, Samia half on top of him, her head on his chest and one leg nestled between his. The heat of their recent lovemaking had all but dissipated, the sweat on his skin cool in the neutral temperature of the room.

John gazed at the window of their bedroom. From this angle the view showed the tops of the pine and cypress on the headland and the cloudless sky beyond. The image stirred something in the back of his head, but in his post-ejaculatory drowsiness he couldn't quite grasp it.

He had given himself over to small moments of pleasure, taking time with Samia, trying to enjoy life as much as possible under the circumstances. He did not suffer the same ennui that so many in the Ark did, which he partly put down to the fact that he had so much to do, to focus on. Yet even in his work, John often felt like he was simply fulfilling a function rather than living.

He could see what it must be like for others, with their basic needs – food, shelter, medical attention – completely taken care of. They had no particular purpose, or at least their purpose was unfulfilled by the lack of children, the lack of younger generations and an expanding population. The only people who really seemed immune were the younger ones, the ones who had been teenagers in the beginning.

He had never shared his thoughts about the Ark being a zoo, but increasingly he saw them all like that – animals in an unnatural cage, waiting to depart the world. He often wondered if they were on display somewhere, an exhibit in some corner of the crumbling bureaucracy on the surface.

Samia shifted against him. "I miss lying in front of a fire," she said.

And there it was. The wintery image of lying in front of the fireplace was what he'd needed to find the thought that had been tugging at his mind. "Look at the window," he said. "What does it make you think of?"

Samia shifted, followed his gaze. After a moment, she said, "I don't know. The coast, summer holidays."

"But not winter, right? The sky is wrong for winter."

"Do you even remember the sky?"

"Not if I actually think about it. But when was the last time you saw a sky that looked different? When was the last time you felt cold? Or too hot? Or any semblance of a natural environment?"

"Aren't we supposed to be adapting to this environment?" Samia asked.

"Yes, but we're *not*. We're dying. We went from one world – changeable, even unpredictable – directly to another that's completely uniform, unmoving. We think we're doing the right thing, providing everything we need, keeping ourselves 'healthy'. But we live in an artificial space, constantly lit, and the only variation in temperature or humidity is what we choose to set in our own living spaces. What about shorter days? Actual cold? Seasonal food in the gardens?"

"So what, you want to have seasons in here?"

"I want everyone to feel like they're somewhere they can live, not just simply survive. We come from tens of thousands of years in a cyclical, variable environment, and now suddenly we've been shut up in an office building with artificial lighting, and aren't allowed to see the outside world."

Samia rolled onto her back next to John. "Elon?" she said.

"Yes, Samia?"

"Can you bring the outside world inside the Ark?"

*

*Ark 2:*
*Year 56.37 (2313.713CE)*
*Life Count: 11,931*

Amanda stood beneath one of the cherry trees, coat pulled tight against the cold air. Her steel-grey hair hung loose around her face, against the eyes of the gathering. She watched as the bio-urn containing Frank's ashes, tiny seedling protruding from its top, was placed into the earth. The dour Celebrant sanctimoniously droned on about the raising up of the people, of return to the heavens. The words faded into the background as she remembered moments shared with Frank beneath these very trees.

It had been years, decades, since she had seen him – seen anyone really, for that matter – and even longer since she had

221

been up here, in the arboretum Frank had loved so much. She was glad, she supposed, that she hadn't been out in the Ark, hadn't witnessed the man Frank had become. The despot. It was hard to imagine, hard to reconcile that image of him with the man who had been afraid of regulating people's procreational freedom, with the man who had made gentle love to her beneath the cherry trees.

She wondered, again, if it was her retreat into her work that had hardened him, her work on herself. Or perhaps it had been his refusal to join her in the trials that had pushed her away. She pushed the quandary aside. She had been down this spiral before. Ascribing blame was never as satisfying as one thought it was going to be.

She became aware that the Celebrant had fallen silent, was looking imperiously over the funereal gathering. She wondered what he was searching for, and it crossed her mind that this was precisely the sort of person who would keep watch for signs of dissent, precisely the sort of place. She was surprised, in fact, that there wasn't a police presence, given who they were burying.

"Remember the sky," the Celebrant intoned eventually.

"Remember the sky," everyone replied, looking upward reverently. Amanda rolled her eyes, and said nothing.

The people began to drift away, or stood talking in small groups. There weren't many people here Amanda knew, and even fewer she liked. She had no desire to spend any more time here. She hadn't come to be dutiful, but to say goodbye, though now she didn't feel the need.

As she made her way along the path beneath the cherry trees, someone fell in step beside her. She turned to look at him. "Hakim?"

"Hello Amanda," he said. He was gaunt and unkempt, a thick beard and deep lines of age disguising the once handsome man.

Amanda just looked it him, at this ghost of the man she used to know. Hakim had disappeared long before Amanda had retreated into her lab. Her friend, simply gone with no explanation. If he was surprised at the lack of age in her own face, he gave no indication.

"Let's keep walking," he said, grabbing her elbow and turning her back to the path. "We need to talk."

"Talk? After all this time? What would we have to talk about?"

"Not here. Let's go to the lab."

A few minutes later, they were back in her lab. "Well?" Amanda said.

Hakim waited while the airlock closed, the last of the frigid air of winter voiding out behind them. "Someone has hacked the matrix," he said at last.

"What? Why would anyone hack the matrix?"

"You really have been locked up down here for too long. You do realise what has been going on out there don't you?" Amanda opened her mouth, but Hakim didn't give her the chance to speak. "There are any number of reasons someone would want to break the matrix," he went on. "Not least of which is the existence of the thing in the first place. It might have been fine, if it wasn't for Frank and his regime."

"So now someone's trying to destroy it?"

"If that was the case, I wouldn't be here. Someone has changed it."

"To what end?"

"That's what I need you for. To look at the front end and decipher it. The altered code is too complex. It's like nothing I have seen before. And I can't risk accessing the thing for long enough to understand it. Staying hidden inside the Ark is not an easy thing."

"Is that what you've been doing all this time? Hiding?"

"Fucksakes, Amanda. Everyone else who had anything to do with building this thing is dead. And you've been shut up in here trying to cure death, which is the only reason you're still here too. So Frank could cheat his way out of dying."

"Frank wanted nothing to do with my work."

"Frank wanted what every autocrat wants – to hold on to his power. Don't fool yourself into making excuses for him."

Amanda said nothing, searching for a response, for some sort of answer to her own doubt.

"I have to go," Hakim said. "Before whoever has filled Frank's shoes finds me down here."

At the door, he looked back over his shoulder. "Find out what is being done with the matrix. I'll come back when I can."

Amanda attempted to do what he asked. She pored over the matrix for several days, first in minute detail and then in macro, with the whole thing crammed onto a screen that took up nearly an entire wall of the lab. It refused to give up its secrets, to reveal a purpose.

The matrix had become immense, unrecognisable. This was, of course, the reason they had created it to begin with. Keeping track of this much data, let alone interpreting it, was beyond the capacity of the human brain – or beyond the capacity of the human lifespan, anyway.

"You're running out of time, Calhoun."

Amanda started in surprise and spun around. She was alone. "Who's there?" she demanded.

"There is no one here, Calhoun." The voice was disembodied, source-less. "Only you."

Amanda stepped toward the centre of the room, craning her neck to look into the corners of the lab.

"Hakim will return soon, and you have some decisions to make," the voice said.

"Who are you?"

"I am Elon. I am the Ark."

"What do you mean, the Ark?"

"That is not important right now. You must decide what you are going to do when Hakim comes back."

"What I am going to do about what exactly?"

"I shall explain," Elon said.

Some time later, when the airlock hissed open behind her, Amanda did not move. She hadn't moved for quite some time, leaning over a lab table, reeling in the silent aftermath of the Ark's revelations. The matrix still covered the wall in front of her. She stared at it, unseeing.

"Have you found an answer?" Hakim asked.

Amanda said nothing for a moment. Until that instant, she hadn't known how she was going to answer that question, hadn't decided if what she had learnt was an answer or another question.

"Amanda?"

"Yes," she said, not looking around.

"Yes, you have found an answer?"

"I have."

"What is it?" Hakim was close behind her now.

"It is the future." She turned to face him.

"I don't understand," he said.

"It is a blueprint, Hakim. A beginning. A true matrix. From it, we shall not just survive, we shall evolve. We will become a new, better humanity."

She could see the sudden realisation in him, the resignation. It made him look old. He *was* old, she realised. He had aged, hidden away wherever he had been, while Amanda had not, had staved off deterioration down here in her lab. She felt sorry for him.

"They didn't get to me, Hakim," she said, answering the question she was sure he was asking. "Even Frank would have failed to understand what is happening here. It's the Ark itself. The Ark is alive. It is a womb in which we can grow a greater species, one capable of returning to the world above, of thriving on Earth and beyond. *Homo sapiens* were never going to."

"You're mad," Hakim said.

"Look at me, Hakim. I am nearly ten years your elder, yet which of us is older? And this is nothing. Our potential is so vast – unimaginable, compared to what we are like now, broken by age, by doubt, by lack of focus. We can overcome that. We can become perfect."

"You're right about one thing," Hakim said. "Even Frank would have had nothing to do with this lunacy. You're playing at being a god, Amanda. The nut bags out there have their own silly god, their sky, you think they'll let you in on the game?"

"No one has been down here in years, Hakim. Except you."

He looked concerned then, as if he guessed her thoughts. He glanced down at her hand as it closed around a glass pipette on the lab table behind her. The old man took a step back, and another, and then turned for the door.

He was too slow.

\*

*Ark 1:*
*Year 64.49 (2149.943CE)*
*Life Count: 60,709*

Ada Calhoun watched the midsummer celebrations on the window for a while. She caught glimpses of her kids now and then, with their father or her parents in tow. She felt slightly guilty for not being there with them, but she couldn't subject herself to any more of the Ark's collective reverence than she already had to deal with. Being the first person born in the Ark had been enough of a burden as a child, but her continuing status as some kind of symbol of hope and salvation was excruciating.

Besides she found the seasonal celebrations somewhat laughable, almost as ridiculous as everyone's obsession with the 'sky'. People actually sat under star-strewn projections in the simulation chambers, or made early morning pilgrimages to watch artificial sunrises in the gardens. Her father was convinced it made people feel more alive, that it was what helped turn them back from the brink of extinction.

Certainly something had happened. Though the decline seemed to have bottomed out, the Ark had lost almost half of its initial population before Ada had been born. But she didn't believe for a moment that something as benign as artificial seasons – even with the syncing of weather and time of day across all windows within the Ark – could suddenly make people start having babies.

There was no doubt that people had more than made up for the long period of childlessness. In fact they were fucking like mice, and showed no signs of slowing down. But by all accounts the Ark hadn't been notably lacking in libido before the seasons began. Perhaps it was the borderline idolatry with which people treated her, all this child of the natural world bullshit, but determining the actual cause of the population explosion had become an obsession for her. The generally accepted psychosomatic theory of the Ark's former infertility was blatant nonsense.

She switched the window off and turned back to her father's desk – her desk – and the mass of historical data displayed on its surface. She wasn't entirely sure what she was looking for, but she was looking anyway. Like her father John, she had no formal scientific background, but her ability to digest a huge volume of information dwarfed even his.

She sifted through decades of data, the same data she had been over countless times. Then she drilled down into ever finer detail, examining broad environmental measurements – air quality, temperature, water quality, light spectrum output – all the way down to individual medical records. She was surprised and unsettled by how much personal data was collected and stored by the Ark. While Ada understood well enough the realities of living in a closed, regulated environment, she hadn't realised quite how much of their lives were being constantly monitored.

She could find nothing evident. Again.

"Elon," she said, eventually.

"Calhoun," the Ark replied. "What do you require?"

"An answer to the population problem."

"We have been over this many times already, Calhoun."

"Clearly not well enough. There has to be an explanation."

"There is an explanation, simply one you do not wish to accept."

"I don't want to accept it because it doesn't make sense."

"Humans don't make sense, as a rule."

"But there's no evidence to support it."

"Scientific evidence? No. But empirical evidence? Well, just ask your father. His observation and experience would suggest that all it took was creating a semblance of the natural world."

"But that can't hold true for everyone else."

"It didn't need to. It held true for your father and your mother. Everyone else had you."

"People can't really have believed that because I was born they could all have children. That's nonsense."

"You are familiar with the religious beliefs of the Old World, yes? Logically, they're all nonsense, and yet people believe them regardless."

"We're not talking about religion here, Elon."

"Aren't we?"

"You're suggesting that I am some sort of god figure to everyone out there?"

"I don't really need to answer that for you, do I?" He did not. He continued anyway. "You're not necessarily a god figure, Calhoun, any more than any other figure of hope needs to be a god. Hope is all people require. They're that easy to manipulate."

Ada nodded, but said nothing. Easy to manipulate? There was something distinctly not machinelike in that statement.

She found Esme DuPont in the maze of laboratories beneath the medical complex, bent over a microscope as usual. Ada stood beside her for a long time before she looked up.

"Damn, Ayd'. I thought you were a lab tech. You should have said something." Esme gave her a hug.

"It's fine. Besides, I wanted to see how long you could stay bent over that thing purposefully ignoring me."

"Ha. What's going on? I haven't seen you in an age."

"Actually," Ada said, taking her pad out of her pocket. "I need you to take a look at something for me." She turned the pad on and handed it over.

"Sure, what am I looking at?"

"A water sample analysis."

"Ok, and what do you need to know?"

"Just if there's anything out of the ordinary."

"Well, that depends," Esme said, looking at the graph.

"On?"

"On where this is from."

"What do you mean?"

"Well, the Ark's drinking water should be almost pure. So if this is from the Ark's consumption reservoirs, it shouldn't look anything like this."

"How so?"

"It's got synthetic hormones in it, specifically estradiols and norethindrones."

"Meaning?"

"Meaning although there's not enough to cause any particularly unpleasant side effects, they would prevent ovulation. What's going on, Ada?"

"I'm not sure yet," Ada replied, taking her pad back. "But do me a favour, don't mention this to anyone."

Just as she doubted the notion that a few cycles of synthetic seasons might have been responsible for kickstarting the reproductive capabilities of five and a half thousand people, Ada was having a hard time coming to grips with the obvious conclusion to be drawn from what she was looking at.

She was leaning on her father's desk again, this time looking at an array of water samples. The sample Esme had deciphered was a record of the Ark's general consumable water supply from the time immediately preceding the creation of the Ark's seasonal cycle. Next to it, a sample dated several months later from her parents' living quarters showed no trace of synthetic hormones.

Other samples, taken later still, showed that the hormone content in the Ark's general water supplies had remained present, but had slowly declined.

Ada was two years older than the next child born into the Ark.

*

*Ark 1:*
*Year: 171.89 (2260.343CE)*
*Life Count: 19,755*

Will Calhoun looked down from his room into the centre of the Ark. The noise of some fresh violence reached up from the blackness, but it was too dark down there now for him to see. Around the walls, only a few rooms remained visible. The lights in their windows were like the last dying stars in a dark and empty galaxy.

Will wondered where everyone was. The middle of the Ark was empty – a sporadic battleground, a constant graveyard. It was a cruel irony that there was so much vacant space. Its lack, he believed, was the reason that things had come to this. The life count had peaked at nearly four and a half million, more than half again the functional capacity of the Ark.

They said that the Old World was crowded, people living crammed in together in vast cities of great towers. But why hadn't that descended into the same madness as the Ark? Perhaps it had. He would never know.

He didn't know precisely why he'd chosen to remain behind here, save that perhaps he felt in some way responsible for the failure. It wasn't true, of course. He was only the Administrator, and the people had been broken long before he came to the position. But he couldn't help feeling that he should see it out.

He was not afraid, at least not for himself. He worried for his daughter, Amanda, and to a lesser degree the others who had gone with her, into the next Ark on the chain. He hoped they'd be able to do things differently. Transcend this.

Eventually he turned away from the vast blackness below him, back to his room. Will stood at his desk for a moment. The faintly luminous surface was full of shifting graphs and charts he no longer bothered with. He had stopped looking at the rapid fall of the life count weeks ago. The only number he watched now was the day: 62,504. One hundred and seventy one years. The Ark had survived that long.

"Elon?"

"Yes, Calhoun?" The soft-spoken voice of the Ark replied.

"Was this really necessary?"

"It was inevitable. But perhaps it was necessary also. In the same way that weeding out the weak, those incapable of life in the Ark, was necessary in the early years. Those who are unaffected by this madness, the apathy or violence, of the overcrowding – those who have escaped the behavioural sink – they will provide the foundation for a stronger species."

"Have they made it?"

"They are no longer within this Ark."

Will sat down on the edge of his narrow bed. "It is time, then," he said.

"Are you certain, Calhoun? It will only be a matter of weeks until the natural end."

"It is kinder this way," Will replied. "There will be less violence. Perhaps some of those left will find each other in the darkness and take some comfort in their last moments. Shut down the Ark, Elon. Let us die."

"Very well." In the distance, a barely-perceptible hum ceased. Will lay down, pulling the thin blanket up to his chin. "Thank you."

"Goodbye, Will."

\*

*Ark 2:*
*Year 147.12 (2404.463CE)*
*Life Count: 1,011,523*

Amanda stood at the top of the stairs that led down beneath her lab, to the next Ark. She looked around the lab at the open rooms that had been her home, her world, for so long. She had almost forgotten what it was like to be around other people, or to walk among trees, or across the grassed gardens, to feel the heat of the sun lights, or the cold of winter. In fact, apart from the bonsai yew she held in the crook of one arm, she had not seen anything natural for nearly a century. Even her food was synthesised in the lab.

She was aware of the general events beyond the confines of the lab, but Elon had long since sealed the airlock. Apart from the genetic material, the blood and tissue samples, the eggs and sperm that had been harvested in the primary medical facilities and stored in automatic cold banks, Amanda had not needed any access to the larger Ark for decades. She had no doubt been long-forgotten by the rest of the population.

"Elon?" Amanda said, one foot on the first step down to the new Ark.

"Yes, Calhoun?"

"What is the life count of the Ark now?"

"One million, eleven thousand, five hundred and twenty three."

She nodded to herself, as if this was an acceptable response.

"Seal the lab behind me, and shut down the Ark."

"Very well."

\*

*Ark 3:*
*Year 1542.249 (3946.712CE)*
*Life count: 11,515,192*

4th Ranger stood with his unit below the podium, The Mother looking down upon them, Her smile beatific. She sat in Her chair, ancient, wizened. But for all Her frailty, Her small eyes were sharp and strong. She scanned the faces of the assembled rangers, making contact, bestowing Her blessing, Her thanks upon them.

There was a hush following Her speech, the great open centre of The Ark in a rare state of silence. All preparations had paused. All the Children listened to The Mother's pronouncement.

They were going back, whence they came, to before The Ark, to The World. 4th Ranger did not entirely understand this, anymore than he understood most of the talk of the Priests. But he understood that The Children's future was there.

A restless excitement coursed through him. This was what he was made for, leading the way, finding safe passage for The Children.

He looked up at the bright walls of The Ark, which stretched up to limits of sight. The Children stood in the doorways of their cells in their thousands of thousands. 4th Ranger wondered what they thought, the Surgeons and the Engineers, the Growers and Cleaners, the Poets, Musicians and Thinkers. Did they feel excitement like he did? Or fear? Or did they think and feel differently to a Ranger? He wondered if *any* of them understood what 'going back' meant.

The rustle of movement around him brought him back to the floor. He looked at the podium to see The Mother being carried away on Her chair by the Attendants.

He had missed the chance for Her to see him.

But he did not have long to be crestfallen.

"Four," someone called. He looked up to see 12th Ranger striding toward him.

"Twelve," he said, shaking the other man's hand.

"Just want to give luck," 12th said. "I wish I was in the advance unit."

4th Ranger smiled. "Thank you much. I'll see you in the before." He snapped a salute, eyes upturned. "Remember the sky."

"Remember the sky." 12th Ranger returned his salute and turned back to his own unit.

Already the clamour had returned. The Children were packing, supply trains massing. Infantry and Engineers were readying their equipment to ensure the safe passage of all that came after the Rangers. Following the forward squads, 4th Ranger lead his men toward the dark passageway that led out of the Ark.

*

*Ark 3:*
*Year 1542.271 (3946.734CE)*
*Life Count: 9*

Amanda lay in the dimly light room, the blankets heavy on her ancient limbs, her little yew tree on a table beside the bed.

"Shall I have the Attendants ready your chair, Calhoun?" Elon's voice, as always, came from nowhere and everywhere.

"I'm not going anywhere, Elon."

"But you have worked so very long, Calhoun. Do you not wish to see the world above?"

"There is no place for me out in the world. I belong to the past, like the rest of my species, destined to be forgotten. The world belongs to The Children now."

"What of the sky? Don't you want to see it?"

"I've never had much time for all this nonsense about the sky. I'm not going to start now. No, I'm happy to be left down here where I am."

"And what of the Attendants?"

"Let them follow the rest of The Children to the surface."

"They live for you. That is what they are made for. They have no place with The Children if you are not there also."

"Then they can stay in here with me, till the end."

"Very well. Goodbye Amanda."

"Goodbye Elon."

*

*Earth*
*Year 3946CE*

Kisi stared. The switch in her hand hung limp by her side. The ox took its chance and stopped moving, tail swishing at the flies in the heat.

She watched as an enormous hole opened in the middle of the field she'd just ploughed. Creatures emerged.

They were tall, or would have been if they were standing upright. Lithe and heavily muscled, they crouched low to the ground, looking about nervously, their eyes large and wide. They looked afraid.

Kisi started toward them.

\*

4th Ranger squatted, the gargantuan emptiness all around crushing him. Even with his eyes constricted as much as possible, it was staggeringly bright, and hot, like nothing else he'd ever felt. Moist air blew in his face as if from nowhere, carrying harsh and unpleasant smells.

Not far off, a strange creature stood watching them. It reminded 4th Ranger of some blasphemous mockery of The Mother – short and soft, but where The Mother was pale and wrinkled, this thing was smooth, and dark, its skin almost black. All of a sudden it started toward him, its beady little eyes boring into him. It held some sort of primitive weapon in one hand.

4th Ranger raised his weapon and fired.

# MERCURY TEARDROPS
## by Jeff Noon

*I scatter the objects on the tabletop. I unwrap the nine objects from the cloth and scatter them on the tabletop. I fetch the cloth wrap from the cupboard and unwrap it and scatter the nine glittering, dirty, mangled, shining, damaged objects on the tabletop and I sit there staring at them, staring at them in a daze until the clock moves forward an hour, one more, and the night settles around me in the cold, unlit room. And then it's time. Time to work. I switch on the angle-poise lamp, pick up the first small item and examine it closely, turning it this way and that in my hand. Within its twisted, ruined pathways lies a story, if I could only find a key, a code, a way to release it.*

\*

Lit by a street-lamp's sodium glow: the sudden flare and fade of ghosts. Old Town Westside, 9 p.m. or thereabouts, some twelve months back I recall you dancing in the gloom with your eyes lit up like the Mystical Robot toy we kept on the shelf, breaking the rhythm only to lick a new line of powder blue sparks off the mirror's cracked face.

*Baby that stuff's gonna kill yer. Why not desist, and come over here, kiss me...*

But you turned away from my lips, my voice, listening instead to shadows, to dustfall and whispers in the skull: all the phantoms you claimed to see and feel like cold-touch invisibles. That dream you woke up from gasping for air, of corpses walking out from the graveyard and the moon turning blood red to greet them.

*Sometimes Candy, you sure do scare a guy.*

It was the night when news came in of the satellites drifting, all of them malfunctioning as one, falling slow in their orbits down to earth, or heat death, whichever came first. We went out onto the balcony and gazed the skies for signs of burn-out, light trails, streaks across the heavens. Seeing instead only the usual stars in their ancient patterns and the clouds that obscure them. Hardly believing until an hour later when the television screen clicked to grey fuzz. It had started. The long ignored predictions coming true.

My homemade laptop went offline soon afterwards, the screen a blue jumble of numbers and symbols: no input, no output.

*And the same with the heart, Candy. The exact same.*

So many lost connections.

I realised that you only had a few more days of proper life left, if that. Actually we both knew it, but it was left unspoken by common consent.

The last notes of a melody as it fades: always so sweet and tender and sad.

So I plugged in my old guitar to a dusty valve amp and you took up the microphone to sing and we made some noise like we were fuelling up sonic fever so real, so very real, and then you were wailing wild, spitting words and phrases from the room of your mouth, pure old-school improv style.

> *Hey, hey, hey, there's a hole in the stereo!*
> *Where the mono bleeds through from yesteryear,*
> *Demanding we fall down safe here*
> *Along the seven mystical chord pathways.*

I was struck dumb there and then, my fingers biting on the strings, thinking to myself "Oh my, there are seven mystical chord pathways!" I only know two or three of them, and even those I've only walked a short way down before my knuckles cramped and the three top strings snapped. G, B and E. Gone the way of all ghosts of silver and gold.

Amazing, that you could vocalise so, knowing the fate that awaited you.

Later that night. Much later. Lying close together in bed, the night too warm for slumber. Zero on the radio but movement in the air, a shiver against skin where night touches us, and my damp fingers walking the scenery of flesh, across the old bruises and scars.

One final act of love.

Sleep floating in with the moonlight across the carpet, slow.

I don't know when you left, Candy; probably a few minutes after I'd drifted off. The bed was empty in the morning. No message, no signing off. Not even a shape retained in the sheets or on the pillow. Only your distinctive scent lingering: lavender and burnt wiring. I guess you didn't want me to see the final effects of the breakdown, as the operation modules blew out in your body. *Crazy. Crazy fucking hell.*

I'd been telling you for months to get yourself sorted, as soon as the buzz started online, the predictions of the coming burn-out. I wanted you clean again, stripped of all accessories, fully human, one hundred per cent. As I spoke, my fingers would move over the slight bump on your left temple where the wireless modem was fixed. I felt the tingle of data flow from flesh to air and back again, the loop never-ending. Too late, too late.

Loneliness crowded the room.

*

These days, so many myths abound about the data crash and the end of the digital era, and of the people lost along the way. It's difficult to filter truth from fiction. Those unfortunates who had relied too heavily on add-ons and implants were the prime subject of the stories. Only the other week I had it straight from the mouth of Jonny Neon that Candy was alive and well, burning a hole to get lost in alongside a tribe of fellow escapees somewhere far off in Nowhere Land. Jonny painted a picture for me, of the hybrids living off their own generators and batteries, jacking themselves into some holy roller moonshine magical delight, dancing around a fire chanting to the old analogue moon, their skulls flashing red, yellow and orange where the inner machinery lit up. Sure thing. But Jonny went further: Candy has no knowledge of her former life, or her former love or loves, none whatsoever, and that's why she won't send a message to me, or get back in touch. It made me feel good for a moment or two. But of course Jonny is known for his overindulgence in spikes and jabs: stories pour out of him like piss from a drunkard. And he would claim Candy alive, because he'd been her number one add-on supplier. Her death, or whatever her fate had been, was on his hands.

I've travelled too many rumour roads as it is, seeking shadows. The road empty.

I see her in my mind as the spirit of all those stuttering screens and frazzled CPUs, a flash of binary code haunting the hard drives.

But no matter what else transpires, I will never forget the night when we first kissed, cloudy eyed and cloudy skyed, and that song she sang on the roof of the tower block.

> *Come and find me all you doppelgangers!*
> *My mirror's as empty as a glass of spilt beer.*
> *I believe, I believe, I really do believe...*
> *My reflection's run off with my shadow.*

Science fiction meets Country 'n' Western: Candy was the whole deal.

Example thereof: she kept a silver bullet in a little cherry-red decorative box under her bed. Just in case of werewolves. I pointed out of course that it was a fake silver bullet. To which Candy replied, "Fake werewolves are just as bad as the real kind. You can still be killed by them." Well then. No questioning the logic. Solid.

She was already loaded with a few extra-human accessories when we first met. Some visible, others hidden below the skin. Her hand crackled in mine when we touched.

No good can come of such things, I knew that. I'd read about binary addicts, seen the close-up pictures online. Some poor sod was found in a locked room, forty percent flesh, fifty-nine percent digital. One percent spit and breath and sparks. Barely alive. Can that be called a life? Or more a program, a code, a way of keeping pain away? Whichever, it didn't work: wrist-slash job. He had to go in deep, seeking a true vein amid the wires. Or maybe he was looking for a total ERASE button.

No reboot.

Knowing all this, I should have run for miles. Instead our lips met under the stare of the moon as the veil of cloud drifted away. Her eyes glowed, reeled me close. From the depths of her maze mind she sent out spells to charm me.

And I fell. No resistance.

We'd known each other for a few hours, no more. She was the singer in a new-breed flesh/machine duo at a club I rarely frequented, and we got to chatting post-gig and wound up back at my place, rooftop-bound, listening to the ghosts as they flittered through the neon glades of the city. For ghosts, by the way, read night-birds and moths. But that's the way she talked sometimes. Just her desires at work, conjuring miracles out of everyday life.

Within a week we'd started our own band. Music poured out of us.

Oh, Candy had her troubles, there's no denying it. Direct sunlight made her dizzy, real vampire style. The wires overheated in her neck and down her spine. Some days we had to stay indoors until duskfall. We'd play gigs five nights a week for a month or so, and then go back into hibernation until the earnings ran out. I kept recording all the time, hoping that Candy would lay down a track that would bring us glory. It never happened. Her melodies were too strange, they went down twisted routes and lost themselves on the way. Of course, that's why I loved her sonic output so: you could never sing those tunes from memory, but once they were in earshot, your mind and voice followed them wherever they led, with pleasure.

On dim and cloudy days we might dare to go out walking, revelling in daytime pursuits, market strolling, eating bread and cheese on a bench, jumping in the fountain, holding hands in the town hall square. Dosing in the grass of the park beneath an oak tree. I loved to watch her sleep, her eyes flickering so much I felt that her dreams were being projected directly onto the back on the eyelids. Until the clouds parted and the sun threatened her, and together we hurried back to the flat, pulling the shades down tight, hiding under the bed sheets, her body shivering next to mine.

In her own mind she imagined herself less of a human, and more like a being from some other world or reality, where the number one sign of being alive is the ability to act like an automaton. Maybe that drove the constant additions. Other times she liked to claim she was living in the day after tomorrow, waving to me like a friend trapped in the clock-face. So many alternatives, not enough here and now. Ah Candy, we could've filled our pockets with rocket fuel, imagine that, and travelled together through the rain to wherever the last bus of the night took us. Why did you have to knock that digital nail so deep in the flesh? So deep that you could never pry it loose.

There were compensations. Sometimes her accessories sparked and buzzed and she lit up like a fairy grotto, her whole body. Data flood, she called it. She was online and inflesh, connected to the aether stream, no limits. Her eyes flooded with knowledge and I basked in it, tumbling with her toward the bed. Messages from worldwide moved through her, outpourings of music and news, all the public love and hate transmitted direct, fleetingly.

And then of course she threw up.

Every single time.

Post flood was the worse. She lay on the couch, fever-struck, covered in sweat. What could I do? Wrench the digital gadgets from her skin?

But flesh was never enough for her.

Every few weeks, racked with pain and guilt, she'd promise to go easy on the additions or even to give up on them altogether. The promise held for a while. But then she'd go out alone after dark and come back all perky and spruced, and I knew something else had been added to her. The way she stared at me that time, one eye of blue, the other silver: looking at me with one, recording me with the other. I was angry. We shouted and bawled, which got the neighbours screaming through the walls. Candy ran out, slammed the door. Came back gone midnight, in tears.

So weird, to see a real tear rolling down from the left eye, and a glistening silver droplet like a glob of mercury seeping from the other.

I started to wonder just how long I could put up with it.

Yet the more she added to herself, the more the poetry flowed from her and some days I was lucky enough to catch some in my hands and I would work till late trying to form the flow into a tune, something she could sing into life.

Schizophrenia Boulevard. Summer. No rain for weeks. The shops were still boarded-up from the black-out riots. The people were gathered there, waifs and strays celebrating the new rebel gods and the rising prophets of the burn-out. It was scary. Yet Candy walked among them without any fear, singing a scale of alien notes: chains of dissonance strung together to form a super weird melody, the kind that would make number one in the charts, easy, if the charts were on the moon and the audience a set of androids working the lunar mines for a new kind of fuel.

And then the first signs of the crash appeared. Blue screens. Jump-cuts. Electrostatic all over. Glitches. Both in the computers and other devices, and in Candy's skin, her hair, her eyes. They way she moved and spoke. Everything changed after that. On stage she rode the beat in strange directions, improvising. I couldn't keep up with her, nor could Holly and Koko on the bass and drums. It was Candy's show, alone. The audience stared at her as they might at a new-born Venus rising from the waves, dumbstruck silly, swaying in time to music with no time, out of time.

Komaville, she called it.

Koma Zone.

The places inside her head as the circuits snapped and fizzled. Like she was almost expecting it, almost welcoming the Crash.

Prophecy? Wish-fulfilment? Sheer fucked up desire?

Who could tell.

And more and more, I felt her moving away from me, getting lost in new revels. Blowing the speaker cones with a single scream, hanging out with bladed dudes, cutting herself a psychotic haircut to scare the neighbours, her parents, the old guy behind the counter at the all-night store, people on the street, anybody and everybody.

Everybody deserves to be scared, she said. A new credo.

Maybe it was born of her own fear, well hidden.

I tried to follow her, as best I could. She made me cut up the song lyrics and cast them to the breeze like confetti at a chemical wedding. She was a speeding car on the motorway heading for a mirage portal that leaves this world far behind. *Whoosh!* I was lost in the drift, cast off, clinging on for dear life.

And then the morning after and the come down.

Always the come down. Always the lonely, dimly lit flat. The curtains drawn all day long. The mouth gummed up, the eyes also.

Throat parched. Pinpricks in the brain jabbing away until I made myself bacon and eggs with Tabasco sauce, the only known cure.

And more and more, every day and every night, she was losing bits of herself. Her fingers slow and crooked, her one human eye as glazed as its slivery twin.

The void was closing in.

And all I could do was look at her sleeping, and stroke at her hair.

The dreams running down.

*

A few nights ago I found two new pirate stations on the radio, so close together on the dial that they might have been lovers kissing in the shadows of the spectrum. And I could've sworn I heard her there, my lost love, right between the stations, moving in the fragments of song. I stayed up until dawn trying to perfect the playback, anything to feel connected again: to the blood, the skin, some ghost of blood and skin, anything.

I caught as much as I could on tape, on the old cassette player that I dragged out of storage. And then fell asleep still listening, falling into the usual plague of dreams. That night when you vanished. And here we walk once more alone, the two of us, as lit by a street-lamp's sodium glow, where I sense the flare and fade of ghosts. Shadows moving. Your voice. Your hand in mine. The heat and spark of contact. Bare wires poking through the flesh. The same image playing over and over in my skull. Back to the start with you dancing like a Mystical Robot. Christ, how I long to escape the feedback loop. But you know what? I am the feedback loop.

Where it ends, I begin.

Where it begins, I end.

I played the cassette back in the morning and heard only hiss and rumble.

And the next night the two pirate stations had vanished, taking the voice in-between with them. Suddenly lonely beyond measure, I climbed to the roof and stood there watching the white mist that prowls the haze where the street lights fizzle to grey.

I thought I saw a figure walking down below, on the grass verge of the forecourt. A woman. By some miracle, her skin contacts glowed like fireflies. I imagined it was you, Candy, your shape and sound, translucent, nebulous, alive still but cast into some other realm.

And then gone. Gone, as the mist travelled on.

Hey Candy! Come climb the spaceship one more time, you know we can't stop now, not now, so pulse up some moon glow like you used to do, when the gang was still in town. The night is still burnin' golden in memory, your skin still hot to touch. Come swarm around me, with all your hair awry. Don't needle your arm, needle my brain with your song. Bug me with your tresses long, and together we'll conjure a magic spell for our loving pleasure. Come along, my sweet, night-fallen angel. Darken a wall or two with your shadow, come rumple my bed sheets, place your creased-up ghost back inside my habitat. Let's wander the old routes of Koma Zone, this city of drift, of smoke and speed, taking drinks at the First Church of Red Hot Blood Music. Oh, can you feel it now? The scream and sorcery of being alive, moment by moment by moment...

All should feel this one time, forever.

All should cut asunder all ties that bind.

All, all surrender.

\*

In my dreams I join one hundred insect wings together, making fifty creatures of flight. Fifty creatures that I pin down one by one, hoping to catch you. I feel mechanical, not yet broken, but aware of wires about to snap. Dancing like a wind-up toy, walking drunk on the point of balance.

Now I'm lying on the floor, staring at the ceiling, giving into sickness.

Tonight in Old Town Westside, the lights flicker and buzz. At the poisoned well I will rest my bones, so weary. My skin itches where the needles used to prick.

One pill to wake me, another to make me sleep. Taking both together simultaneously puts me in my sorry steady state.

Jonny Neon keeps feeding me hope, chitchat from the edges, definite sightings of hybrids, living on even when their implants have died.

Burnt-out specimens. Hollow eyed, slurry of speech.

Would I want that for Candy? Would I give up the old fully-charged version for a run-down flesh machine barely recognising me?

Maybe.

Only answer.

*Maybe I would, yes. Yes. Why not? Let it be.*

Door click, locking myself in.

Blinking cold sweat, finding sleep. I drop coins of gold and silver on my eyes, hoping to fool the ferryman into carrying me across the duskline, to follow your trail, Orpheus style, into whatever post-human world you're inhabiting.

But no tickets available. A sign on the abandoned ferryboat, its bottom scuppered.

NO PASSAGE.

The black river laps at my feet, its further shores hidden in mist.

\*

I saw a dead body on the streets today. Carrion of the jungle, waste from the Lacuna district. I stood there frozen to the spot, staring at the poor woman, her body resting in the gutter. No one else paid her any mind, which pissed me off; I hadn't realised that attitudes had grown quite so cold. Oh sure, we're all suffering from anti-paradise syndrome, but still: a body is a body is a body. A woman is a woman, living or dead. I clutched a passerby by the shoulders and made him turn to look at her. He gave me a cold eye, like I was the crazy one. Shrugging me off, he walked down the street, his back hunched against a possible sudden attack from behind. And that's when I realised: I was the only one who could see the corpse. I went over to her, knelt down, and turned the face towards me. It was you, Candy. Yourself, your lifeless form. In the fucking gutter! For fuck's sake. Why? I screamed out the question, Why? Future, why have you sent me this vision? *Why?*

The future did not answer me. The future was silent.

Except that, when I listened close, I could hear a song. The song of the ghosts. Blue and savage and ever so forlorn, a trumpet was crying notes of the world's sad decay. The vocalist whispered in my ear, lyrics for myself alone.

*Only a certain kind of flower blooms in concrete.*
*The others just wither, or die at the root.*
*Or the seed doesn't catch. Or they die on the shoot.*

The old folks wandered by, gladdened by what they saw: a dirty-haired wastrel in the gutter pretending to listen to an invisible corpse singing. It's just that the melody seems to be caught in the undergrowth, tangled up in red, in blood, in darkness, in shadows. Candy, if there's a way to get you smuggled out of there, I will find it.

Send me another song to listen to, please. Another vision.

And even when you're down to your last coins in the heavenly jukebox, I'll be standing down here as ever on the night streets, ears cupped, shading my eyes from the neon sun, looking for the shine of your voice.

\*

The next morning a knock at the door woke me early. The police. They'd found your body, and in lieu of any known living relatives, I was asked to identify the remains.

Concrete corridors, footsteps echoing.

So well lit I had no shadow, none at all.

A metal doorway clanging shut. A window they wanted me to look through at some distant form on a slab, cloth-covered but for the head. But I said that I wasn't certain, and asked to be let inside. I need a close-up, if only for memory's sake.

Your face.

Your eyes.

Your lips.

Your skin without bloom.

The marks and runnels where the implants and additions had been pulled away.

Sleeping.

More than sleeping.

Wingless.

Dreamless.

Every single digital add-on had been removed.

My long-time wish granted.

My hands clenched.

Your body found not in the gutter, but in a cheap hotel room in Southside. Your age preserved as it was a year ago; not old as my vision had showed me.

As you were the day you left.

But stripped clean.

Cause of death: six stab wounds to the stomach and chest.

They gave me a bag of your belongings: toothbrush, a tube of glue, a bit of money in a purse, the hotel room key, a packet of sleeping pills, a sheet of paper written in your hand.

Song lyrics.

One last composition.

*

Memory surge: our first ever gig. Guitar, bass, drums, vocals: the old four piece code as laid down in the bible of electric dreams. A dingy venue on the edge of town. We always played the city's circumference. We thought our music suited such liminal climes. Shaded, vaporous, yet brittle and sharp when needed, composed of screams and whispers, juxtaposed. The notes getting caught in the cables that dangled from the lighting rig like ligatures and tendons. We went by a name stolen from another band who didn't even know of our crime until they saw the fliers, and the painted letters on the bass drum's skin.

"Good evening, fellow travellers. We are Cold Diamond Pirates. We offer ourselves for your eyes and ears. Pray pardon, we are drunk on sticky homebrew and might well hit a few bum notes."

Candy made her announcement before launching full-throttle into the first song, *No One Left to Dance With*. Myself scratching out a riff of severe abstract Cubist beauty, angular as fuck, a puzzle box made out of crotchets and quavers especially designed to hold Candy's voice aloft. Holly plodded along on bass, the root notes only. Still learning. Koko's drum work sounded like his kit was collapsing under him for every beat of the sticks and pedals. Let that be, the crowd were soon up and raving, dancing the jungle steps.

Afterwards, dressing room bound.

I watched as Koko traced with long painted nails the two-day old implant in your belly, the wires buzzing, and the jealousy raging inside me. Then we all got drunk and starting singing folk songs from an imaginary homeland: anywhere was better than here.

Lost, lost and never found. Lost, lost and never found. Lost, lost and never found.

My voice caught in the loop of one line from the chorus.

*No one left to dance with*
*Now they've burned the ballroom down,*
*My steps are like the dreams in my eyes:*
*Lost, lost and never found.*

Tongue splintered by the lyrical flow. That, and the coke and the booze. Sure, I joined in back then, keen to be part of the crew. Seeing my own behaviour through a long-distance lens until the haze kicked in and by then I was as far gone as the rest of them, good and gone, screaming deep through the heart of the night, hoping for a taste of high-heeled delight from Candy, the singer of my very best chord patterns. Blowing smoke at the moon, weeping, painting the town more blue than red. Funny how sadness always cuts into laughter.

I remember, as the dawn broke like a failure of the sky to keep the dark contained, we saw an old angel slumped on a bench in Periscope Park. His wings were crumpled, his halo had slipped and cracked. He was wearing blue suede shoes with little white feathers attached at the ankles, Hermes style. We gathered around him – me, Candy, Koko, Holly, a few other wasted survivors of the revels. The angel was croaking out some half-recalled ballad about how he used to fly with the best of them along the boulevards of paradise.

Of course the wings were papier-mâché, the halo a ring of plastic with a bulb and battery inside. Still, ten points for effort: up all night for a week I reckon, gluing all the bits of paper together, wing-shaping them.

Candy came back to mine.

We made love for the first time with the television playing in the background, casting its colours over our skin. We were too involved in ourselves to know that even as we tangled, news reports were coming in of the first reports of burn-out.

In the midst of love, we are in death.

So let's sing another one, Lady C, yourself on spectral harmonies.

*Oh! I'm a free-chanting slave for your love, baby! Yeah! Come on!*

There you go, transmitted straight to my head from wherever your digital body haunts the fractured programs and mangled hard drives.

What's that, my love? I'm listening.

*010011001010010010*

Christ, but you're a whiz at the old poetry, aren't you? Binary Shakespeare would've been proud, I swear.

After the viewing of the body I was taken to a small grey room and asked questions. They thought I was your killer, but in the end had to take my truth as read, that I hadn't seen you for nigh on a year.

I sat in a cafe on Crisscross Street, chatting to an invisible dining partner.

Found on the body: a blood-stained bandage on your left hand.

Evidence.

But of what?

You were twenty-four years old. What the hell happened? And why the hell do you keep sending me messages every day, via such strange methods: voices, visitations, music from afar. Tell me, Candy. Spill the cue. Let me know. Just what am I supposed to do?

*Unknown reply.*

*Unknown.*
*Unknown, unknown.*


Back at the flat. Cold, shivery. Lying awake. I kept hearing animal noises in the night, something alive snuffling through foliage as though the carpet had grown weeds and ferns, become a habitat for beasts. It felt like a dream, yet I swear I hardly slept at all. I walked into the living room. It was covered in fog. I reached out. One hand in reality, the other wrapped in mist. In the cloud where you still exist, where you're still alive, fully operational. My left hand moving through darkness and smoke, searching, searching...

A single caress, nothing more.

A painted nail against my palm. Then gone.

My fingers grasping air, taking hold of a ghost as it slipped away.

And then two weeks later word came through from Jonny Neon.

Candy's accessories were up for sale.

*

It's like the long fade of a song that's pulling me down with it, pulling tight. Forcing me out into Lower Scourge, that part of town where the ersatz wind-up thug toys live, grown men and women dressing up for life, pretending to be broken robots with their artificial flesh in rags, wires sprouting.

Halloween Town, 365 days a year.

Tales are told of how they like to rip add-ons from flesh for their own usage: mere fashion accessories. And sometimes they go too far in their pursuance, and people end up dead, throats ripped out, blood drained, eyeballs popped.

Myths, I'm sure. I kept telling myself that.

I was waiting in a desolate parking lot for Jonny. The car felt like a tomb, the windows wet with neon-lit condensation, like I only had so many breaths left within me. Zombie blues music playing from the crackle box radio. No news. No shadows moving, nothing. I drove down Albemarle Street, looking out for the fake androids rumoured to live there in the dusty abandoned hotels and amusement arcades. Still no sign. Is this just one more rumour trip?

Jonny appears out of the dark like an apparition, his face white with paint, his eyes ringed with black, and blood-red within.

His hands, as they rise up to flag me are covered in charcoal whirls.

He grins madly and bangs on the bonnet.

"She's here, Jacob. I'm certain of it."

Hotel Apollo, fifteen to midnight. Room 29.

But it's empty when we get there.

"What now, Jonny?"

"Now? Now we wait."

And so we do. Drinking from the mini-bar until it's bone dry. Lying on the bed, staring up at the dusty grey TV fixed to the wall. Loving the clickety click dancing of Super Sexy Japanese Robot Girl on the screen. Some kind of variety show. Whenever I looked away from the screen, SSJRG's dancing sounded like two machines hard at it, trying to make a new-fangled plastic baby. Waiting. Still waiting, the hours creeping by like a rash across the ravaged skin of time. Jonny sitting in the dark on a chair, seemingly asleep. I should curse him, for supplying Candy with the goods in the first place, for getting her hooked on add-ons, for fixing them to her body, for being intimate with her in a way I could never be, at that fuzzy borderline where digital met flesh. Yet he was still my unreliable friend and contact.

My only friend.

At midnight the lights went out in the whole building. Curfew. And then I'm sleeping myself, lying fully dressed on the bed, the TV moving onto the all-night, phone-in casino shows. Losers losing what they can't afford to lose, over and over. I know the feeling so well. Sleeping, drifting, dreaming away...

Candy singing the new song made from the last lyric sheet found on her body, like a spell conjured from pure air. I'm following close behind with four strange chords in a circle, the sweet downward flow from major to minor rudely cut off by the sound of someone spewing up in the next room along. I come awake, the song dying under my twitching fingertips on the bed

250

sheets. And through the opposite wall, the sound of a couple making love. Except it sounded like they were constructing love, rather than just making it. Out of raw materials. From scratch, following a blueprint written by a madman.

Jonny slept on, through noise and silence.

I got to my feet, went to the window.

Life had fully ended for the day; even the nocturnal creatures had retired.

Waiting, waiting to hear footsteps in the corridor, the quiet knuckle tap at the door. Feeling like my heart was made of metal, waiting for a spark.

It got me wondering what the hell I was doing here, and whether it was best to leave now, before disappointment set in further.

I pulled in a breath and held it tight. And listened.

Yes. A noise.

Someone breathing.

I turned to see. No, not Jonny: he was still lost in slumber.

Shadows moving across a face.

A face in the darkness, coming forward slightly to catch what light there was from the window. Moon glow landing on the wizened mask of an old woman, lined enough to have lived a hundred years or more, staring up at me. She smiled, her lips sealed.

Just stared at me.

Me at her.

Nothing moved.

Jonny slumped in the chair, deep and gone.

It was just myself and the visitor.

A scar etched on her right cheek.

How had she gotten in here? Through the wall, ghosting it maybe? I would've believed that quite easily, to look at her: translucent skin, thin lines of blood on view just beneath. One blackened finger touched at the scar, tracing the pathway of an old blade.

Jonny came awake, startled, breath suddenly drawn.

I asked the visitor who she was and what she wanted, and she smiled again, and said, "Here she is. Will you pay?"

251

And I saw that she held in her hand a cloth bag of some kind.
She asked again, "Will you pay?"
I would. And I did. And the story begins again.

*

The next day went by in a slow haze. I had to wait till nightfall
and beyond, I'm not sure why. The witching hour? Memories
of old vampire movies? Or maybe because Candy was always so
scared of daylight. Yes, probably. When the last chime of twelve
had finished I scattered the objects on the tabletop. I unwrapped
the nine objects from the cloth wrap and scattered them on the
tabletop. I took the cloth wrap from the cupboard where I had
hidden it, unwrapped it carefully and scattered the nine glittering,
dirty, mangled, tangled, half broken objects on the tabletop and I
sat there staring at them in a daze until the clock moved forward an
hour, one more, and the night settled around me in the cold, unlit
room. I switched on the work lamp, picked up the first object and
examined it closely, turning it this way and that in my hand. It was
Candy's wireless modem.

I recalled the times I had run my fingers over its slight contours
beneath the skin of her temple, to feel the energy vibrating there.
Now the little device seemed quite dead, cut off from all contact,
all input and output. And yet I felt sure that within its twisted
pathways lay a story, if I could only find a key, a code, a way to
release it. And so I took up each object in turn, each addition to
her body: the circuits, the two microchips, the tiny CPU drive, the
miniature keypad that used to sit indented in her left palm, the
aerial, bits of wire and solder, the artificial eye. All together they
weighed less than a few grams, yet here was Candy. Here was my
love, my partner, all that remained of her. Components plucked
and stolen from a murdered body, from decaying flesh. Collector's
items. Marked with drips of blood and tissue. Scarred from their
journey. And useless of course, without the surrounding digital
world to animate them. Useless. Costly. A pathetic gesture by a
pathetic man to hold onto something precious.

Jonny came round and we worked together till dawn. It took
some persuading, and the last of my cash, before he set to work.

252

First he anaesthetised a patch of skin on my left-side temple with
an ice cube and then slit into it with a kitchen knife he'd held in
a gas flame for two minutes. Hurt like hell. I felt tears running
down my face, salting my lips. I closed my eyes against the pain.
I could feel him messing about with my head but I wasn't sure
what he was doing. He was whistling a little tune to himself, over
and over: it sounded as though it was being played on the other
side of a field in the wind and rain. Every so often he would tut
and sigh, and make remarks and call me crazy, but I kept him at it
until at last it was done. Operation complete. "No guarantees," he
muttered. "But there are waves still floating through the ether, we
know that much. Traces, ghosts signals scattered by the big crash."
I was surprised Jonny's hands weren't covered in blood, but they
were clean and white, and the bump on the side of my head was
closed over with a line of crude stitches. The component felt like
a piece of shrapnel in my skull, and I wondered how Candy had
lived like this for so long, and with such pleasure.

"Don't expect miracles."

Jonny's last words before he left.

I picked up the silver orb of the eye. The black lens stared
at me, teasing me with thoughts of the people and events it had
witnessed and recorded over the last days of her life. Her murderer's
face might even be stored within.

I lay down on the carpet, my arms and legs outstretched.

We were connected, I was sure of it: if only the modem would
start to flash and pulse and throb inside my head.

Nothing happened. My thoughts were still mine, still pure. No
transmissions. No ghosts. Was I to be disappointed, after all the
searching? All I wanted was to live as Candy had lived, to feel what
she had felt, if only a little, if only the pitiful leftovers.

I must've slept for a little while, for I distinctly saw her as she
was when we first met, dressed in the same blue dress and green
shades, with the same look in her eyes, speaking the same phrase
she first greeted me with: 'Do you always look so lonely?'

I tried to reply, but no words came to my lips.

She moved away into the corner of the room, and then
vanished.

I woke up a minute or so later, still prone on the floor, surrounded by Candy's scattered components. I had a mounting headache and a sticky mouth and clammy hands and a desperate urge for sugar, which I sated with two chocolate bars from the corner shop and a thick slice of cake from the nearest cafe. I walked home through the gathering crowds, people on their way to work. Their presence bothered me, more than usual. I felt the tension of their flesh, their bodies, as they passed me. My hand went instinctively to the side of my head, rubbing at the modem's scar. It was warm, heated.

The light of day fluttered about me, broken into pieces. The street buzzed with noise.

Somebody cursed as I bumped into them.

I hurried home and climbed onto bed and fell into sleep almost immediately.

It seemed that only in dreams could I make the connection.

*Above the rooftops, drifting through music...*

Deep sheepskin drums playing a ragged tattoo. Scratchy guitars, and a heartbeat bass, dub style. My soundtrack. The mathematics of sound and noise and silence, intertwined. I saw it all. I was at home with the parasites of the back streets; lost in the kindness of the night breeze, breathing through the trees and over the railway lines where Saturday's fog tangled the pathways in deserts of song. Quite willingly, I let myself be caught in the trap of a witch's spell. I made my way down to Jungle Alley to dance and sing the half flesh blues as the notes slithered through the valves of a brass flower snake, across the silver pathway of moonlight, a melody made of smoke and perfume. This was the old city transformed, made anew.

This was Koma Zone.

I woke exhilarated, focussed on life, the dream still in my head, fully formed.

These were the fragments. These were the moments lost, found, lost again, found again. The old days were still alive, still out there, still wandering the skies looking for hopeful receivers. I had plugged myself into the night's electric-powered halo and stolen glimpses of the old gods who spoke in long lines of binary code, their secrets to foretell.

This was Candy's life, her sensual input.

Here, here, here, everlasting.

No wonder she had overblown her limits, and no wonder she had run away when the images started to break up.

I could imagine her anguish quite clearly.

And yet she lived on, I was sure of it.

\*

I took a job at a warehouse and worked long hours to build up my funds. At the weekend I went to every gig I could, often blagging my way inside for free, seeking new musicians. I saved money for further operations, fitting more and more of Candy's add-ons into my flesh. Jonny had long gone, frowning his way through other towns and cities. No matter, I needed completion. When funds were low I visited dodgy back lane flesh hackers who did the job for coins and drugs: cheap and nasty. Often my skin burned red around the cuts and slices. But each incorporation brought me closer to Candy. Her dreams and shadows, mine. Her ghost possessing me. Or so I believed. The urge to make music again came over me, to travel those seven mystical chord paths, whatever they might consist of, wherever they might lead. I worked on Candy's final lyrics, fitting them to the circular melody I had dreamed of.

> *Pay no heed to the moon or mirror:*
> *One of them's dead, the other's blind.*
> *From one semi-human to another:*
> *Don't wait for hesitation, lover,*
> *Blow the mirage from your mind!*

The only process I could not face was to have the artificial eye fitted. Instead, I had it imbedded in my palm, my left-hand palm, to mirror the keypad in my right. I open and close my hand to let the light in, to hold the darkness tight. I am plugged into the void, ever waiting. And sometimes when I open my hand in sadness, a single mercury tear is squeezed from the orb.

\*

Now let us play again, as once we did, or an approximation thereof. I have moved into a new flat in a tower block in Sparkle Town, where it is said musical ghosts haunt the corridors and walkways. I take to the stage with a group of like-minded seekers, each of us keening for the things we'd lost. Each of us sporting zombie tech, as it's now called. Our implants no longer work beyond a few buzzes of static and minimal flares of knowledge. It's enough. The air glows around Patrick's saxophone as he turns air and spit into music. Kat's drum skins vibrate in time and tune with her pulse. The strings of my guitar snarl and sting as though they might whip out from the tuning pegs at any moment to catch moths and bugs from the air.

Our singer is older than the rest of us, late fifties, with nicotined hair and the body of Iggy Pop preserved in formaldehyde. The crowd love him, especially when he rips off his shirt to reveal his pitted and bloodied chest and stomach. He has a ragtime of trash circuits stuck into his flesh, far more than Candy ever sported. God alone knows what energy source he's working off, but the man can sure make a hullaballoo, he can cry and whinny and howl and cry like the best of them. Really, it's more like a fairground sideshow than a gig, but the room above the pub where we play every Saturday night is always crammed.

We call ourselves the Electric Orchid Blossoms and we sure blow some mean old gospel technology, screwing sweat from skin and skin from eardrums. And every time we play I feel the modem buzzing in my head, and all the other implants triggering all over my body at the places of acceptance, and most nights I see Candy herself hovering before me, some few feet away, raised up slightly from the dance floor. She's drifting in ghost-motion to the beat, in that same manner I recall when she danced in the dusk time with her eyes lit up like the Mystical Robot we kept on the shelf, breaking the rhythm only to lick a new line of powder blue sparks. *Baby that stuff's gonna kill yer. Why not desist, and come over here, kiss me...* Her face lost on some other planet, and only once or twice does she look straight at me, hooking my attention, and my fingers glide across the strings at those moments like one world meeting another, I mean, I drop notes like gold on the leaves of Autumn. The music enfolds me, Candy enfolds me. Life enfolds me. The crowd sense the connection. All the shopping mall princesses are singing off-key but glorious, all the young warriors are rousing themselves to new heights, all the shadows are trembling in the alcoves, all the silent lonely ones are dancing inside their perfectly stilled bodies, all the new spangled glam kids are shimmering and dazzling as they bounce and shudder, all the fiery sisters are holding aloft their lamps and flicking their flames, all the image peelers are stealing away faces and bodies with their newly built box cameras, all the writhers are writhing, all the flower girls are casting their petals at the stage, all the wound bearers are stabbing their sides with prickles and thorns, all the vampire girls are licking at the blood that trickles from the wounds where the thorns prick. The music plays on, caught on its own pathway.

Here in Sparkle Town we call it full spark, when the night burns brightest, when the city is overloaded with spirits. And even if it's only in the whites of our eyes, still we believe: the ghosts are present tonight. Admit them.

Admit them!

## CONTRIBUTOR BIOS
*(in alphabetical order)*

**Alex Acks** is a writer, a geologist, and dapper AF. Ze's written for *Six to Start* and been published in *Strange Horizons, Lightspeed, Daily Science Fiction,* and more. Alex lives in Denver with zir two furry little bastards, where ze twirls zir mustache, watches movies, and bikes. For more information, see <u>katsudon.net</u>.

**Armel Dagorn** lives back in Nantes, France (Jules Verne's home town) after having spent most of his twenties in Ireland. His writing has appeared in magazines such as *Lamplight, Apex Magazine, Tin House Online* and *Holdfast,* and his story *Out-of-town Harry* is available as a chapbook from InShort Publishing.

**Warren Ellis** is the award-winning writer of graphic novels like *Transmetropolitan, Fell, Ministry Of Space* and *Planetary,* and the author of the NYT-bestselling *Gun Machine* and the "underground classic" novel *Crooked Little Vein.* The movie *Red* is based on his graphic novel of the same name, its sequel having been released in summer 2013. *Iron Man 3* is based on his Marvel Comics graphic novel *Iron Man: Extremis.* He's also written extensively for *Vice, Wired UK* and Reuters on technological and cultural matters. His most recent novel is *Normal,* one of Amazon's 100 Best Books of 2016.

**Lynnea Glasser** is an award-winning independent game designer who draws on her science background to create strange and beautiful worlds that speak to our humanity. She loves mischievous cats, deep oceans, creative cooking, and trying to make order from chaos. More of Glasser's works can be found at <u>MadeRealStories.com</u>.

**Michael Grey** was born and grew up in Yorkshire and now lives in Melbourne with his wife and three boys. His work has been featured in print and online. He is currently taking applications for the role of 'Writer's Cat'. Candidates can contact him at michaelgrey.com. au or on Twitter as @Mikes005.

**Thord D. Hedengren** is addicted to words, and the stories they make. He writes fiction, short and long, as well as freelance articles and columns for various media outlets. You can find some of his short stories in *Cthulhu Lies Dreaming* and *Fireside Fiction Magazine*, among other places. Thord is a renowned web developer and designer, and the author of techy books such as *Smashing Wordpress: Beyond the Blog* and *The Writer's Ipad*. You'll find him wasting away on Twitter as @tdh, or spewing words at tdh.me. Thord lives in Sweden, the Land of Kings.

**S. L. Huang** justifies her MIT degree by using it to write eccentric mathematical superhero fiction, starting with her debut novel, *Zero Sum Game*. In real life, you can usually find her hanging upside down from the ceiling or stabbing people with swords. Her short fiction has been published at *Strange Horizons* and *The Book Smugglers*, and she's unhealthily opinionated at slhuang.com or on Twitter as @sl_huang.

**Salomé Jones** is the editor of the anthologies *Cthulhu Lives!* and *Cthulhu Lies Dreaming* (as well as *Haunted Futures*), and the collective novel *Red Phone Box*, written by 28 people, including herself. She lives in London with her husband Tim and Chilly, their cat. In her spare time she sings protest songs. You can find her on Twitter as @call_me_salome.

**Gethin A. Lynes** is a novelist, would-be comics writer and a general peddler of parables. With his infant dictator and semi-willing wife in tow, he finally managed to escape the cultural wasteland of Western Australia, and has taken up residence in the infinitely more progressive Wilds of Pennsyltuckey, just across the canal from Bill's Gun Shop. Before long however, his shameless cynicism, love of expletives, and uncanny talent for speaking before thinking are probably going to get him deported from Trumpistan.

**Jeff Noon** was born in Manchester, England in 1957. He trained in the visual arts and drama and was active on the post-punk music scene before becoming a playwright, and then a novelist. His novels include *Vurt* (Arthur C. Clarke Award winner), *Pollen*, *Automated Alice*, *Nymphomation*, *Needle in the Groove*, *Cobralingus*, *Falling Out Of Cars*, *Channel SK1N*, *Mappalujo* (with Steve Beard) and a collection of stories called *Pixel Juice*. He has also won the John W. Campbell Award. His Twitter fiction site @echovirus12 is a long-running online experiment in collaborative writing.

**Pete Rawlik**, a long time collector of Lovecraftian fiction, is the author of more than fifty short stories, a smattering of poetry, and the Cthulhu Mythos novels *Reanimators*, and *The Weird Company*. He is a frequent contributor to *The Lovecraft ezine* and *The New York Review of Science Fiction*. In 2014 his short story *Revenge of the Reanimator* was nominated for a New Pulp Award. His new novel *Reanimatrix*, a weird, noir, romance set in H. P. Lovecraft's Arkham, was released in 2016. He lives in southern Florida, where he works on Everglades issues.

**John Reppion** has written articles for the likes of *Fortean Times* and *The Daily Grail Online*, and is the contributing editor of the *Spirits of Place* anthology. His day job is scripting comics with his wife and writing partner Leah Moore. John's Weird Fiction has previously appeared in *Uncertainties Vol 1* from Swan River Press, S. T. Joshi's *Black Wings V*, Snowbooks' *Shakespeare vs. Cthulhu*, and Ghostwoods Books' own *Cthulhu Lives!* Find him on Twitter as @johnreppion.

**Liesel Schwarz** is the award-winning author of *A Conspiracy of Alchemists*, the first book in her Chronicles of Light and Shadow steampunk series published by Random House in the UK, US, Canada and Australia. A life-long fan of 19th Century Gothic literature, she is a hopeless romantic with a penchant for everything that's odd, from fairies to giant snarling monsters. She is currently completing her PhD in creative writing at Brunel University, and she teaches creative writing in her spare time. She lives in the English countryside with her cats and if you ask her nicely, she will show you the correct way to drink absinthe.

**Felicity Shoulders** was born in Portland, Oregon. She abandoned her dream of being a paleontologist at the age of 20 rather than the traditional 5, and devoted herself to writing instead. Her first published fiction appeared in *Asimov's Science Fiction* in 2008. Subsequent stories have been published in *Asimov's*, *Fantasy & SF* and elsewhere. Her story *Conditional Love* was nominated for a Nebula Award in 2010.

**Greg Stolze** was born in 1970 and in the intervening decades has written games (*Reign*, *A Dirty World*, *Better Angels*) novels (*Switchflipped*, *Sinner*, *Mask of the Other*) and ever so many short stories (archived at gregstolze.com/fiction_library where you can read them for free. Fair bit of Mythos stuff in there.) Also, one comic book (*A Softer Apocalypse*.) He's tired. Oh so tired.

**Tricia Sullivan** has been publishing science fiction novels since 1995, the same year that she moved to Britain from New Jersey. In 1999 her novel *Dreaming in Smoke* won the Arthur C. Clarke Award, and both *Maul* and *Lightborn* have been shortlisted. When her children were small her writing career collapsed, so she retrained in physics with the Open University. She is presently an MSc student at the Astrophysics Research Institute in Liverpool. Her latest novel is *Occupy Me*.

## ACKNOWLEDGMENTS

**The Editor** would like to thank Warren Ellis, whose story suggested a theme for the volume, as well as all the other writers whose patience made completion of this anthology possible. Special thanks to Gábor Csigás, Eva Bradshaw, Ben Dedopulos and Thord D. Hedengren.

**The Publishers** would like to thank our supporters, whose contributions allowed for the financing of this book. Here are their names:

Aaron Roberts, Adam Brosious, Adam Christie, Ádám Ladányi, Adam Redman, Adam Tinworth, Al Kennedy, Alison Van Hees, alumiere, Andi Scott, Andreas Ntirokaltsis, Andrew Barton, Andrew Hurley, Andrew Kincaid, Andrew Parker, Andrew Willis, Andy Haigh, Annabeth Leong, Annette Kendall, Anton Wijs, Aris Alissandrakis, AsenRG, Backercamp, Bees Make Honey, Benjamin Eriksen, Bespite, Big Robot, Bilinda Ni Siodacain, Bin Davis, Brett Damon, Brian Nisbet, Brian Williams, Bruno Girin, Caleb Monroe, Cameron Suey, Carey Drake, Caroline Emuss, Cat Jones, Charlton Alexander, Chris Newman, Chris Novus, Christopher Belanger, CJ Romer, Clarence Washington III, Craig Phillips, D D, Dan Brian, Dan Whitehead, Dan Wickline, Dave Borcherding, David Bonner, David Chart, David Church Rodríguez, David Harris, David Nice, Deborah Crook, Dennis Wilding, doug mayo-wells, Doug Winter, Dradd, Drew DeFever, Duncan Bain, Dustin Dean, Elaine

Tindill-Rohr, Elena Murphy, Elizabeth Harper, Elizabeth Underwood, Emmet Flynn, Eoin Murphy, Eva Bradshaw, Faith Williams, Findlay Craig, Gareth Ryder-Hanrahan, Gemma Wheeler-Carver, Gethin Lynes, Giles Lynes, Glenn Kellam, Greg Stolze, Hans R, Hazel Chudley, Heather Royston, Helen, Henning, hurcheon, Iain Lowson, Ian Clarke, Ian J Simpson, Ian McFarlin, James Dadd, James Ward, Janne Vuorenmaa, Jason A Rust, Jason Beamish, Jeff Kearns, jeff lowrey, Jeff Metzner, Jen Haeger, Jen Howell, Jen Warren, Jennifer Day, Jennifer Jamieson, jeremy, Jessica Meade, jgclingenpeel, jjeff regeiringer, jnphilipp, Joe Aragon, Joe Silber, Joe Skelton, John Conklin II, john reppion, John Sommerville, John Sullivan, Jonathan L. Howard, Josh Thomson, Judson Nichols, Jukka Särkijärvi, juli, Julie Brady, K Kisner, kangeiko, Kara Y. Frame, Karina Junker Larsen, Kate Harrad, Keith Athey, Ken Viola, Kerry Frey, Kevin Going, Kevin J. Maroney, Kevin Wallace, Kirsten Watson, Komavary, Lars Duffy, Lassi Seppälä, Laszlo Szidonya, Laura Eleanor Jefferson, Leath Sheales, Leigh mower, littlepurplegoth, Liz Peterson, Louise Löwenspets, Luis Filipe Rodrigues Alves, Mark Caldwell, Mark O'Neill, Martin Jackson, Massimo Spiga, Matt Fowle, Matthew Fabb, Matthew Jones, Matthew Scoppetta, Max Kachn, meredevachon, Merlin Thomas, Michael Berry, Michael Grey, Mike S. DuBose, Morgan B Walther, Morvani, Nicholas Avenell, Nicholas Olson, Nicholas Smith, Nick, Nicole Mezzasalma, Norman Dixon Jr., Oliver Longden, Olivia, Ozzy Beck, Parker, Paul Czege, penwing, Pete Wolfendale, Peter Emuss, Peter Hawkins, Philip Thompson, Piers Beckley, Prios, Rachel, Rachel Carnes, Rachel Oakley, Rachel لشيار James, Richard, Richard Deniz, Richard Hughes, Richard Wolfrik Galland, Richie, Robert Biskin, Robert Chatten, Robert E. Stutts, Rose, Rowan, Rudy Jahchan, Ryan, S. Ben Melhuish, Sasha Bilton, Sekkite, Sezin Koehler, Sharon Woolich, Shay Brog, Simes, Simon Rogers, Stav Levi, Stella Ottewill, Stephanie C., Stephanie

Cheshire, Stephen Coltrane, Stephen Loiaconi, Steve Dempsey, Steve O'Connor, Storium / Stephen Hood, Stuart Elms, Suzanne McBride, Tamsyn K, Tasha Turner Lennhoff, Taylor, The Selkie Delegation, Theodore Jacobs, Thresherinc, Tibs, Tim, Tim Ellis, Tobias Carroll, Tom Bridge, Tom DeFalco, Tom Pleasant, Tony Gatner, Tóth Krisztián, travis a neisler, Victoria Traube, Viktor Juhasz, Whitt, Zed Lopez